BLESS
HER
DEAD
HEART

THE RIGHTE🕱US SERIES

BLESS HER DEAD HEART

MEG COLLETT

To Elle
You're in my dreams

CHAPTER 1

LOEY GRACE KEENE TUMBLED CLEAN off her porch when the tornado sirens screamed to life.

She landed in a hydrangea bush with an explosion of white blossoms, and the ruined cartilage in her bad knee popped as it bore all her weight. The sirens drowned out her agonized cry.

She simply lay there, her heart in her mouth, her knee pulsing as she waited for the twister to suck her up, up, up into the ominous green sky.

Her grandmother had always said green skies meant the Devil was coming.

Gran would have kicked her in the butt for being so simpleminded as to lie in a bush while the tornado sirens wailed. After all, the chickens were still out and the laundry hung on the line, likely flapping in the wind like white flags of surrender. Loey had lived in the South her entire life—never left and never would either—and she'd been raised on the commandments of a good Southern woman: a well kept house is a well kept soul; say nothing if you can't say anything nice; pour two rings of salt around a grave just in case the first should fail; and never, *ever* let clean sheets get rained on.

She pried herself out of the hydrangeas, hobbling on one leg, and craned her head skyward. The first splat of rain landed on her cheek. Beefy clouds hung low and churned with

1

sickness while the wind whipped the weathervane around so fast it was a blur of rusted metal atop the red barn.

From the pasture beside the barn, Butters whinnied in fright. He loped down the fence line with his ears pinned back. The herd of pygmy goats bleated and scampered toward the barn. From behind the screen door at her back, Dewey woofed.

"It's okay, Dew," she murmured, eyes on the sky, her hair twisting over her shoulders. Her gaze followed the line of clouds away from her farm and down the sloping hay pasture toward Blackmore Baptist and Cemetery, her home not-so-far-from home.

One cloud rotated directly over the white clapboard church, nestled at the bottom of the hill near the main road, which descended in a series of switchbacks toward town. The funnel cloud's hooked tail reached down in whipping tendrils, and debris at the base of the growing twister swirled, the ground tearing apart in a dust storm. The bell in the church steeple clanged in terror.

She should have gone inside and hunkered down in the bathtub with Dewey. Instead, she watched the twister finish forming itself like it was a handsome stranger swaggering into town with a six-shooter on his hip and a black cowboy hat pulled low over dark eyes. She didn't know what had inspired the vision, but she saw it in that monstrous storm.

The Devil wasn't coming. He was already here.

The church lights were on, and a white Ford Explorer sat outside. Pastor Briggs was preparing his Sunday sermon, his reading glasses low on his small nose, his frail body hunched over his Bible and the cup of weak tea on the pew beside him. Surely, he'd heard the sirens wailing from town and tucked himself into the church cellar.

But he sometimes took out his hearing aids and set them beside his notebook. He said not hearing the outside world helped him listen closer for God's whispers.

Thunder boomed, lightning cracked, and a yowl pierced through the racket, snapping Loey out of her reverie. Boltz, the world's unluckiest cat, skittered around the corner of her old farmhouse, his hair sizzling, his tail scorched black and smoking. *Again.* He ran a touch crooked from the last time lightning had struck him, back in the spring during the storm that had knocked down the big hundred-year-old sycamore in the town square.

She scrambled onto her porch to take shelter. Dewey, big as a horse, jumped against her screen door with a *Hurry up, Mom* bark. As she reached for the latch, the wind stopped dead. The temperature dropped, and the roiling clouds stilled. Her ears popped deep inside her head. Dewey growled.

Between the siren's wails that rose and lowered in pitch, someone screamed into the empty-air silence.

She whirled around right as the sirens drowned out the scream, but in the cemetery, where the scream had sounded from, lights flickered. She blinked and they vanished.

The twister howled louder than a train over rusted rails as it crashed down on the chipped pavement of Devil's Maw Road beyond the church. The sirens pitched low again, and as the tornado trundled away, she caught the last few notes of the scream before it died off completely.

She ran for the church with a lurching gait.

The sloping hill carried her down quickly—too quickly; she almost fell head over heels. The pain in her knee amplified such that her stomach heaved, but she kept limping in her long-legged gallop, the knee-high grass slapping at her worn jeans. Her boots skidded over loose bits of dirt as she sprinted into the churchyard.

The church's pine doors were splintered down the middle and hung crookedly from their hinges. She barreled through them and straight into the church. Glass and wooden shards broke beneath her boots.

"Pastor Briggs?"

The stained glass windows her great-great-grandfather had soldered himself were blown out. Purple, red, blue, and green glass littered the wooden planks between the overturned and misaligned pews.

The unmistakable stench of sulfur tainted the air. She pinched her nose.

A ripping sound tore through the broken windows. Loey flinched. It came again, as loud and painful as a shotgun fired right beside her.

"Pastor Briggs?"

She hurried down the aisle, dodging pews. With her breath stuck in her throat, she rushed out of the church's back door and into the graveyard. Expecting the air to be cleaner outside, she sucked in a deep breath.

She gagged.

The sulfur stank stronger back here.

In the wake of the twister's wind, the trees had been stripped bare of leaves and branches littered the graveyard. Blooms from the graveyard's flowers blew between the headstones in tiny flashes of color. The older mausoleums stood intact, their delicate stone walls plastered with damp leaves and errant petals. Overall, the damage was minimal, given the twister had touched down mere feet from the cemetery.

She hurried along the brick path with patches of moss and weeds sprouting between the cracks. Around her, headstones poked up from the ground like stone teeth from an old man's gums. The sirens stuttered to a stop, though their echoes still rang in her ears. Only her boots clapping over the bricks broke the cemetery's silence. Through the hedge beside her, lights flashed again, firefly quick. She scrubbed her eyes to clear away the lights. Now was not the time for an ocular migraine.

She rounded a tall, untrimmed hedge and charged into the heart of the graveyard.

Her attention swept toward the giant tree looming over the cemetery. "Pastor Br—"

The words died in her throat. She clapped a hand over her mouth to hold in her scream. She'd found Pastor Briggs, and he wouldn't be answering her anytime soon.

From the branches of the poplar tree, which had stood vigil over Righteous's only cemetery since the town had been nothing more than a patch of dust with a few graves, hung Pastor Briggs, stark naked.

Hung wasn't the right word. *Skewered*, her brain provided.

He was pinned high in the tree, his arms and legs dangling limply. He wore one leather loafer, his other foot bare, with blood dripping from his pale toes. He'd been impaled, shish-kebab style, on the thickest branch of the leafless tree, whose bare limbs had curled like gnarled bones around its bloody prize.

The branch protruded from his narrow belly. Loey's gaze drifted higher, above the limb, to his chest. A whimper slipped between her fingers, and a wrecking-ball sense of déjà vu crashed through her.

Through the tufts of gray hair, his skin was burned in a pattern Loey recognized too well. Those two parallel, slashing lines with a single curving arc like an elaborate *H* had haunted her nightmares, her weakest moments, and even the times she almost forgot about the night she discovered her friend dying on the playground, this same symbol burned into his chest.

Any hope that Briggs's poor form was not the second murdered body she'd discovered in six years was dashed by the headstone beneath him. It belonged to Townsend Rose—Righteous's founder. On it, a simple sentence was written in blood with a scrawling hand.

"I'm back and I ain't forgotten."

CHAPTER 2

WEDNESDAY MORNING, LOEY EASED THE paint-chipped, rusted blue Ford into her usual parking spot in the alley beside Deadly Sin Roasters, the only coffee shop in Righteous.

The farm truck choked out a sigh as she cut the engine. Grabbing her bag, she threw her shoulder against the door, the hinges screeching madly when it sprang open. As she climbed out of the truck, careful with her bad knee, she swung her gaze away from the side mirror, lest she glimpse the scars on her cheek and the downward pull of her mouth's left corner, which made drinking sweet tea and kissing young men messy. They were reminders of an accident Loey only thought about in her nightmares.

But she did catch the briefest glimpse of her brand new nose ring, the one she'd gotten in the city only a week ago, the one everyone in town kept telling her had ruined her pretty face. She'd never hear the end of it if they also knew about the spray of delicate peony blooms tattooed across her shoulder.

It wasn't that she was rebellious or the type for tattoos and nose rings; she was just tired of people looking at her scars and giving her pitying glances. If they wanted something to look at then she'd give them something to look at.

She slammed the door shut without bothering to lock it.

No one locked anything in Righteous; it wasn't the way of things.

Then again, people getting impaled on tree limbs wasn't the way of things, either. Except that had happened two nights ago. She still couldn't decide if the killer or the twister had hauled Briggs's small body up into the tree. She'd had a lot of time to think about it too, given she wasn't sleeping none too much.

Since finding Briggs and calling the police, who had been responding to calls from all over the valley after the twister, she'd split her time between the police station, the coffee shop, and her house. When she did sleep, she only had nightmares about playgrounds and symbols. Folton Terry Jr., with his claw-like hands and dry skin, was cropping up in her dreams again too, and she knew why.

Poor Pastor Briggs, the sweet old man who'd baptized her as a child, was dead because of her. The killer who'd left Leigh Parker's body hanging in the playground the night of the high school Christmas formal dance over six years ago had returned.

Along the sidewalk running the length of Main Street, the pharmacy, post office, art gallery, and second-hand boutique were all quiet this early in the morning, the storefronts dark beneath the streetlamps' soft light peeking through the fog. It was too early for even Mr. Weebly to be on the empty streets delivering the day's mail.

Like the church and cemetery, the town proper had suffered little from the first tornado to touch down in Righteous in decades. The brick shops' glass windows were all intact. The American flags hanging from every streetlight remained in place, flapping in the early morning breeze. The bits and bobs of trash that had blown through town after the storm had long since been cleared away.

Loey rubbed her eyes and stifled another yawn, exhaustion

mingling with a deeply rooted sense of dread.

It's happening all over again, a voice whispered in her head. *And it's all your fault.*

Suddenly so wide awake she might never sleep again, she turned back toward the coffee shop's front door.

A man stood in the middle of the road with his back to her, a shadow amidst the light from the streetlamps. His legs were wide apart as if a great wind might gust through town and push him over. His wide shoulders tapered down to narrow hips. He wore dark clothes, and his hair brushed his shoulders in a waterfall of ash. A cattleman hat sat on his head, which, coupled with his long coat, made him look like a cowboy from one of Pap's favorite old westerns.

Loey's boots scuffed against the sidewalk's concrete. The sound drew the man's attention, but he didn't act surprised to find her standing there as he faced her fully. In fact, his eyes found her so quickly in the morning's darkness that she had the impression he'd known she was behind him the entire time. He stared until a warning chill built at the back of her neck.

"Ma'am," he drawled in a thick southern accent that carried down the street. Fingers touching the brim of his hat, he dipped his chin.

"Good morning." The hello wasn't in her normal, friendly pitch, nor was it followed by the best version of her ruined smile. A good Southern woman always had a smile for everyone, but something about this stranger had Loey gripping the straps of her purse tighter as he ambled down the middle of the road, not heeding the perfectly good sidewalk beside him.

Although, he didn't strike her as the sidewalk type.

"Don't seem to be much good to this morning, what with this fog and all."

He drew close enough for her to make out his hard jaw and harder eyes, which were black as the ink in her Bible. His almost pretty mouth could've eased her unexplained nerves if not for the fact that it perched beneath a nose that had been broken its fair share of times.

"A cold front," she blurted.

"Pardon?" The stranger stared steadily at her in a way Loey didn't appreciate. His midnight eyes lingered on her scars in a terribly unabashed manner before turning to her nose ring.

"It followed the storm in from the mountains." She studied him closer too, forcing herself to consider what exactly it was about him that made her back teeth clench. "You're not from around here. Were you in town during the storm?"

"Lucky enough to have missed it. I've been traveling all night from Savannah, and my phone said this was the only coffee shop in town. You work here?"

He angled his chin, a minuscule movement as if he were rationing his body's motions, toward the door marked with a skeleton drinking coffee beneath the shop's name. Her grandmother had rebuked the logo as macabre, but her grandfather had loved it. He'd smile every time he saw it, and Gran would smile every time Pap smiled, so neither one of them had changed the sign, even if it flustered Righteous's never-miss-a-Sunday-church do-gooders.

Not that they could complain much. The Keenes never missed a Sunday service either, especially when Gran and Pap had been alive. Since they'd passed, Loey kept attending because that was what you did in Righteous, and because Gran and Pap would be disappointed in her if she didn't.

She checked her watch. It had belonged to Gran. The thin leather strap was frayed, and the gold watch face was chipped, but she kept it clean and gleaming. She considered the time, biting her lip. A man *had* just been murdered, and her letting a stranger into her store before shops hours was probably stupid, but if he was dangerous, Dale would be coming by at

10

any moment. Then again, if he was simply the type to loiter in streets, she could make a sale. He might set her teeth on edge, but this was Righteous after all.

"Technically, we're not open yet, but …" She looked up and found him staring at her mouth, where she'd been biting her lip.

Heat spread out from her collarbones.

Now *she* was staring at *his* mouth. What in good heavens was wrong with her? He could be Pastor Briggs's killer for all she knew. "I mean, if you want to wait, I can get some coffee started."

"That would be much appreciated."

She found the shop's key on her ring before turning her back to the stranger, which made her feel intensely vulnerable, and facing the door. "I didn't catch your name. I'm Loey Grace Keene."

He said something she didn't hear above the jingle-jangle of her keys against the lock.

She glanced back at him. He hadn't come any closer as if he'd sensed her nerves. It only made her feel marginally better about letting him into her store.

"What was that?"

"It's Jeronimo. Jeronimo James." At her surprised expression, he added, "Family name."

"We have a lot of those around here."

She unlocked the door and pushed it open, the rusty bell chiming overhead. She hit the light switch, swathing the quaint store in patchy light from the dust-covered bulbs overhead.

The shop had been Pap's pride and joy. It comprised a hodgepodge of clustered leather sofas and stately wingback chairs, and floor-to-ceiling bookshelves lined two of the four walls, the shelves bowed under the weight of the books that added a musty smell to the air. Her grandfather used to pull out a book at random and flip the pages beneath his nose, inhaling the scent of old paper. *"Magic,"* he'd tell her. *"Pure magic."*

Rugs covered the floor at random angles. Tables, all from yard sales, dotted the space between. The old-fashioned counter had gilded edges and age-spotted glass. Above the cash register, on the crumbling brick wall, a massive chalkboard depicted all the store's offerings. When the shop had first opened back when she was in high school, Loey had spent hours on the script, precisely planning and writing each word with care under her grandfather's appraising eye. "Mocha" and "cappuccino" and "Shiner's latte" and "Gran's biscuit" were all written in white, slanted cursive.

"Damn fine," Pap had told her when she'd finished the board. Gran had swatted his arm, her cheeks flushed. *"Watch that mouth, Harlan."*

Jeronimo, respecting her space or perhaps just curious, started exploring the shop. She flipped the Closed sign to Open, drew back the blinds, and went behind the counter. Pulling on the stained and faded apron Pap had always worn, she fell into coffee-making mode, which involved a series of steps, like a fine dance, that Pap had taught her when she was old enough to sit on the counter and pretend to help. She picked the darkest, strongest roast, because Jeronimo looked like a dark and strong kind of man, and ground them into a coarse grit. The smell of fresh grounds pervaded the small store to mix and mingle with the soft leather and old books. It was the perfume of her childhood and her present. Often, it was the only thing that could calm her frayed nerves, but even the shop's special comfort couldn't put her at ease of late.

She prepped the massive black coffee maker before dumping in the fresh grounds. She started up the machine and wiped the first of many leftover grounds on her apron as she looked up at the stranger prowling her store.

"Where are you from, then, Jeronimo?" she asked because it was rude not to and it helped her ignore her nerves.

His name tasted like an acidic Colombian roast with smoky, volcanic undertones, something unusual and foreign. Something that would always surprise her, no matter how many times she'd tasted it. The way her skin prickled told her she shouldn't like the sound of his name so much.

He walked around the edges of the bookshelves, his eyes on the spines, and said, "Savannah most recently. I move around a lot, but my family's from here."

She raised her eyebrows. "Really? What's your kin's names?"

"They've been dead a long time."

"*Pardon?*"

He paused in his examination of her shop. There was the slightest movement beneath the faded threads of his shirt that could have been a shrug. The rest of him remained hyper-still. "My grandparents left in the fifties. The only Jameses left in this town are in the cemetery."

The coffee machine gurgled, but she kept her eyes on him. He ran his finger along the back of a green velvet chair in desperate need of reupholstering. His dark eyes shifted to the macramé tapestries she'd hung around the shop. He stepped over to the nearest one and leaned in to examine the complicated knotted pattern she'd spent hours on.

"Macramé," she offered in the resounding drum of his silence.

"Looks intricate."

Talking about her art, which she sold enough in town and online to help with some of her loan payments, had never been her strong suit. She just loved tying knots. If she hadn't worked on a tapestry in a while, she would look down to find her fingers twitching as if tying an imaginary thread.

"It's something to do, I guess. My grandmother taught me before she ..."

Died seemed too familiar a word to say to a stranger, especially one as unnerving as Jeronimo. Her uneasiness captured his attention from the tapestry.

"I'm sorry. When did she pass?"

Loey's spine stiffened. "This March, in a car accident. It took both Gran and Pap. Anyway," she said, focusing on getting more information out of him, "you picked an unfortunate time to visit. There was a murder a couple nights ago during the storm."

An instantaneous shroud of anger dropped over his face, turning all those hard angles into edges sharp as the limestone cliffs of Shiner's Ridge. "So I've seen."

All her previous unease swept back at his sudden change in mood. Her gaze fell to the shotgun that had set below the cash register since the shop's opening day and likely wouldn't fire anyway. A stronger woman would've questioned him, but Loey just wanted him gone. She quickly poured his coffee into a disposable thermos. "Coffee's ready."

He dropped a handful of crumpled cash onto the counter before taking the offered cup. When he looked up at her with a nod, his anger had completely dissolved, leaving her to wonder if she'd misjudged the emotion.

Instead of leaving as she'd expected—and hoped—he hesitated. With his tanned and long-fingered hand, his fingernails trimmed short and square, he reached into the inner pocket of his jacket, where something paper-like rustled against his fingers. "There's something—"

The bell above the shop's door let out a staccato chime.

Dale Rose-Jinks, Loey's best friend since elementary school, gusted in harder than any tornado in her designer clothes, curled blonde hair, and perfectly done-up face. "What is *with* this fog? So creepy and shit—oh, who's this?"

She drew up short in the center of the shop, her summer storm–blue eyes locked on Jeronimo.

He dropped his hand from his jacket and nodded at her. "Jeronimo James, ma'am. Pleasure to have your acquaintance."

A smile beamed onto Dale's perfect mouth. "The pleasure is all mine, I promise. I'm Dale Rose," she said, leaving off her married name.

With his coffee in hand, Jeronimo passed Dale with a tip of his hat that sent her eyebrows spiking into her soft golden curls. She shot Loey a *who's this* glance.

"Sorry for your troubles, Miss Keene. You ladies have a good day now."

The bell sang out his departure, and the shop door slapped shut against the morning's first rays of sunlight peeking above the valley on the eastern outskirts of town.

Loey stared at the door, her heart fluttering and her belly tightening. She couldn't tell if the sensations sweeping over her were pleasant or disconcerting, like she couldn't tell if the man who'd caused them was friend or foe.

"Jeronimo James." Dale whistled low. "With a name like that, he should be a Wild West gunslinger with a swagger that can get a girl pregnant just watching him cross the street."

Outside, a gust of wind rattled the door. A chill at the base of Loey's neck spilled down her spine. She shivered.

"Someone walk over your grave?" Gran would've asked if she'd been there.

CHAPTER 3

AUGUST 15, 2011

THE FIRST DAY OF SENIOR year smelled like fresh possibilities.

The brick school at the edge of town had been renovated over the summer. Fresh paint and new floors adorned the low-lying structure. The lawn was freshly cut and the flower beds filled with blooming azaleas and pansies. The bushes were trimmed beneath the gleaming windows the teachers had decorated. Behind the school, a shiny red slide had been installed in the playground. Kids kicked their legs on the swings in a competition to see who could fly the highest before the first bell.

Loey adjusted her backpack and double-checked her assigned locker. The seniors, all thirty-six of them, had lockers toward the front of the building, where the big windows let in splotches of morning sunlight that zigzagged across the linoleum as the trees outside shifted in the breeze. She found her locker right beside the art history classroom, her first class every day.

A rangy boy stood at her locker with its padlock held in his too-large hand. Frowning in concentration, he studied its numbered dial.

She walked up to him, a huge first-day smile on her face. "I think that's my locker."

"Oh." A lock of red hair flopped over his green eyes. "I musta got the numbers wrong."

She recognized the boy from his bashful stutter. His height had thrown her off, along with his clear skin and new clothes.

"Leigh Parker!" she said. "I didn't recognize you. Goodness, you must have grown two feet over the summer."

He peeked at her through his shaggy hair. She had the urge to push it away from his face and pat his shoulder. Leigh had always had the hunched look of a stray pup down on its luck, though that wasn't unusual for kids from Little Cricket Trailer Park.

"Growth spurt, my momma said." He grinned. "My locker's right next to yours, I guess."

She glanced at his schedule clenched in his hand. "You're right there." She pointed to the locker to the left of hers. "But these padlocks are tricky. Do you want me to help you? I got pretty good at undoing them last year because mine always stuck."

Tension unwound from his shoulders. He'd always been the slowest kid in math, struggling to put the numbers together right, and she didn't want him to feel embarrassed on the first day when he couldn't open his locker.

"I'm putting my lock inside my locker once I open it." His grin stretched big enough to reveal bright red gums as if he'd scrubbed his teeth too hard this morning. "Ain't no reason to lock anything up in Righteous."

"That's a good plan. What's your code?"

He offered her the paper, and after glancing at his numbers, she got to work on his padlock. She purposefully fumbled it a couple of times before she moved on to hers.

"Do you need any help with yours?" he asked, setting his backpack inside the metal cabinet.

She didn't, but she handed him her class schedule anyway. "Can you read me the numbers?"

She pretended to take her time as he stutteringly read the code to her padlock. When her locker finally sprang open, it was almost time for the first bell.

"Thanks, Leigh. What's your first class?"

He checked his schedule, searching for the right line. He frowned hard with concentration as he read, "Art history with Mr. Terry. Who's he? He wasn't here last year."

"He moved here over the summer from Memphis. He was nominated as a deacon last Sunday at church. Speaking of, you should come by sometime. We would love to have you—"

"Hey, ho bagel!" A hand slapped Loey's jean-clad butt.

She rolled her eyes as her best friend pranced up next to her. "Morning, Dale."

Cross, Dale's older brother, strolled behind her with a few of his football friends in tow, including the team's quarterback, Travis Jinks. He'd been chasing after Dale ever since middle school and she'd finally given in over summer break, much to her mother's horror. Roses did not mingle with Jinkses. Not after Dale's great-grandpa had brought ruin to the Jinks iron empire back in the fifties.

Loey's friends crowded around her and Leigh's lockers. As they did, Leigh shrank away, disappearing behind his uncut hair.

Born and raised in Little Cricket Trailer Park, Leigh was an expert at becoming invisible. In that westernmost part of town cast in the shadow of the Appalachians, it was best to hide first and ask questions later. All the crime in Righteous came from Little Cricket—at least the crime that made the papers.

Dale was saying something, but Loey interrupted her before Leigh could fold himself away for good. "Look at Leigh, y'all!" She grabbed his arm. "He's grown three feet over the summer!"

Dale shifted her gaze to Leigh. She cocked her head and examined him with a sweeping floor-to-brow look.

"Holy shit, Leigh Parker. You did grow. Look at you." She slapped her brother's arm to pull his attention away from his football friends. "Hey, Cross, look at Leigh Parker here. He's grown six feet over the summer. Maybe he should try out for the football team. Then Travis might have someone to throw to."

Cross threw his head back and laughed. Beside him, Travis slung his arm around Dale's neck, hugging her tight against him. She wrapped her arms around his waist.

The first bell rang, and around them, students slammed lockers and surged like salmon in a river toward their classrooms.

"I've heard y'all Little Cricket boys are as fast as you're skinny," Travis called above the cacophony. "If not, our defense could always use some target practice."

"Screw you, Travis." Cross smacked his back, causing Travis to stumble forward. He then shot Leigh a crooked grin. "Don't listen to him, Leigh. Try out."

"Both of you need to calm down," Loey said. "Leigh would be great on the team."

"Yeah," Dale added, "and it's not like the team is winning any state titles."

Travis laughed and squeezed Dale tight against him. "You're right, babe. It sure as shit would be nice to have someone other than Butterhands here to pass to." He hooked his arm around Cross's neck and pulled him and Dale down the hall toward their classroom.

Mouth open in awe, Leigh watched them walk away. "Do you really think I could make the team?"

Before Loey could answer, the door beside their lockers swung open. Folton Terry Jr. stepped out of the classroom wearing khakis and a shirt buttoned all the way up to his throat. His glasses were round, and his hair was shockingly white, though he couldn't be older than thirty-five. Dry skin flaked around his mouth.

"Don't want to be late now." He smiled at them with too-small square teeth. "You must be Loey Keene and Leigh Parker. I memorized last year's yearbook so I'd know everyone's name on the first day. Come inside. I won't bite."

Loey smiled, forcing herself to look away from his dry skin, and walked into the classroom.

As she passed him, he leaned down and stage-whispered, "At least not too hard."

CHAPTER 4

WITH HER POUTY LIPS, DIMPLED chin, and slate-blue eyes, Dale Rose-Jinks was easily the prettiest girl in Righteous, but something else lurked behind her empty smile. It whispered out of her like a cautious wind blowing across a person's skin as they stared at her. It was off-putting, and Dale knew it. She liked it that way.

As her best friend, Loey knew the hollow parts in Dale, though she hid them from everyone else well. As a Rose—the richest family in Righteous—and a former Miss Tennessee pageant queen, Dale was a master at hiding behind a mask of beauty and wealth, with empty eyes most people mistook for dimness. Opposite of dim, Dale was whip-smart, and she knew every wayward word ever spoken about her because her ear was always on the heartbeat of this town. Unfortunately, there were a lot of untoward things spoken about her, especially after her senior year in high school when everything had changed. After that, people didn't look at Dale the same no more, and she took every judging glance like a stone she could pick up and hold to her chest, collecting them until she built towering walls around her heart.

"… more worried about missing church than they are about the preacher being impaled by an actual branch through his actual chest. That's what my dear, sweet mother said about missing a service this Sunday. Like, *really?* Pastor Briggs is *dead.*"

Loey tried not to cringe as she restocked the counter display for the countless time that morning. The shop had slowed, and only a few customers talked over their chai lattes and cappuccinos. From her stool opposite the counter, Dale swung her bare legs back and forth, her elbow on the counter, her chin resting in her hand.

"I mean," she continued, used to Loey's silences, "thank *goodness* I tried some new recipes last night, or else we couldn't have kept up. Murder's great for the coffee business, though."

This time, Loey couldn't fight back the cringe. To steer her friend away from talk of Briggs, which was causing her stomach to burn, she said, "Is Travis still complaining about you helping here so much?"

Dale harrumphed. She sounded like her mother, Darlene Verity Rose, when she made that noise, though Loey would never dare tell her. Dale had been at war with her mother ever since the first trimester when Darlene couldn't even think of sweet tea without kneeling over a toilet. To this day, she wouldn't drink it and she never let Dale forget it.

"You know Travis. If he can bitch about it, he will. Where did these men get the notion that having their women working and earnin' money would make their penises shrink? As if I'm only good for cooking and popping out babies. He asked me *again* last night about getting pregnant. Can you believe it? He would have to put it in me to get me pregnant, and I doubt he can stay hard enough for that. I literally take my birth control in front of him every morning, and the idiot doesn't know. He thinks we're *unlucky.*"

Loey's stomach twisted with searing heat. She'd had too much coffee today and wasn't thinking straight. This line of conversation wasn't much better than talk of murder. She stared at a jelly-dotted scone, seeing blood, her mind tangling around memories of high school and the present, all that guilt and terror and horror carving out one endless void.

Dale had stopped speaking. A silent Dale was like a skinny cop in Righteous—it didn't exist.

Loey met Dale's eyes through the counter's glass. "What?"

Dale crossed her arms. Her shoulders were bare, her flouncy pink top cropped short of exposing her stomach above her high-waisted denim shorts. Loey could never pull something like that off. Not because she lacked Dale's perfect tan, but because she couldn't imagine not wearing her typical uniform of t-shirts and Wranglers.

"She's a cowgirl through and through," Pap would say when Gran tried to get Loey to wear a dress. *"Cowgirls don't need to dress pretty. They've got horses to work."*

"You haven't talked about what it was like to find him," Dale said.

Loey finished stocking the counter and stretched her back. She wrinkled her nose instead of speaking, which was typical for them. They could have entire conversations with hand gestures and eye rolls.

"I *know*," Dale said, "but you have to. It's weird if you don't." The sharpness in her eyes revealed how little slipped by her. *"Are* you okay?"

Loey swallowed. As she pictured Briggs in the tree, the biscuit she'd forced herself to eat after the morning rush burbled in her stomach. The bloody words, which the town mercifully didn't know about since the police hadn't released the detail to the public yet, flashed neon red across her memory. And the symbol that was so familiar, etched deep into her mind, told her all she needed to know.

"What if it has something to do with Leigh?" she asked, speaking her deepest fear aloud.

"It can't."

"But the symbol—"

"Loey Grace." Dale's eyelashes batted rapidly as if she was seeing all the things she wasn't saying flash across her mind. It was her surest sign of anger. "That was *years* ago. You're confusing the two."

Dale had never seen the symbol on Leigh's chest, but Loey had seen it up close. She'd been the one on that playground, screaming for help as the boy whose hand she held died.

"But what if it's—"

"It's *not*."

"Dale," Loey growled like a coon caught in a trap, and that got her best friend's attention. Dale didn't have many friends aside from Loey and Cross because most people were terrified of her. But Loey could bite back just as sharply as Dale. "What if Briggs's death was our fault? What if it was Leigh's killer who wrote that message? Don't you feel guilty?"

"It's a coincidence. That's all," Dale said, softer now. "Besides, a good Southern woman should always feel guilty. What better reason for guilt than a pastor's murder?"

"You can't really believe that."

"I can believe whatever I want." Dale flicked her hair over her shoulder and shrugged. Just like that, Dale the Pageant Queen had taken over. "Let it go."

"He was murdered, Dale."

"So what?"

Loey turned her back on her best friend to wipe down the back counter. Sometimes, Dale scared her real bad.

"Tell me more about Tall, Dark, and Handsome. What else did he say before I got here? Did he like your nose ring? Better yet, did he make your nose tingle?" Dale waggled her eyebrows at her last question. She knew Loey's nose tingled when she was turned on.

The bell above the door chimed, saving Loey from her best friend. On a wave of humid summer air thick as wool, Righteous's sheriff and the mayor walked in. Sheriff Burl Jinks cast a brief wave in his daughter-in-law's direction.

"… keep this thing from getting national attention," Mayor Goody was in the middle of saying. "That's the last thing we need, you hear me?"

"Yes, Mayor."

Burl hitched up his belt to arrange his bulk behind the table. Mayor Goody crossed her legs, her red high-heeled toe bobbing up and down like a squirrel on crack cocaine.

As Loey started on their usual orders, their conversation drifted over to the counter.

"The town doesn't need to know the grim details of a good man's death. Those stay sealed up tight, and you make sure your deputies know that. If they leak even a tiny detail, I'll see to it they don't work in this town again."

If Mayor Goody's words chewed into Sheriff Burl Jinks any, he didn't show it. He was a tree trunk of a man, his weathered skin harder than bark beneath his tan police uniform. He scratched the back of his neck.

At the counter, Dale deftly changed their conversation to the strawberry donuts she'd made last night, her voice taking on an air of ditsy chatter to cover up their eavesdropping. As Dale pretended to chatter on, Loey's mind sprang to the stranger she'd met this morning. She absently nodded along, her hands busy with the tasks of making coffee, and decided the stranger's unsettling nature warranted a conversation with the sheriff.

"Now Mayor," Burl said, his voice like loose gravel at the back of his throat, "you know I can't control what that liberal bitch at *The Righteous Daily* prints. She's got her fangs in it and won't let go. She's already been by the station twice. She's gotta be on the rag."

Mayor Goody leaned in, her bobbing toe stilling its assault on the air and her lacquered fingernails inching across the table as if they wanted to wrap around Burl's neck. "Tabitha is a smart journalist, and she smells a story. Not everything a woman does is connected to her period, Burl. Though I'm sure those hookers you pay to bleed on you would insist otherwise, since you provide them with such fine job security."

Dale choked and hid it with a subtle cough. Wrapped up in their conversation, the sheriff and the mayor didn't notice.

Burl's cheeks bloomed red, but he stuffed down his retort, those gagged-back words likely chewing up his insides. Mayor Goody was the only one keeping the sheriff in check; she was also the only reason he hadn't been relieved of his duties after his hooker scandal earlier that year. Though that latest debacle had been the one that broke the camel's back for Mrs. Jinks. She'd left with half of nothing that was left of the Jinks's estate and hadn't looked back.

"What would you suggest I do about her questions, then, Mayor?" he asked too sweetly to be sincere.

"I suggest you figure that out before her stories make national headlines. If that happens, you can kiss your reelection goodbye."

Loey hurriedly finished up their coffees and rushed over to their table before one of them could storm off. Dale hissed something at her as she sped off, but Loey ignored her.

"Morning, Mayor," she said. She set the coffees, both black and bitter without a touch of sweetness, before them. If they didn't hate each other so much, Loey figured they'd be dating now that Burl's divorce was finalized. "Sheriff Jinks. How's the investigation going?"

Burl sighed, sounding like a bear waking from hibernation. "Nothing's changed since the last time you asked that, Loey Grace."

Loey flashed a smile. If she had a nickel for every smile she had to force in the wake of a man speaking down to her, she would have far fewer debt collectors calling. "That's what I wanted to mention. Someone came by the shop today. A total stranger. He said his name was—"

"Jeronimo James?" Mayor Goody supplied.

"Um, yeah. How did you know?"

"He stopped by the station this morning," Sheriff Jinks said. "He wanted access to old town records at the courthouse. He studies theology, and he's here on research business. Something about old cemeteries."

Loey crossed her arms. "That doesn't seem suspicious to you? Cemetery research business? After I found a body *in a cemetery?*"

"We get those academics 'round here all the time. It doesn't make him a suspect."

"It should!"

"Loey Grace," Burl warned. It was the same warning tone she'd heard many times since Monday evening. Luckily, Burl Jinks had never scared her and never would.

"It's the same symbol. I know it. It's the same person who killed Leigh Parker."

"Leigh's killer is in jail." Burl's fingers tightened around the mug, splashing coffee over the rim. His eyes cut to Dale, who sat back at the counter, humming to herself. "How can you even mention Folton around her? After what she went through? Your grandmother would be ashamed."

At the mention of Folton's name, Loey's body flushed ice cold, but she knew Gran would never be ashamed of her. "But the symbols—"

"We have no reason to believe Sheriff Jinks got the wrong man back then, and we have even less reason to believe these two murders are connected now." Mayor Goody's stunning hazel-gray eyes set off her rich black skin. People had talked about having a black mayor, especially one with a white mother, but her actions in office had put that talk to bed, leaving no room for murmurs.

"That's what I've been trying to tell her," Burl grumbled.

Mayor Goody stood and swung her laptop bag over her shoulder. "Thanks for the coffee, Loey. Put it on my tab." She cast her gaze down to Burl. "Call my office if anything changes."

She left the shop with a goodbye to Dale. Back at the table with Burl, Loey scooped up the mayor's untouched coffee, a waste if she'd ever seen one, and stomped back behind the counter. She dumped the mug and all in the sink.

"I told you," Dale said.

Only when the mayor was a safe distance down the sidewalk did Burl lumber over to the counter with his tail tucked between his legs. He set his mostly full coffee mug on the countertop. "Dale, you seen my son around today?"

"He went into the office early this morning," she said with a smile. The ring on her left hand gleamed in the sparse light. She'd married Travis Jinks right out of college, almost two years ago. It was long enough for Loey to know that when Dale said Travis had gone into the office early, it meant he hadn't come home last night.

"He works too hard," Burl said, puffing out his chest. Word was Burl wanted Travis to run for county commissioner. Next stop, mayor. That would really stick it to Mayor Goody. No one dared mention to him a Jinks in office would never happen, not after their family's fall from grace.

Dale kept smiling. "I tell him the same thing."

Travis did not work hard at his job. He worked hard at other things. Things that kept him out at night. Sometimes, Loey thought the apple hadn't fallen far from the tree, but

Gran would have deemed such a thought unkind. Loey made a mental note to pray about it Sunday.

Burl paid for his coffee, and Loey put the money in the register. With a nod, the sheriff started to leave.

"Sheriff?" Loey began.

Dale's smile frosted over, her icy eyes on Loey in warning. Loey ignored her.

Burl turned back reluctantly. "Yes?"

"The message on Townsend's grave made it sound like the killer was returning. You have to entertain the possibility that there's a serial killer."

"This is Righteous." His voice shifted, his words clipped. "We don't have serial killers in Righteous."

"But what about a copycat killer?"

"I'm sorry you found the good preacher like that," Burl said to her. His eyes were kind, his big-bear presence warm, and his hard tone forgotten. He was a good sheriff when he wasn't getting caught with hookers. "But don't stick your nose where it don't belong. You might lose it."

"Yes, sir," Loey mumbled.

He kissed Dale's cheek and invited her and Travis to dinner before leaving.

I'm back and I ain't forgotten.

Unlike Sheriff Burl and Mayor Goody, she knew they hadn't caught a murderer all those years ago.

A serial killer walked free in Righteous, and she would have to be the one to catch him.

CHAPTER 5

SEPTEMBER 21, 2011

L OEY WORE THE BURNT ORANGE dress Dale had picked out for her presentation in art history on Fauvism, which, as Dale had said, was a Crayola wet dream. Loey's legs were clad in knit stockings to ward off fall's nippy air, and her hair hung in loose curls over her shoulders thanks to Dale's ministrations that morning. She had a touch of makeup on her eyes and cheeks, with mascara, black as a crow's feather, making her lashes look long. She felt *pretty*, and Matt Everton had kept staring at her in pre-cal.

Her presentation went perfectly. She didn't stammer once. As she gathered up her bag at the end of class, the other students filing out, her mind was already on meeting up with Dale at her place to "study" for history, when really, they'd be texting boys.

She all but danced toward the classroom door.

"Loey." Mr. Terry smiled at her from his desk.

"Yes, Mr. Terry?"

His smile widened to reveal a row of crooked bottom teeth. "Good presentation today. I liked your take on neo-impressionism's influences on the Fauve artists. Very forward-thinking of you."

"Thank you, sir."

She tried to leave, thinking the conversation over, but the

wheels of Mr. Terry's desk chair squealed over the linoleum as he stood. She paused at the end of a desk. He crossed to the classroom door and shut it, blocking out the clamor of the students as they prepared to spill out into the parking lot.

"But we need to talk about your last test."

He pushed up his glasses as if he were nervous. Her stomach flipped. She *had* made a 72 on the last test, which was almost failing. She hadn't studied enough, choosing instead to ride Tempest through the back pasture that butted up against Shiner's Ridge. On the way back to the barn, she'd released the reins, letting Tempest take off across the field, her hooves flying over the ground, and she'd clutched the mare's wild mane, inhaling Tempest's scent, like a summer thunderstorm, somehow terrifying and reassuring at the same time. Loey had closed her eyes, smiling like a loon, never happier, and imagined they were flying. Pap had met her at the barn, his eyes shining, and helped her unsaddle Tempest in his quiet way. *"She's your forever girl,"* he'd told Loey with a pat on Tempest's neck.

"I'm sorry, Mr. Terry. It won't happen again."

"Do you need tutoring?"

He walked closer, his reedy frame taller than she'd expected. His chinos stopped at the top of his ankles and his sweater had leather patches on the elbows. Loey had thought her best friend silly for thinking him creepy—until now.

"Loey?"

He towered over her, so close she smelled the garlic potatoes he'd had for lunch. He had the beginnings of a pimple right beside his left nostril. She avoided staring at the dry patches around his mouth, where the skin flaked off.

"I'm fi-fine, Mr. Terry. Have a good afternoon."

She went to slip by him, but his hand wrapped around her arm. She told herself it was a friendly touch, but his fingers tightened. Her flesh dimpled beneath his fingertips, and his fingernails, too long for a man, dug into her skin. She whimpered.

He pulled her back in front of him.

The classroom had no windows, aside from the square one in the door.

She yanked on her arm, and she was strong, having pulled Tempest back from a gallop enough times that her biceps were well developed, but she couldn't pull away from Mr. Terry.

"When I'm tutoring you after class," he murmured on a cloud of garlic breath, "you can call me Folton."

The fingers of Folton's other hand hooked underneath the neckline of her dress beside her collarbone. Her heart thrummed like a hummingbird trapped beneath a skylight, thrashing its body against the glass, thinking itself free, only to find itself trapped.

His fingernails scratched her as he pushed his hand farther down her dress, bunching the material. He was breathing harder, panting against her face, and she was crying. Her arm hurt in his grip.

"If you tell anyone about this, I'll say you came up to me," he whispered against her ear, his body trembling, his hardness pressed against her hip, "and ran your hand over my cock"—he wrenched her hand down to that hardness and used her hand to viciously rub himself—"and pulled up your dress. I'll say you came on to me, and everyone will think you're a dirty slut."

He bent her over the desk. The tear clinging to the tip of her nose splashed onto the pages of her paper, a written version of her presentation, and blurred the ink of the printed words.

She squeezed her eyes shut and imagined she and Tempest were flying again as her entire world changed.

CHAPTER 6

L IVING ON A FARM, LOEY had battled many a foul
creature, but she'd never met the likes of Sophia, Blanche,
Dorothy, and Rose.

They were the Golden Girls of laying hens and had been
Gran's darlings. They bickered and squawked and flocked
around like single old ladies living together and getting on
each other's last nerve. But in times of crisis, like when their
precious eggs were about to be stolen, they banded together as
only the fastest of friends could do and stared down their foe.

Which today was Loey and her hand.

She jerked away with a hiss as Blanche pecked her wrist.
Roosting beside the gray and white speckled hen, Sophia,
a haughty Golden Comet the color of spun honey, chirped
indignantly.

"Fine." Loey held up her hands, her wicker egg basket
empty on her arm. "Keep them. I wasn't hungry anyway."

She backed out of the henhouse with her eye on Dorothy,
who liked to flog at Loey's heels like a ticked-off Chihuahua
with nothing to lose. Gran had always had a special touch
with the hens, but Loey had never mastered it.

Safely outside, she closed the door and hung her empty
basket on the hook.

"One day," she grumbled, "you'll be brave enough to have

eggs for breakfast again."

Dewey lifted his head from his paws, drool stretching from his lips, and huffed.

"It's not my fault. They're mean, and those beaks hurt."

He settled his head back down, already tired from holding it up. Another thing Loey understood. Her entire body ached. She was too scared of the nightmares to sleep, but she planned to dig into her chores with relish today, thoroughly exhaust herself, and then fall into bed without a drop of energy to dream, because tomorrow, Briggs's funeral would surely stir up old ghosts.

She freshened the goats' water, put hay out for Butters, swept the barn aisle, tidied the tack room, and sprayed weed killer along the fence lines. The late afternoon sun beat down against her back until beads of sweat rolled into the waistband of her jeans. Even this late into the summer, humidity thickened the air, and the scent of honeysuckles sat high up in her nose. Gran's cherry blossom willows released their blooms like snow across the yard. Dewey slept on the porch, watching her work. High in the barn's loft, Boltz paced, his half-bald tail flicking as he tracked a mouse. In their coop, the Golden Girls pecked the ground for bugs, and the little goats bounced around on stiff legs like cartoon cartons.

I'm back and I ain't forgotten.

Those words drifted between the trees on a breeze blowing straight down from Shiner's Ridge. Pausing to stretch out her stiff knee, she glanced down the hill toward the church. A cop cruiser was parked in Pastor Briggs's spot. The deputy was likely Matt Everton. Gran would have pushed her out the door with coffee and a sandwich, instructing her to be sweet and smile a lot at the young, single man, but Gran wasn't here and Matt wasn't that good in bed anyhow.

As she went to turn away, she thought she saw lights

flicker in the cemetery, similar to the night she found Briggs. But they were gone quickly enough that she chalked it up to a headache and reminded herself to take her medicine before the migraine took hold.

A thick rumble drew her attention to the winding gravel drive leading up to the farmhouse. She recognized the machine kicking up dust from Pap's old *Easyriders* magazines. A 1929 Indian 101 Scout with olive paint, a leather saddle, low handlebars, and well cared for, glinting chrome. The man steered one-handed, with no helmet, his ashen hair a calling card. His leather jacket flapped open in the wind he created from his careless speed, his eyes hidden behind black aviator sunglasses.

When Jeronimo pulled to a stop in her drive and stood up his bike, Loey glanced toward her house, where her shotgun leaned against the wall behind the front door. Dewey, her second-best protection, also lay within the house, cooling off from the afternoon heat.

The stranger might have won over Burl with his heavy drawl and good manners, but Loey wasn't convinced. She refused to be the type of woman who let a handsome face and sexy motorcycle buy her trust.

Jeronimo pulled off his shades as he walked over. "Afternoon, ma'am."

Loey shielded her eyes against the sun. "What brings you up Devil's Maw?"

His gaze lifted to the ridge behind her and the Appalachians beyond. He considered them like they were old friends, his black eyes squinted against the late afternoon sunlight, his shoulders relaxed beneath his black shirt. "Sheriff Jinks was kind enough to send me your way when I mentioned I was here to study the cemetery."

Loey gritted her teeth. Of course Burl had. He'd hear

from her tomorrow at the funeral. But she saw an opportunity to get more information from the stranger. Maybe something that would put Burl onto Jeronimo's scent.

Too bad Jeronimo isn't a hooker who likes it kinky, then Burl would be interested.

She pushed the thought away. She'd have to pray about that one too.

She'd been quiet for too long, and Jeronimo's expression had turned confused. "Maybe it's a bad time? I can come back—"

"No, no, not at all. What can I help you with?"

"Well now," he drawled, and she wondered if he was playing up the accent. The accompanying smile seemed put on as well. "Almost everyone I spoke with in town said when it comes to Blackmore Baptist, a Keene's who I should talk to."

"Old traditions." She batted the air like she could wave away the silly notions of old men and women. He wasn't the only one who could put it on. "The church is on Keene land, but it's the town's through and through."

Jeronimo explained no further, as if waiting for her to answer a question he hadn't spoken. She got the feeling he did that a lot.

"But if you want to talk, I have lemonade on the counter and leftover zucchini bread from the shop."

He tipped an imaginary hat. "I'd be obliged."

She smiled and headed toward the house, rolling her eyes when her back was to him. A southern accent and southern manners to boot. Gran would have been impressed if not for the machine he'd ridden in on.

The motorcycle, though, did enhance the image of a killer she was conjuring around Righteous's newcomer.

She opened her screen door to find Dewey sitting perfectly still inside. His eyes tracked Jeronimo as he came in behind her. It had been a long time since a man had followed her inside her house, and she didn't count her and Matt stumbling drunkenly through the screen door.

"Big dog," he observed.

"He's a mastiff and a touch aggressive, so you might—"

Dewey swayed his big body over to Jeronimo, tail wagging. He offered his giant head for petting. She glared at the traitor.

"He's not so bad." Jeronimo scratched Dewey in the spot behind his ears that made his back leg thump.

With a glance at her shotgun, her only faithful protector, she said, "Kitchen's this way."

As they passed the living room, he paused. She hesitated to see what had caught his attention. One of her macramé pieces lay on the floor of the room.

"Work in progress," she told him, feeling nervous as he ran his eyes over the knots she'd started last night.

"How long will this take you?"

She didn't like him staring so intently at the tapestry, like he was seeing bits of her soul in the bound threads. "A few weeks. Anyway, ready for that lemonade?"

She hurried into the kitchen, forcing him to follow or be left behind. The tapestries had been her grandmother's thing, but after the accident, tying those knots for hours every night had felt like Loey was binding Gran and Pap's memory to her soul. It was old lore that people tied a knot to remember something important, but to Loey, it was a governing truth. She worked until her fingers ached because she didn't want to forget even the smallest detail.

Once he'd settled in at her table with Dewey sprawled across his boots, she poured him a glass of lemonade from the porcelain pitcher. She pulled out Gran's good plates meant only for company and the loaf of zucchini bread from the bread box. She divvied up the slices of bread, arranged them on the plates, and grabbed a glass of lemonade for herself before taking a seat opposite Jeronimo.

"What's that there?"

He lifted his chin toward the kitchen's big window over the farmhouse sink. An old blue mason jar of dirt perched between her herbs.

"My grandmother was a superstitious woman. She kept jars like that all over the house, especially on the windowsills. It's holy ground. Well, it's dirt from beneath the church. Call it holy ground if you want. But most people around these parts keep similar jars in their houses to keep out evil spirits."

"And do you believe?"

She couldn't *not* believe after being raised by Gran. But those jars of dirt, and all the other things scattered throughout the house, along with Gran's weird sayings, had become such a part of Loey that it wasn't a question of belief, but of who she was. That was the way of things in the South. Faith was a way of life, not a choice.

At least Loey didn't remember ever choosing.

So, it was easier to answer, "More or less," and then change the subject. "Speaking of the church, what did you want to talk about?"

"I thought I might ask for a tour of the cemetery." His put-on smile returned, crooked this time, and his eyes looked like he might even wink at her. "I could buy us dinner after, if you wanted."

He spoke the words like he was doing her a favor and she'd never taken to charity. She held in a sharp remark, and said instead, "The cemetery is still a crime scene until the funeral tomorrow."

The words sounded harsh even to her ears. A good woman would've softened them with an apology. She didn't.

His smile disappeared so easily she knew she'd been right

to think it was fake. Deep furrows rutted in his brow. "That's a shame."

Yeah, such a shame the pastor was murdered so brutally that it's affecting your plans, she thought.

"But," she said, trying to play nice, "if you want to know about the traditions, I can tell you about them now."

His shoulders relaxed a fraction. Easier now, he said, "I'd appreciate that."

He pulled out a well-loved spiral notepad and pen from his jacket's inner pocket, the motion reminding her of the first time they'd met.

Somehow, the action had seemed so sinister in her recollection, like maybe instead of the paper she'd heard rustle, he'd been reaching for a gun to shoot her. Now, she reckoned he'd been wanting to take notes.

He clicked his pen open and held it over the page. "The salt," he started, "what's that for?"

"Two rings in case the first should fail," she said, the words like a nursery rhyme, "are poured around the grave. They're kept in place through the first night, even if a tent has to be put up to protect them from the rain."

"Interesting." Though he said the word like it was the furthest thing from it. He'd also forgotten to take notes. "Why's that?"

"The souls, in case they try to leak through."

Tourists often meandered through Righteous, hoping to catch a glimpse of the infamous cemetery. A sign and a donation box had been mounted at the front gate with directions for parking and a warning to head back down Devil's Maw before dark. The people of Righteous thought little of their peculiar ways, so long as those ways got them to Heaven. They weren't above making cash off it either. Sometimes, Loey even gave tours of the cemetery for the more interested tourists.

Typically, that sentence, *in case they try to leak through,* won her more shock and awe, sometimes gasps. It got her an eyebrow twitch from Jeronimo.

"Leak where?"

"Here and there. Shouldn't you be taking notes?"

He put his pen down as if to spite her, or possibly as a challenge. "I heard a weapon is also put in the casket. Is that true?"

Loey took a deep breath and started ticking off the traditions on her fingers like she was naming a grocery list.

"Everyone is buried with their weapon of choice." Her grandparents had been buried with a sawed-off shotgun and a hunter's blade passed down from her great-great-grandfather, Knox Keene, who'd called this town home since the late 1800s. "Caskets are made from the pine right off Shiner's Ridge and put eight feet into the ground instead of six. Bells are attached to a string that threads down a pipe into the grave, through the casket's lid, and tied to the departed's finger, in case he or she should wake. Though we haven't buried anyone alive in Righteous in decades."

He inclined his head. The way his black eyes gleamed at her suggested this was the closest he'd come to a real smile around her. "Did your grandmother teach you these traditions?"

Her face must have revealed the pain that erupted at every casual mention of her grandparents, because he amended, "I'm sorry. Their passing was sudden."

She mentally gathered up her undone pain before it spilled across the table.

"No, it's all right. It's still rather …" She was going to say "fresh," but the word conjured up the memory of dirt heaped over a fresh grave.

"My condolences, ma'am. Were you raised by your grandparents?"

His questions cut to the point. Weren't they supposed to

be talking about the cemetery? Why did it feel like he was researching *her*?

She took a long drink of lemonade to stall while she collected herself. When she set down the glass, she stared into the cloudy liquid and said, "My mother, Evelyn, didn't stick around long after having me once she graduated high school. I haven't seen her since, and I don't care to. She hurt my grandparents real bad when she left. She didn't even have the good grace to show up at their funeral."

She hadn't meant to speak about herself, especially to a stranger who could be the killer she sought, but she'd opened her mouth and the words had delivered themselves. Maybe it was the quiet way Jeronimo listened, his expression devoid of judgment, which was as rare as unsweetened tea in this town. If the situation were different, she could have appreciated that about him.

"Sounds like you were better off with your grandparents, then. I haven't been in town long, but I've already heard many good things about the Keenes."

"Thanks." She tucked into her smile with extra force, as if she could make it sincere the harder she smiled. "So, why Righteous?"

He considered her words for a while, and mulled over his own before he allowed himself to utter them.

"Part of me wanted to see where my family had come from," he said. His voice almost sounded raspy with emotion, but his eyes were too flat for such notions. "My research has taken me all over, but I ain't seen tradition quite like what you've got here in Righteous."

"It really is something."

Her words must have sounded too sardonic, because they'd caught his interest. He leaned forward in his seat. "Then why do you stay?"

It had been a long time—the summer after high school graduation—since someone had asked her why she'd stayed in Righteous. Though that conversation, with Dale, had been far different, because the reasons keeping Loey in Righteous were not ones she would reveal to a stranger. They'd been nearly impossible to utter to Dale, to say them aloud, to say, *"I'm trapped."*

That conversation so long ago was the first and only time Loey had ever understood why her mother had run from Righteous and abandoned her three-month-old baby to her parents. Thankfully, the trapped feeling had abated, and Loey could say with almost complete honesty that she only felt trapped sometimes—most days, she might have even chosen to stay if she'd had the choice.

But she gave Jeronimo the Hallmark-card answer. "For all its silly traditions, Righteous is a good town. I'd rather put up with the gossip, the scandals, and the odd tornado than leave."

The interest in his eyes deadened. She sensed she'd disappointed him.

"Silly traditions, huh?"

Maybe she'd hurt his feelings. He was here to study those silly traditions, after all. A big part of her, bigger than she wanted to admit, was frustrated with herself for letting him down. She mentally kicked herself. She was supposed to be collecting information on him to give to Burl, and she had nothing.

Before she could think of a probing question, he threw her off by asking, "Do you ever read Revelations?"

She had, once, but it had given her nightmares of pale horses and men who were Death. But something in his tone made her want to lie. "Sometimes. Why?"

His eyes drifted to the jar of dirt on her sill. She couldn't look away from what she saw in his gaze: pain and sadness and a long life, though his exact age was hard to gauge because of his tan face and squint-wrinkled eyes.

"Sad reading, ain't it?"

Her spine tingled. "You could say that."

"Seems to me, if what He says in Revelations is coming, we're gonna need all the help we can get. Silly traditions or not." His eyes flicked one last time to the jar on her windowsill.

Her mind fumbled for a response. Truth was, nobody in Righteous spoke like him. Conversations ran shallow in this town, with responses spoken out of habit and not thought. Loey wasn't prepared for this.

"Better get going, then," he said before she could think of anything. He stood with a tip of his head. "Thanks for having me."

"Er, you're welcome." She fumbled with her chair.

Dewey scrambled to his feet, tail thumping against the table's legs.

"Could I ask one more thing of you?"

She wrapped her arms around her waist as if to ward off a chill. "Sure."

"Can I have your permission to attend the funeral tomorrow? I don't want to be uncouth, but I'd like to pay my respects since I plan on staying in town for a bit."

Her fingers dug into the flesh right beneath her ribs. Was he hoping to get one last glance at his victim? Either way, his presence tomorrow would prompt Burl to check out Jeronimo's past.

She turned on her smile and ignored the way he considered the scarred corner of her lips. "I think that's a great idea."

She walked him out and watched him drive down Devil's Maw on his motorcycle. He took the wooden cross-marked turns like a local. When she went back inside to tidy up, she found his plate of zucchini bread and lemonade untouched.

Later that evening, Loey limped down the field toward the church. She carried two heaping bouquets of wildflowers she'd picked around the outskirts of the horse pasture. Blue and yellow blooms kissed the tips of bent green stems. They made her hands itch and her nose twitch from the pollen, but they'd been Gran's favorite, and Pap had always planted a few extra seedlings in the spring to make Gran smile whenever she looked out her kitchen window.

At the bottom of the hill, she met the cemetery's outer fence. Vines and wisteria covered the curling black wrought iron. The gate, as old as Righteous, creaked beneath her hand as she pushed through. She walked the narrow path toward her grandparents' graves, keeping her head down.

The shadows stretched long this late in the evening. The last rays of sunlight illuminated the sky behind strips of cumulus clouds. On the breeze, she smelled the flowers that had been blooming in this cemetery for a century and a half, ever since the first bodies had fertilized them. Gardenias and heaping azalea bushes, lilies of the valley and heady chrysanthemums. A perfume of death, apologies, and atonement, Loey considered them. In the summer, she and Gran had often spent their evenings weeding, pruning, and deadheading the wasted blooms. With her grandmother gone, the cemetery's care had landed solely on her, and the overgrown hedges, weed-ridden bushes, and errant vines spoke of the care the place needed.

"You there," someone called from behind her.

Matt Everton hurried up the path that connected to the cemetery's front gates. He removed his hand from his pistol when he recognized her.

"Nice, Matt," she said with a huff of annoyance.

"Sorry, Loey. Couldn't tell it was you in these shadows."

He glanced toward the tall trees shading the graves. "It gets dark in here awfully fast."

"Scared?" It was easy to tease her high school crush. She knew Matt well, almost too well at this point. He'd asked her to marry him once, back when he was at the University of Tennessee and she was helping Gran at the coffee shop while taking the only online class she could afford.

Her medical bills, especially the dental reconstructive surgery, had eaten up her entire college tuition fund, stranding her in Righteous. And when the college fund had run out and the bills had pressed her hard up against her grandparents' Medicare, she'd taken out loans.

Matt had said something she'd missed and he was staring at her, waiting for an answer.

"I'm sorry, what was that?"

Matt's cheeks reddened. He didn't quite look her in the eye as he said, "I like your nose ring. It's pretty."

"Oh, well thanks." She waved the flowers over her shoulder. "Better head on before it gets too dark."

His shoulders slumped. He said his goodbyes and walked back down the path with his head down.

When her grandparents' graves came into view, she paused on the path. A fresh bouquet of cheap carnations already adorned the soft earth in front of their headstone. Loey frowned. She hadn't brought the flowers. She walked closer and crouched, her left knee still tender, by the bouquet. The flowers smelled like a grocery store's freezer, but the bouquet had been carefully picked; not a bloom was withered.

Gran had always said it was unlucky to remove flowers from a grave, so with a shrug, Loey added her bouquet to the small heap. Once she'd arranged the flowers prettily, she settled back to sit on the ground, her boots near their stone.

Harlan Nolan Flint and Ellery Mabel Keene
1947-2018
Beloved wife and husband
Tenders in this life and beyond

Loey hadn't known about the "tending" part, but it was an old Keene family tradition. The phrase marked all the family's headstones around Gran and Pap's. One day, it would mark Loey's too.

As she often did, she lost track of time out in the graveyard. Most young girls played on swings and teeter-totters, but she had spent her childhood here in Blackmore Cemetery. She knew its paths and hidey-holes like she knew the lines on her palm. When the cicadas clamored deep in the woods of Shiner's Ridge and the sky was russet red and tired, Loey stood and swiped at the back of her jeans.

The animals needed to be fed, and so did she, according to the low growl in her stomach. With a farewell glance at her grandparents, she limped back up the path toward the center of the cemetery.

On impulse, she walked by the oldest graves and the poplar where she'd found Briggs. Here, the lilting headstones were slabs of unpolished rock, the words barely legible. Gran had taught her how to keep the lettering from wearing by using soft bristle brushes to clean out the crevices. But looking at the old stones now, Loey resolved to come back down and polish them up.

As she walked on, the wind shifted and brought the faintest chiming of a bell. The sound came whisper-like on the wind, more like a thing to be felt than heard. She stuttered to a stop, frozen. Her eyes stretched wide.

The chiming came again from a few feet away.

Near a simple headstone, a brass bell trilled in the breeze, its song like soft notes of laughter.

Loey's feet carried her to the grave of their own accord. She crouched in front of the chipped headstone and blew at the rock to clear away the dust.

Jeronimo James
1927-1956

She pressed her hand against the rock as if to feel for a heartbeat.

Hadn't he said he had family in Righteous? That Jeronimo was a family name? Even without brushing off the surrounding graves, she saw many of them contained the same last name. Frederick, Nelson, Ruth Ann, Beulah, and Bartholomew all neighbored Jeronimo's headstone.

The wind gusted again, the strongest of the evening so far. Across the oldest graves, countless bells pealed.

Loey jerked to her feet, and her arms went numb with fear. Her vision slanted, and between one blink and the next, the cemetery was filled with thousands of lights, strung out in fine, flickering lines. Then they were gone, and her head was spinning with a pressing headache.

"The dead are talking," her grandmother would have said. *"Are you listening?"*

CHAPTER 7

PASTOR BRIGGS'S FUNERAL BROUGHT OUT the entire town. When the preacher of the only Baptist church around these parts died, his funeral became an all-day event.

It started that Friday morning at the coffee shop. Coffee was on the house, as Gran would have wanted, and Dale had prepared all her best pastries, breakfast sandwiches, and donuts. The bell above the door didn't sit still, its chime becoming the day's mourning song. By lunch, the townspeople had moved to the rectory, where more food was laid out in Pastor Briggs's former home. Everyone helped pack up his belongings, which would be distributed to the local Goodwill as he had no family. By afternoon, the townspeople had made their way across the field to the church, which Loey had decorated with heaps of flowers as if Guilt itself had laid out every bud, bloom, and steam. Thankfully, the windows had been replaced in time for the service. After the service, Briggs would be laid to rest near the heart of the cemetery and the tree in which Loey had found him.

She kept that to herself.

Outside the church, everyone gathered in clumps as the last details of the funeral were ironed out inside. A visiting preacher from Memphis had come in to officiate, even though word had spread about a certain stranger's background in theology.

"It's weird, right?" Loey whispered.

She cut her eyes to Jeronimo's form across the churchyard. He stood beneath the shade tree, talking to Sheriff Jinks and Mayor Goody. Today, his ash-blond hair softened his ruggedness. He'd swept it back in a disheveled way that even had the old biddies stealing peeks. He wore a simple white shirt tucked into black slacks sculpted for his backside.

"I think it's actually really sweet," Dale said.

"Killers like to return to the scene of the crime. It gets them off."

Dale smoothed the swishing swell of her dark purple skirt that made her pale skin look moonlit even though the late afternoon sun cast slants of sunbeams across the churchyard. "First of all, you've watched too much *Criminal Minds*. Secondly, if we're talking about getting off—"

"We're not," Loey begged.

"—then we need to speak about those puppy-dog looks Matt Everton keeps giving you. Like, what did your vagina *do* to him?"

"Don't look at him. He'll know we're talking about him."

"What are you two whispering about now?" Cross Rose, Dale's brother and Righteous's most eligible ineligible bachelor, joined Loey and Dale at the edge of the yard. He wore a gray suit that set off his blue eyes, his finely chiseled face gleaming from a fresh shave. They were less than a year apart in age—Dale, the older sister, took protecting Cross to an entirely new level—but they acted more like twins.

"Loey thinks that tall drink of water over there talking with Burl and the mayor killed Briggs." Dale didn't even try to hide her chin lift in Jeronimo's direction.

Loey hushed her before Ms. Ida May overheard.

Ms. Ida May was the head of the old biddies—the women who were widowed, never married, or married to men who'd rather spend their days fishing and their nights in a recliner. They flocked as one, chattering like crows on a telephone line. They knew everything happening in Righteous, often before it happened, and they bore the burden of being the town's gossip-harbingers like Sisyphus with his rock. They spoke highly of themselves and their duty to keep Righteous righteous to anyone who would listen and especially to those, like Dale, who wouldn't.

Cross followed Dale's gaze to Jeronimo. His mouth popped as his jaw dropped. "Holy *shit*."

"It's creepy he's here. Does no one else see that? He's not even from Righteous."

"Oh please." Dale fanned herself with the pamphlet for Pastor Briggs's services. As if on instinct, Cross started fanning her with his thin fold of paper too. "Let it go, Loey Grace. You'll give yourself wrinkles."

"Isn't that dress too short for a funeral, Dale?" a shrill voice asked from behind Loey.

They all faced the fire with forced smiles.

"I like to catch a breeze, Ms. Ida May," Dale said, simpering.

Loey spoke quickly before Dale could get in a fight with an elderly lady. "Afternoon, Ms. Ida May. You look awfully nice today."

"Oh, Loey, dear," Ms. Ida May said, her attention swinging away from Dale to land on Loey. Instantly her eyes fell to the silver ring hooked around Loey's nostril. She tisked. "Such a shame you did that. You'll have a hole in your nose forever now. And what would Ellery say? She'd be so disappointed you ruined your God-given body."

Loey's cheeks hurt from the weight of her smile. Her God-given body had been ruined a long time ago, even before the accident that had scarred her. It had been ruined in a classroom, after school, by a man with no soul.

As for Gran's approval, she wouldn't have minded, not after she'd prayed about it for a few weeks. But she wasn't here, and Loey figured God had far bigger troubles to fret over than her nose ring and tattoos.

"Your casseroles have been a real lifesaver," she said instead of engaging in a hopeless debate with an elderly woman who would die by her notions of a proper Southern woman.

Ms. Ida May took Loey's hand and squeezed hard. For a brief second, her rheumy eyes swam with tears. "Ellery was the finest woman I knew. You let me know if you need anything, you hear? You've been looking thin since their passing."

That was the crux of Righteous: its people could damn you in one sentence and redeem you the next. They were the greatest people Loey knew, but they were also the worst. And she could never love them any less.

Loey gently squeezed the old woman's hand in return. "I will. Thank you."

"Now," Ms. Ida May said, dropping Loey's hand, "where's this young preacher man I keep hearing so much about?"

Loey tried not to grimace. "I don't think he's actually a preacher—"

"Pish-posh." Ms. Ida May swayed. Her teeth had yellowed with age, much like the rest of her. "Burl! Burl Jinks! Bring that fine man over here to talk to me."

Beneath the willow tree, the sheriff glanced up from his conversation with Jeronimo and Mayor Goody. Both men looked first to Ms. Ida May then to the young people standing at her side. Mayor Goody gave her goodbyes to them with a nod before moving away, lest Ms. Ida May call for her as well. Ensnared, Jeronimo and Burl walked over.

"What was that, ma'am?" Burl asked politely. Even at a

funeral, he wore his uniform to remind folks who they were voting for in September.

"I was mentioning to these fine young people and Dale that I heard our visitor was a preacher."

"Thank you, ma'am," Jeronimo drawled, dipping his chin, "but I haven't spent much time preaching. I normally have my nose in a book."

"What a waste, if you ask me, but those books are mighty lucky."

Loey fought back an eye roll.

"Jeronimo," Dale said, resting her hand on his arm, "I'd like you to meet my brother, Cross Rose."

"Good to meet you, Jeronimo." Cross shook Jeronimo's hand, his grip tight enough to grind bones. Why men needed to test each other in such ways had always baffled Loey.

Jeronimo's lips gave the impression of a smile toward the siblings. "Those are some interesting names. Old family ones?"

Dale hooked her arm through Cross's and curtsied prettily. "Oh, you know, Jesus and NASCAR."

Jeronimo's face was as empty as a smokehouse in June. "I'm afraid I'm not familiar with…" He paused and his eyes slid to Loey. "NASCAR."

Dale spluttered, Cross barked out a laugh, and Burl blustered in shock. But Jeronimo stared at Loey as if she had the answers rather than the crowd gathered around him.

"They don't have NASCAR in Savannah?" Loey challenged, refusing to bow beneath his unrelenting focus.

His lips angled out farther, nearing a smile. "I find excitement in other ways."

Loey's nose tingled as it often did when she was turned on. She fought the urge to rub it because Dale was smirking at her with a look in her eyes that said she knew exactly what was happening.

"It might be macabre timing," Ms. Ida May stage-whispered, leaning in closer to Jeronimo, her eyes cutting toward the church, "but we could use a preacher. Poor Mr. Briggs. Bless his soul."

"I wouldn't want to presume—"

"Now, now, we would love to hear you preach one Sunday. Maybe this Sunday?" Jeronimo opened his mouth to respond, but Ms. Ida May wasn't finished. "I don't see why you couldn't stay in the rectory either, seeing as you're here to study the cemetery. No use in a good house sittin' empty."

"That would be convenient," Jeronimo said with that put-on drawl of his.

"It's what poor Pastor Briggs's would've wanted." Ms. Ida May pressed a thick-fingered hand to her bosom. "Right, Loey Grace?"

Everyone's gaze swung to her, even Jeronimo's. He hadn't fought much to explain his purpose in town. In fact, he'd resisted Ms. Ida May's suggestion so weakly Loey wondered if he wasn't searching for a way into town life. What better way than as the new preacher?

Through clenched teeth, Loey said, "I think it's a great idea. Next Sunday sounds fine. Totally fine."

"It would be an honor." Jeronimo dipped his chin. All he needed was a hat to tip.

The bell gonged in the church steeple. Its trills trickled through the yard and down Devil's Maw into town, spilling across the valley like sunlight. Loey had always loved the sound, but as she followed the other mourners into the church to lay Pastor Briggs to rest, it reminded her of the cemetery's much tinier bells tolling last night, and her skin tightened around her bones.

Once settled in the pew beside Dale, who sat beside Travis and Burl, she glanced over her shoulder. Mr. and Mrs. Rose sat behind her, their shoulders untouching, the ice between them enough to make Cross's expression a permanent grimace. He nodded at Loey. Behind the Roses, the rest of the town was all in place in their typical pews. Toward the back, her eyes found Jeronimo against the wall since all the pews in the small church were full. He brought two fingers to his forehead in a subtle salute, as if they were going off to war together.

Loey doubted they were fighting on the same side.

CHAPTER 8

ATER THAT EVENING, LOEY CARRIED her sandals up her porch, her feet aching from the day and her knee swelling beneath the hem of her simple black dress. Dewey greeted her at the door with a slobber and a whack of his tail when she didn't follow him fast enough to dump kibble into his bowl. She put out food for Boltz, wherever he was. At the back door, she slipped her feet into her boots to check on the barn animals.

She followed the trail down to the barn, the front light buzzing above the open doors. Mosquitoes hummed in the night air, and bats swooped low, their silhouettes darting across the ground.

Out of habit, she glanced down the hill toward the church and the cemetery. The funeral for Pastor Briggs had dredged up the memories of laying her grandparents to rest only a few months prior. The day seemed to never end, and it had worn her down to a thin ribbon of raw nerves—

Loey froze on the path.

A beam of light bounced between the headstones. She waited for the light to disappear, indicating another headache was underway, but the concentrated beam kept swinging back and forth through the trees and foliage in the cemetery.

Someone was down there with a flashlight, and the hour was too late for them to be up to anything good. It had to be Jeronimo, returning to the crime scene, like she'd thought. She'd tried to tell Burl after the funeral, but he'd brushed her off again.

Whirling around, she raced back into the house, and like any good Southern woman worth her salt, she grabbed her shotgun, whistled for her dog, and took off back outside.

There wasn't any time to dig her phone out of the lint-covered bottom of her purse. Besides, by the time Burl pried himself out of his recliner, where he was no doubt installed and intoxicated, Jeronimo would be long gone.

Without wasting another second, she rushed down the back hill, not yet worried about concealing the sounds of her footsteps as the tall grass hissed against her bare legs, her dress tangling behind her. If she caught the real killer, she could make things right. Or as right as they could be, considering it was her fault Briggs was dead. But Jeronimo wouldn't get away with skewering anyone else.

Part of her questioned how Jeronimo could have been around town during Leigh's murder all those years ago, but she shoved the niggling thought aside and ran faster, the weight of her guilt propelling her down the hill, away from her house, and toward the church and cemetery.

The hem of her dress snagged and ripped, but she sprinted toward the swinging flashlight beam. Dewey thundered beside her, a growl low in his throat, his massive form eating up the ground.

The killer wasn't getting away. Not this time. Not again.

At the cemetery's gate, she sat her shotgun inside the fence, propped against the wisteria vines, and eased herself through. The metal screeched on its hinges. She flinched but kept moving. Grabbing her shotgun, she started down the brick path, Dewey leading the way, his hackles raised, his head low in challenge.

They wound toward the center of the cemetery where Loey had been only a couple of hours before. Dewey slowed. She raised her gun and looked around.

The shadows shifted. The moonlight filtered through the clouds, and the shadows became solid objects. Gravestones. Plastic flowers trapped in their plastic vases. The juniper trees standing sentinel in the windless night. And through them all, the shape of a person moved on silent feet. They were tall and broad-shouldered with tapered hips.

The trespasser could have been any man, but Loey instantly knew him by that rolling hip swagger.

Even in the dead of night, alone in a graveyard, he walked like he had something to prove to every pair of ovaries within a twenty-mile radius. She'd known that man was trouble from the very beginning.

Loey hid herself and Dewey behind an oak tree far enough away to watch as he walked beneath a hemlock and into the moonlight. Wrinkles fanned out from his eyes as he squinted at the grave he'd stopped beside. From its fresh mound of dirt, Loey knew it belonged to Pastor Briggs.

He crouched. His hand descended onto the pile of dirt, fingers splayed across the earth. The headstone hadn't been brought in, but a simple wooden cross marked Briggs's resting place. Dangling from the cross was a delicate brass bell, to which a small string was attached. The end of it, Loey knew, would be tied around Pastor Briggs's still finger.

Jeronimo was careful not to disturb the thick lines of salt forming two concentric circles around the grave. Loey had poured them herself for Pastor Briggs, seeing as he had no other family.

Two, those of Righteous said, *just in case the first should fail.*

He tapped the brass bell suspended above the grave, making it chime out.

Dewey twitched, and she grabbed his collar to keep him from bounding into the light. After a quiet beat, Jeronimo continued through the graveyard like he knew every misaligned brick, offshoot path, and shortcut, which he took straight to the church's back door.

She followed, hoping to catch him in the act of something criminal, but flooring her completely, he bent over and stuck his hand into the iron shoehorn to pull out the church's spare key. He unlocked the door and strolled right in as if he owned the place.

Loey waited for a few short breaths before following him inside. Dewey padded softly behind her.

Jeronimo set his flashlight aside. The moonlight streamed in through the new windows, casting enough light for Loey to see him run his hand along the old wooden pulpit carved in the shape of a cross. It had been in this church since Knox Keene had hewn it from a chestnut tree's massive trunk. He'd built this building in the early 1900s and placed that pulpit right at the front, and she couldn't stand to watch Jeronimo touch it like he understood the miracle of its existence in this town founded on the profits of Townsend Rose's tree-logging empire.

She didn't have time to wait. She had to do something before he wiggled his way out of this.

"Put your hands up where I can see 'em."

Jeronimo didn't jump or flinch in surprise. He stood still, his back mostly to her, his palm resting on the pulpit. Then he slowly faced her, his hands rising into the air. The moonlight through the windows played a strange trick, making his face look younger. His hair was in a disheveled state, and his day's growth of beard took a decade off his tanned face. His dark eyes shimmered.

"Loey," he said, accent thick on her name as if he knew all its curving vowels intimately. "Why am I not surprised?"

"Returning to the crime scene, I take it?"

"Didn't think it was a crime scene no more. You caught me doing some research." He gave that imperceptible shrug again as if he couldn't bring himself to put too much effort into the motion. "Since I'm moving into the rectory, I didn't think looking around would do no harm."

Loey kept her gun steady on her target like Pap had taught her. "Tell me what you're really doing down here. Are you the killer? Did you murder Briggs? Where were you in 2011? What does the name Leigh Parker mean to you?"

"I have no clue what you're talking about." His voice was flat and dry, but she got the impression that, on the inside, he was smiling at her. Laughing at her.

"I'm calling the cops," she bluffed.

"You're not doing that."

"Why not?"

"I can give you something you want."

Loey snorted. "I doubt I want anything you've got."

"You sure about that? What if I said the preacher's death wasn't the first murder of this kind in this town?"

"That could just be a lucky guess."

"But I couldn't guess the symbol burned into his chest, could I?"

Her palms sweated against the stock of the gun. At her feet, Dewey whined. "That seems like something only the killer would know."

"Or someone who was sent here to bring the killer to justice."

Her heart tried to beat out of her chest, and she could barely focus over the ringing in her ears. "Who sent you?"

His eyes glinted in the moonlight. He didn't answer.

"Tell me or I'm calling Burl right now."

She figured he was bluffing to stall while he figured out a

way to silence her. But she wasn't prepared for the next words out of his mouth.

"Your grandparents."

She jerked the gun higher, aiming for his face, though the tip of the gun shook from her head to toe trembling. "You're a dirty liar. Don't you talk about them."

"They died like Briggs died, at the hand of the same killer." He paused, an almost smile on his face. "They were murdered."

She pumped the shotgun. "Shut up!"

"I can prove it."

"How?" she growled. Dewey pressed against her legs.

"I have a letter in my pocket." With his hands still raised, he pointed to his shirt pocket, where the thick outline of folded paper made a square against the material. "I'm going to reach for it, okay?"

It couldn't be a gun, so she nodded, her tongue too thick to speak.

Moving slowly, as if for her mental benefit and not because she held a shotgun, he pulled out the paper.

"Put it on the ground and slide it over. Don't move."

"I have to move to put it on the ground, Loey Grace."

"Fine," she snapped, feeling sick and unsteady. Was it her imagination, or did she smell Estée Lauder perfume? "Move real slow."

He crouched. The piece of paper slid cleanly across the church's wooden planks to her feet. Keeping the gun leveled despite her trembling hands, she dipped down and grabbed the page.

"Don't move," she told Jeronimo again.

He'd lowered his hands, but he waited, unmoving, as she unfolded the page.

The motion stirred up the stationery's scent. Estée Lauder, familiar as the ache in Loey's chest. Her eyes flooded with tears. They made it hard to see the stark black ink on the page, but she'd recognize that handwriting anywhere. It was slashing and harried, as if scrawled in a rush, but it was Gran's through and through.

She read.

Mr. James,

I pray this finds you quick. Our plan to seal the Seam has failed. Something much stronger than Bartholomew is ripping tatters all over. We believe it's trying to tear its way free. It must be stopped before the Seam is torn wide open and all its shadows spill into our town. The Tenders can't handle this on our own. It's just Harlan and me left. We need you more than ever.

Please. Come quick.

Ellery Keene

Loey read it through twice. She'd started on the third pass when Jeronimo said, "They sent me. The letter is proof."

She lifted her gaze. He was so still he couldn't be real. The page rustled in her hand, and tears dripped from her chin. Dewey whined again, her sudden change of emotion confusing him.

"This can't be real."

Jeronimo groaned and raked a hand through his hair. "Come on. It's her handwriting. Hell, that perfume has been following me around since I opened the damn letter. You know it's hers."

The nose of the shotgun had lowered as she'd read, but she didn't have the strength to raise it and hold on to the letter at the same time. He was right about the letter being undeniably Gran's, but she knew none of the words it contained.

"What's the Seam? Or Tenders? Who is Bartholomew?"

Her voice quaked like her hand trembled. Coldness spread out from her bones.

Outside, the wind kicked up. Tiny peals of laughter, like hundreds of bells trilling in time, slipped through the cracks in the church's wooden walls. She could have sworn lights were dancing in time to the bells out there between the graves.

"We're gonna have to do this the hard way, ain't we?"

Loey looked away from the nearest window to see that Jeronimo had closed the distance between them by half, and she hadn't seen him move.

She jerked the gun upright, crumpling the letter against the barrel. "Don't move!"

He cocked his head, animal-like, his eyes as black as the deepest shadows Loey had ever seen. She stumbled back a step. Dewey growled.

"Jeronimo," she whispered, wavering in her warning. "Don't make me shoot you."

"Too late."

He moved viper quick toward her, his dark eyes shifting to something darker, something that belonged to the night. Dewey barked in alarm.

She pulled the trigger.

CHAPTER 9

THE SHOTGUN RECOILED, AND SHE stumbled back into a pew. Dewey's barking and the shotgun's blast left her ears ringing.

It was a shock to shoot and for the decision to have been so quick and easy. For a split second, she was ashamed of herself. Killing a man should have been harder. She would have to pray about that.

But Jeronimo didn't fall.

He looked down at the hole blooming in his stomach, a dark pit with no blood or sinew or pink flesh, all the things she had expected a shotgun blast to produce.

He brought his focus back to her. "Do you believe me now?"

She'd *shot* him. Pulled the trigger. Felt the kick. The knowing of taking a life. She'd seen that lead tear into him and the jolt of his hard body taking the impact.

Yet he tugged at the tattered edges of his shirt and poked his fingers into the cavern of his belly, sticking most of his hand into the buckshot hole. She'd shot him from a close enough range that the pellets hadn't spread. The shot had been concentrated in one spot, creating one gaping hole.

He should have been dead.

He should, at the very least, have been bleeding.

"Wh-what…" Her teeth chattered too hard for her to finish the sentence.

A loud *thunk* shook the planks at her feet. She'd dropped her shotgun. Dewey's sagging jowls peeled back over his teeth, and he never took his eyes off Jeronimo.

"What am I?" Jeronimo finished for her. His voice reached her as if from down a tunnel. "I can't answer that. Not because I'm lying, but because I don't know."

"Wh—"

"Why am I not dead? I wish I could say it's because you're a lousy shot, but you're right, this shoulda killed me."

Loey staggered around the pew to retreat a couple steps. Dewey kept close, keeping his body between her and Jeronimo. A strange keening noise came from her mouth. She might have been going into shock.

Jeronimo stalked after her and bent to pick up her gun. He unloaded it, slinging two shells out of the chamber, and tossed it aside. It hit a pew then fell onto the floor. Dewey barked at the racket.

"Hush up," Jeronimo growled back at the dog.

Dewey quieted, but he didn't back away. His body twitched with rage.

"You… you…"

"Can't die." His brow furrowed as he considered his next words. "Seeing as I don't have a soul."

That was it. Loey whirled around, crashed into a pew, and tore off down the aisle. Dewey raced past her with a sharp bark to lead the way.

She'd reached the church doors when Jeronimo called out, "I guess you don't want to bring their killer to justice."

The words were a trap. She prided herself on being smart, but still, she glanced back. He'd retreated back to the front of the church and sank onto the step before the pulpit. He'd leaned back, his hand on his belly and his head tipped down, his eyes cast into the shadows of his shaggy hair.

He looked as if he'd fallen straight from Heaven. It was probably blasphemy for him to recline against the pulpit like that.

"Are you an angel?"

Her question surprised him. He snorted out a laugh, but the noise cost him. Grimacing, he grabbed his belly. "Hard to be an angel when you've lost your soul, honey."

"Don't call me honey," Loey snapped, and her tone or the way she rounded on him must have surprised him more than her asking if he was an angel, because he sat up straighter and regarded her with somber eyes.

Dewey sounded off another bark from outside the church, as if telling her this was a bad idea, to hurry up and run away. But she ignored him, ignored reason. Unlike her gun, she hadn't dropped Gran's letter. Its buttery soft page felt creamy against her palm.

She held it up. "How did you get this?"

"Your generation can't have forgotten how the mail works?"

"Stop dancing around the truth. Tell me."

"Your grandparents are—were—Tenders, as most Keenes from these parts were, but the tatters in the Seam are being ripped too large. They needed my help."

The word *Tenders* recalled her grandparents' headstone and all the other stones around it. *Tenders in this life and beyond.* A family tradition, those words.

"What are Tenders?"

"They keep the world's threads bound tight to separate this world from various pocket worlds. Tenders all over the world mind their Seams and patch up any tatters. If a rip gets too big, things can slip across the Seam."

"And the Seam?"

He lifted a shoulder. A shrug, maybe, but with Jeronimo,

she couldn't tell. "It's what the current generation calls it, but it's nothing more than a barrier. We have one right here in Righteous separating the town from a small pocket world."

"What's in the pocket world?" The questions came out of her mouth, but her voice didn't sound like her own. She felt outside her body, out in the cemetery with the Keenes' headstones and the tolling bells and the firefly lights.

Jeronimo glanced at the church windows as if he could feel beyond the walls too. He stared outside for a long moment. "I don't know. Never seen the other side."

"There's a headstone in the cemetery with your name on it."

He didn't blink.

A man would have blinked.

"What is in the ground beneath that headstone?"

When he didn't answer, she stared at the hole in his belly. Finally, she dragged her gaze back to his face and whispered, "This is crazy."

The corner of his mouth hooked into the most crooked of crooked smiles, but it wasn't mischievous or mocking. It matched the dark sadness in his eyes. "Things would be much easier if I were the murderer you so desperately needed me to be, wouldn't they?"

She wanted to argue she wasn't desperate, but she felt too unhinged to press the point of her sanity. "My grandparents died in a car accident."

He shook his head. "They didn't."

He was lying, but why? She was still standing here, but why?

"I'm calling the cops. I'm going. Now."

"You're not calling those cops, because you're going to help me bring the killer to justice."

"Why would I help you?" She wished her voice didn't sound so small.

"You're the last Keene," he said as if it were the simplest

thing in the world. "You have to Tend the Seam after I take care of my... after I take care of what's ripping holes from the other side. You're the only one left."

The only one left. She still couldn't think about her grandparents' deaths, not without feeling as if the ground was dropping out from underneath her. But wasn't that loss? Hadn't she learned that lesson? But now was not the time to fall apart. She could do that later, behind closed doors. And Gran had taught her better than to crumble with fear but to stand tall in the face of it. The thought gave her much needed strength.

"How do I know you're not ripping these holes?"

"I guess you'll have to trust me. But barring that, trust your grandmother. She sent for me. Why would she do that if I was the one ripping holes in her precious Seam? I'm the only one who can stop my... stop the thing in there."

Her eyes narrowed. "That's the second time you've stumbled over that. Who's in there?"

"He's the one who's been killing all these people," he said as if he'd spoken the words countless times. "Your grandparents. Briggs. Likely countless others."

Her mind flashed to Leigh and the symbol, to Briggs and the tree and the message.

"Who is he?"

Jeronimo slouched as if suddenly drained. "My brother, Bartholomew."

"My grandparents sent for you to kill your brother?"

"No, they sent for me to finish the job. I tried to kill him in '56."

She thought of his headstone, the one that said he'd died in 1956.

Moonlight fell over Jeronimo, framing him in a silver glow. Again, she wondered if he wasn't an angel. But hearing him say those impossible things, she wondered if he wasn't the Devil instead. A devil wouldn't have a soul.

She met his eyes with trepidation. She wanted to want to look away. She didn't.

"Tell me."

CHAPTER 10

APRIL 7, 1956

ERONIMO HAD ALWAYS BEEN HARD on his brother Bartholomew. Too hard, probably, but their Paw had fallen onto a blade in one of Townsend Rose's mills when the boys were little, and no one was around to keep them straight. Momma was always working herself to the bone, and when she wasn't on her feet or at the mill, she was dead asleep. Barty had been too young when Paw died and didn't understand why Momma wasn't around much. So Barty grew into a man with a chip on his shoulder, thinking no one loved him and no one cared, and he probably hated Jeronimo for knowing Momma before she was skin and bones and used-up breath.

Barty looked for Momma's love in whichever woman was loose enough to have him, in Righteous or the town over or the one over from that. He didn't care what valley or mountain he had to climb for the promise of pussy on the other side.

Jeronimo didn't mind his brother's endless search, so long as it didn't interfere with the family business.

They had a deal. Jeronimo made the shine up the ridge and Barty ran it from the back of Paw's old pickup, which Barty had torn apart and put back together with piecemeal parts he'd salvaged from all over. 'Neath that old rusted hood was a mean machine that could spr⋯ wings and fly down

And it about needed to, as business took right off when Blackmore Baptist got it in their heads that the James brothers' shine was holy water that allowed them to commune with the holy spirit and caused miraculous healings. After that, there wasn't enough time in the day to take their money. It was a good time to be a James. Even Momma started wearing the new dresses Barty bought for her.

No one could compete with the brothers' shine. They'd cornered the market, and if a man wanted to make any coin, he had to ship his shine out to the Carolinas' borders, and nobody was willing to risk that. One by one, those other late-night still fires on Shiner's Ridge went out.

Shiner's Ridge belonged to the brothers. Whispered tales of booby traps and spirits up in the hills kept out smarter men. Only fools ventured up the ridge to steal the secret of the brothers' shine. They never came back down.

Then Frankie Rose roared through town in her daddy's 1940 Ford Coupe and blew a cloud of dust straight into ol' Barty's heart. At the time, they didn't know she was one of Townsend Rose's younguns. Jeronimo had pegged her as a pennied-up honey with a wild streak.

God bless him, but when it came to Frankie Rose in those early days, he didn't get much right.

After she hooked up with Barty, they split the runs, and then Frankie got better at racing the roads than Barty. She'd hoot and holler around those tight mountain switchbacks, ridin' that clutch and shifting like the Devil himself were giving chase. The more she drank of the liquid thunder, the faster she drove. Faster than the brothers deserved.

She became the best runner south of the Virginias. She'd take that old Ford with jars filled to the till and rattle her way to every barn, whorehouse, and church paying for the brothers' salvation. She needn't worry about no revenuers neither. Because when Frankie smiled, she could get away with murder.

And get away with murder she did. She and Barty spent a lot of time with shovels up on Shiner's Ridge.

Maybe she liked Bartholomew's justice or maybe she liked the smell of blood like Barty did or maybe she was scared. Maybe it was all of them. But she got her hands bloody same as Barty. They were thick as thieves, bound by blood and secrets.

Jeronimo let them have their fun. He had his own trouble to deal with. His business had drawn the eye of every lawman in the South, and one particular revenuer from West Virginia was poking around the streets of Righteous, hell-bent on bolstering his career with the arrest of a great James brother. With his arrival, Jeronimo had taken to living on Shiner's Ridge, hiding out in the woods with a bullet for any wayward man who had it in his head to bring down the kingpin.

It was a hard time for Jeronimo up in those woods. The loneliness rooted in deep with the paranoia in his head. Voices traveled on the wind and faces peered out from between the trees. He'd convinced himself that something evil lived on the ridge with him, and when he drank his shine, he saw that evil in the shadows and in the water's reflection staring back at him. It talked to him, and he liked none of what it said.

That darkness was rutted so deep in his heart that it took him a while to notice Barty and Frankie hadn't been around to pick up the deposits of shine he'd left in their squirrel holes scattered around the ridge. By the number of jars, they hadn't been around in days.

Jeronimo didn't need to venture far to find out why his brother hadn't picked up the jars. From up on the northwestern face of the ridge, he made his way down to the spring that fed Little Cricket Creek. It was those creek waters that gave his shine its magical properties, and he guarded that water like it was his own lifeblood running over the smooth river rocks.

But it wasn't his blood he found in the creek that day.

It was Frankie.

She'd been made to suffer on purpose, bled until not a drop was left in her. Her mouth was stretched wide in a silent scream, and her hazel eyes were foggy with bloat. Her contorted body bobbed in the water, her dress snagged on a root.

Seeing her like that—seeing any woman like that—wasn't right. Wasn't nothing right about it.

Jeronimo was a good deal crazy by that point, thanks to the woods and the shine. Standing over Frankie's body, he was madder than he'd ever been. He trembled with a dark rage that woulda scared the evilest of men.

Jeronimo knew who'd killed her too.

How could Barty kill Frankie when she'd smiled at him like he hung the damn moon? He'd had to hate her to kill her like that.

If Barty had been there right then, right beside Jeronimo, he'd have killed him with his hands. Slow, too, so he'd suffer like he'd made Frankie suffer.

Jeronimo shimmied down that bloody creek at a run that was as silent as it was wild. He could move through those woods like a vapor, which was how he snuck up on Barty at their main moonshine still, right as the storm clouds blustered up over the ridge.

As thunder rattled the mountains, Jeronimo drew his hunting knife from the sheath on his belt.

Barty turned at the sound of metal whisper-kissing leather.

Lightning sparked overhead. The air smelled of fire. Thunder crashed like God's fist against the ground. Then the rain came down in sheets, pelting the trees like buckshot.

Storms on Shiner's Ridge weren't nothin' to trifle with.

Men with good sense woulda taken to lower ground, far from water and the giant metal moonshine still that sat in the clearing between the trees.

But the brothers stared each other down, Jeronimo's knife held between them.

"You found her too, then," Barty shouted above the storm. Rain ran in rivers down his face. He looked thin and pale. His eyes were wide with terror.

Barty took Jeronimo's silence as confirmation.

"Oh God." He wrapped his arm around his middle and sagged to his knees. "Oh God. She's really gone? Sh-she tried to tell me… she tried to stop… Oh God." He hiccupped and choked on his words. His shoulders shook beneath the weight of his sins.

"I didn't listen," he continued. "I couldn't stop, and she tried to stop me. Told me I wasn't doin' it for the right reasons no more. I tried, JJ. God, I fuckin' tried, ya know? I knew I shouldn'ta involved her. But the blood. It… it felt so good when it sprayed on me." His muscles twitched hard enough to make his hands jerk. He fell silent.

"You went too far, Barty," Jeronimo said between cracks of thunder. He smelled fire somewhere up the ridge. He'd be lucky if all his stills weren't burned out in the morning.

Barty nodded once. His shoulders drooped.

"It shouldn'ta been her."

Barty nodded again at his brother's words.

Jeronimo walked up to his brother and put the knife to his throat. He wanted to make him suffer like Frankie had suffered, but when it came time to make the choice, he couldn't.

Barty was a killer and the worst of men, but he was still Jeronimo's brother. Pressing the sharp metal edge against his throat, he could only picture Barty on Momma's hip, fat fists tangled in her hair as she sang to him.

Barty trembled, but he held his head back, exposing his neck like a brave man.

"I won't stop if you don't stop me." His throat bobbed as he spoke. The knife broke the skin and drew the first drop of blood. "Thank you, brother."

Crimson dripped down his throat from the knick. Lightning struck right beside them, splitting an old oak clean in half. The tree toppled with a great groan from deep in the earth. It fell on top of the still, and the metal screamed beneath the weight in time to the thunder.

The storm couldn't get no closer. Perhaps Jeronimo would die up here tonight too. He wouldn't mind. He thought he heard Barty say something about lawmen, but more thunder cast out his words, and Jeronimo wasn't in no mood to listen anyway.

"I'm sorry, Barty."

He drew the knife across his brother's throat, but the world tore apart before he could finish the cut.

Lightning struck the still. The still, filled with shine, exploded.

White light burst across Jeronimo's vision. Heat beat down on him, and he was in the air, falling ass over hat. He hit something hard, knocking the wind out of him, and then lay still.

When the ringing in his ears cleared and he could make some sense of what was happening, he heard Barty gurgling, drowning in his own blood and suffering, even though Jeronimo had intended to make his death fast.

"JJ?" Barty hacked out, calling for his brother like he was a kid again.

An animal screamed nearby. *Panther*, Jeronimo thought as light edged into his vision. Nothing else could scream like that, and he knew better than most that big cats stalked these woods.

He blinked into a light that illuminated the ripped-open world.

The trees had been uprooted or bent clean in half. The still was on fire, burning blue flames and giving off a heat Jeronimo had never known. There, his little brother burned, his entire body engulfed in flames and beyond recognition. He screamed and burned and screamed some more. His silhouette lurched against the too-bright flames.

"JJ!" His voice sounded right beside Jeronimo's ear, but it must have been God speaking because Barty was still screaming as he burned in the fire.

Jeronimo turned away from the flames toward the sound of his brother's voice and saw God standing in a light far different from the fire's light. This light flickered and flashed, pure and soft. From the other side of it, God called Jeronimo home with his brother's voice.

But Jeronimo had never believed in God. Never wanted to be like those good Baptists who got shine-drunk on Sundays and called it worship.

"JJ!"

The feeling came back to Jeronimo's body, and he sat up, but he did not reach for God's hand.

The light ballooned out then contracted until it was a single point that seared into Jeronimo's vision. He shielded his eyes.

When the world fell silent again, he dropped his hand. The rain had stopped, and the storm had moved down toward Righteous, the thunder muffled. Beside him, the creek burbled. Higher up the ridge, an owl hooted.

Only hunks of bent metal, shards of bark, and hanks of trees marked where the still had stood. His brother was gone. He hadn't even left a charred outline on the ground.

The stars came out overhead, and the world went on like nothing had happened.

Jeronimo got to his feet. His heart stuttered through each labored beat. His shirt caught on something. When he twisted around, he saw a jagged slit of metal sticking straight through his side. Its shining, clean tip protruded from his back.

He wrapped his hand around the curled edge and yanked it free from him as if he were tugging a rusted nail from a board. The metal released with a wet suck.

Jeronimo waited for the pain to hit him, and when it didn't, he chalked it up to shock. A wound like that, through his gut and insides, would kill him quick. While he still could, he looked around for any sign of his brother.

His knife lay near the creek bed, blood gleaming on its blade.

Sulfur choked the air right up.

Jeronimo walked, without stumbling, to the still. There he saw a line. Not a physical line on the ground, but a line between the destruction of the still's explosion—the mangled trees and sulfur-tainted air—and across the creek, where the trees stood tall, their leaves dripping rainwater. It was as if a wall had protected that side from the blast.

"JJ." The whisper came from that pristine side. "JJ."

Jeronimo reeled back and fell to the ground. He scrambled away from the line. Piss spread across the front of his pants. He trembled as he stared, waiting for his dead brother to appear out of thin air.

When nothing happened, he looked down at where the metal had torn into him. His shirt hung in tatters, but no blood had spoiled its threads. His heart pounded, but not from pain. Though he might be dead already, he felt alive enough.

He lifted his shirt's tail and stared down at his belly. The wound was already closing. No blood. No guts. That injury should have killed him, but his flesh hadn't even puckered with annoyance.

He was alive, and his brother was gone.

"JJ," came that whisper from the other side again.

He scrambled to his feet and tore off down the ridge as his brother called his name into the haunted winds of Shiner's Ridge.

CHAPTER 11

JERONIMO HAD BARELY FINISHED TELLING Loey his story when the ground shook.

The rumble vibrated deep in her bones. Dust fluttered down from the ceiling, and the pews wobbled across the floor. Dewey's toes scrambled across the floor for purchase. She grabbed onto the nearest pew, her wide eyes on Jeronimo, reclined against the pulpit as if he'd expected the ground to shake beneath him. A shadow rolled from his nostril. He swiped at it, smearing blood across his jaw.

The earthquake only lasted ten seconds, but it felt like forever. All the while, his nose continued to bleed. He hadn't bled from the gunshot wound, but an earthquake had given him a nosebleed?

As the church settled, she took a moment to find her voice. "Wh-what was that?"

Jeronimo rolled his eyes. She almost barked out a laugh at the sight of such a trite gesture on his stoic face.

"Barty's always been one for dramatics."

"Your brother did that?"

"He heard me."

She didn't believe him. Not really. She didn't even know if she believed his story of murder and Tenders and threads holding the world together and bad things bent on ripping through to freedom even if part of his story was in her grandmother's handwriting. But the fact his brother had heard Jeronimo's tale was almost too much.

Or it would have been if the earth hadn't shaken again.

It was a brief aftershock, but staring at Jeronimo, his dark eyes on her, Loey knew the truth: Bartholomew James had heard them speaking ill of the dead—or nearly dead.

"But what happened to him? Where did he go?" She whispered her question as if Bartholomew might not hear.

"Across the Seam, into a stitched-up pocket of the world where only shadows and forgotten things exist. And Barty, now."

"Is he... *dead?*" she whispered.

A muscle in Jeronimo's jaw twitched. "He was close to dyin'. I think that's why the Seam took him, like it takes souls if they're not salted. But his body is over there with his soul. He's alive like you and me, but caught in another place."

Slowly, like she was reiterating something crazy—because it was crazy that a living and breathing person could be caught and dragged into a pocket world—she said, "He's stuck in there."

Jeronimo nodded.

"How were you not trapped over there too?"

"Luck, I guess," he said, words clipped like short flashes of lightning during a summer storm. "In the instant of the explosion, Barty and I both died. The Seam tried to take us, but something went wrong. It took all of Barty, yet it only took my soul. I've always figured it was 'cause I got blown too far away."

"And that's why you can't die."

"So it would seem." Jeronimo swiped off the last of the drying blood from his nosebleed.

She pointed to his face. "Why is that happening? You didn't bleed when I shot you."

"It's Barty. Something about him being close to me

through the Seam and my soul being over there. It's the only time I ever bleed."

Loey felt like she was submerged in icy water, the surface as black as the water below her, such that she didn't know which way was up. "But my grandparents' letter said something stronger than Barty is ripping the Seam."

Jeronimo unfolded himself from the ground and stood to his full height. He seemed so much taller now. "They were wrong. It has to be Barty. That message on Pastor Briggs's grave was meant for me. My brother wants revenge, and he's trying to tear his way free to find it."

"But how is he killing people from the other side of the Seam?"

"The symbol you saw is from an ancient form of mountain magic. Tenders have used it in these parts since they started caring for the Seam, but those symbols can also kill and hurt. If Barty's strong enough or close enough when the Seam rips, he can reach through and inscribe that symbol on someone's skin. It kills them quickly."

"Like Pastor Briggs?"

Jeronimo dipped his chin. "It's not just Barty that can rip the Seam, but also highly chaotic natural events like the tornado. The pastor was too close at the wrong time."

"And…" The sentence formed in her head, causing her heart to gallop. "And my grandparents? He killed them too?"

"They were trying to stop him by sealing the Seam for good. I don't know how close they came—Seams don't want to be sealed—but they must have gotten close enough that Barty went after them. I'm sorry I didn't make it here in time."

She flinched. She was sorry too. So sorry she could have sunk through the church floor and into the earth and lain there forever. But she pushed on.

"What about a murder years ago? A young boy with a

similar symbol on his body?"

Jeronimo spread his hands wide. "If that boy had a symbol on his chest like Briggs, then it was Barty too."

Loey sank onto the bench. Dewey put his head in her lap. She spread the letter out on her leg and stared at Gran's handwriting.

"A man," she whispered, "was arrested for Leigh's murder. He was innocent."

"He was," Jeronimo answered as if her words had been a question. But they were a statement. She knew the truth. She'd known it long before tonight.

"And my grandparents knew," she said, finding her way through all the revelations of Seams and Tenders and vengeful brothers to a darker truth. "They knew he was innocent."

Jeronimo studied her as if he didn't understand the turn her questions had taken. "With that symbol, they woulda known it was Barty."

But they'd let the sheriff arrest Folton Terry Jr. anyway. He'd gone to prison for a crime he didn't commit. Her grandparents weren't bad people, not like her. They wouldn't have allowed it, not unless they'd known what Folton had done to her and why she'd framed him for Leigh's murder.

"Loey?" Jeronimo asked slowly, his voice uncertain, like he didn't know where she'd gone.

But she'd gone back to 2011, to Folton's classroom, and she was sinking into the truth that her grandparents had always known and they'd borne her secret with her. They'd allowed Folton to go to prison for Leigh's murder because she'd needed justice, and they'd respected her desperate need for no one to know, even them. Maybe they'd hoped she would tell them when she was ready. But they'd run out of time.

In the South, a truth like that, once out, could never come back. You were always tainted, always different. Loey had seen that plain enough with Dale, after she'd lied to the cops and told them Folton had molested her for so long. It was why she'd married Travis, why she kept her chin held so high in defiance to all the lingering stares, why her mother hated her and her father never came home from the city.

But now there was a secret so huge it spanned across an entire family. A secret so big that Gran had sent for an impossible stranger who couldn't die to help her and Pap instead of asking their own granddaughter.

She ran her hands over Dewey's soft, wrinkled face. Why hadn't they told her this? Why trust a stranger and not their own granddaughter?

Because they didn't think you were strong enough. You couldn't even tell the truth about what Folton did to you. You made your best friend shoulder the burden.

She thought back through the night, to the letter and the secrets, but she landed back on Folton and her grandparents knowing what he'd done. "Did they see me as weak and pathetic? Were they ashamed of me?"

She hadn't realized she'd asked the questions aloud until Jeronimo answered, "No, Loey. That's not it at all. They wanted to protect you. They didn't want you to be a Tender. They were trying to seal the Seam for good so no one else, no other Keene, would have to be trapped in this town again, taking care of those damn threads."

"They told you that?"

His jaw flexed. "No, they didn't. I only heard from them once, in that letter. Because of what I am, I stay far removed from Tenders. If others learned of my existence, it could be dangerous for everyone. But I've lived long enough to know your grandparents wanted more for you. It's the only reason they would try something as crazy as sealing the Seam."

After high school and Folton, the accident and the

surgeries that burned through all that money so quickly, she'd lived small. Most people in towns like Righteous lived small, but Loey's existence was different than her neighbor's pure and simple lives. She needed to go unnoticed, to pass through each day without taking up any space. She wanted to never be seen by a bad man ever again. It was why she didn't feel trapped in Righteous all that much anymore; she doubted she'd have the will to exist anywhere else.

Her grandparents had always understood that need without her ever having to speak it. They were her soft place to land, her quiet place. But they'd seen what she hadn't: her smallness had turned into weakness over the years. And when they'd needed her most, she hadn't been strong enough to help shoulder the burden.

"I need your help," he pushed. "You need to do this for your grandparents, to finish what they started."

She recoiled as if his words were stinging wasps. She'd barely wrapped her head around the quite literal shifting of the very foundation on which her life was built. There was no room inside of her to consider undertaking the tasks her grandparents had left unfinished.

"I… I need to think. This is all too much."

Jeronimo's eyes flashed as black as the night outside the church. "What the hell is there to think about? I have to kill Barty and you have to learn how to Tend the Seam. I have to get out of this town."

Gone was the fake, flirty stereotype. Here was the real Jeronimo James, and his intensity unnerved her just as it had the first time she met him.

"I need some time."

"You don't understand, I can't stay here," he growled.

She stood, clutching a pew to keep from falling back down. The letter rustled in her grip. It tethered her to all her shortcomings and all the ways she'd failed her grandparents. They'd needed her and she'd been too weak. She knew nothing about Tending—she couldn't even tend to the flowers in the cemetery.

The only magic Gran had taught her was the special sort of magic found in a simple life. A life of living right, doing right, and praying for anything falling short of that. Yet all along, Gran and Pap had been holding Righteous's threads together.

Had her mother known? Was that why she'd left and never come back? The thought spun Loey completely off the rails.

"I have to go," she told Jeronimo.

She stumbled away. Dewey followed.

"Loey, wait," Jeronimo called.

She crashed through the church's front doors and staggered down the steps. The night air contained a hint of autumn bite. She shuddered, her thin dress doing nothing to ward off the chill.

"Loey!"

She turned back.

Jeronimo stood framed by the church's pine doors. Above him, the steeple formed a pointed cross. He made no other move to follow her.

"Check the mirrors."

She shook her head. "What?"

"Your grandparents were Tenders. They would have protected their home. Check the mirrors. You'll see. You'll see they were protecting you."

CHAPTER 12

THE KEENE HOUSE WAS A place of contradictions.
The house smelled of comforting must, like a grandparents' house should, and Gran's perfume. Everything had a place and every place had a thing. Books were mounded in corners, as the oak bookshelves Pap had constructed long ago were full. Mirrors hung in more spots than pictures, such that you could almost always catch your reflection. Iron dragonflies hung at angles over thresholds, and petals were pressed between pages in books. There were locked doors and lead mirrors in which her reflection never quite added up. Rugs were piled sometimes two or three thick, all at haphazard angles, or so Loey had thought until at twelve years old, she'd found a trapdoor beneath one that led into the cellar. The discovery had transformed her childhood home into a mystery for her to solve. Yet no matter how much she explored, there was always something new to discover. Fireplaces with no chimneys, hollow walls in wrong places, and closets with back doors. And those were just the things a person could touch and see and smell.

The rules of the Keene house were even more peculiar.

Doors were always kept closed, never left open, especially at night. Black-eyed peas were kept in pockets. Iron trinkets could only be above windows, never left around willy-nilly.

Books were things to be treasured and dog-eared and loved with notes in the corners for the next reader to find. Pictures were handled with care, though Loey had found fewer than five photos of her mother in the entire house. There were none of her father, a man she'd never known and whom no one spoke of. A pinch of salt was never thrown over a shoulder but sprinkled across thresholds to keep out the Devil. In the summer, black-eyed Susans and butterfly weeds permeated the air in a violent competition with the scent of apple fritters and fried chocolate pies. Outside, the trees grew tall and strong. The weak ones were culled, and the ones struck by lightning were adorned with glass trinkets of the dead. The house always welcomed the downtrodden, the lost, and the broken, whether that be stray cats, cast-out puppies, or people, like the young boy in Loey's second-grade class who'd only been in Righteous long enough to be moved to another foster family.

The Keene house was unusual to anyone but a Keene, and Loey found its peculiarities as familiar as family members.

After a night when her entire world had been upended and shaken until all her spare parts had fallen from her pockets, she walked through the house and inhaled its perfume, and felt safer for it.

Dewey went straight to his food bowl to finish his dinner, the excitement of the night forgotten. Boltz mewled and rubbed against Dewey's legs as the big dog slopped up his meal. Loey downed a glass of sweet tea and headed straight to the hall bathroom. She turned on the lights and bent over the sink. She splashed water on her face to pull herself back from the brink of numbness. Over the sink, she opened the medicine cabinet, took out two headache pills, and swallowed them dry.

She closed the cabinet door. Without letting herself think about it long enough to doubt herself, she ran her fingers along the edges of the cabinet and checked the door and the shelves. When she found nothing, she stepped back and stared at herself.

Her eyes were wide. Even now, she looked frightened. Her face was pale, her scars pink against the gray wash of her complexion. Her cheekbones stuck out more than normal. Ms. Ida May was right; she had gotten thinner. Her eyes, brown and boring, looked too big for her face. The silver ring in her nostril glinted sharply, making her face look even starker for its shininess. She touched her mouth and traced the pull of her lips where the metal panel had tried to rip her face clean off.

Don't let her see the mare hit the ground.

To this day, the words haunted her. The memory of the rag the paramedics had laid over her face, not for her benefit but to keep the spectators from screaming as the paramedics hauled her to the ambulance, came back so clearly. She felt its wetness, soaked through with her blood, over her mouth. She recalled how it had turned her breathing into a damp, hot thing, the fabric sticky as the blood dried and she screamed.

"Stop," she told herself before she fell into the void. "Just stop."

She went to turn off the lights, but she paused. She hadn't checked *behind* the mirrored cabinet. With her fingers on the switch, she looked back at the mirror, staring sidelong at her reflection. She could check now and be done with the task.

And then what would she do? Go to bed and pretend tonight had never happened? Smile at Jeronimo tomorrow and pretend she didn't know what he meant if he asked about the night she'd shot him in a church and he'd revealed to her a family secret?

Was she such a coward?

She latched her fingers around the cabinet's edges. She jerked at it, but it didn't budge. She struggled, ripping and tugging and grunting, until it tore free. She stumbled backward and nearly toppled headlong in the claw-foot tub, with the cabinet and half the drywall behind it in hand.

She righted herself and lowered the cabinet. The wallpaper surrounding the cabinet was torn, and hunks of drywall had crumbled onto the vanity. There was nothing there.

She was a crazy woman. She heaved out a breath. Who was she anymore?

After tonight, she had no idea.

She hefted up the cabinet, her toiletries rattling around inside, and went to set it on the vanity. She'd rehang it tomorrow after patching the drywall too, or else she'd always know the hole was back there, forcing her to remember this night and how crazy she'd been to rip the cabinet clean off the wall.

A scrap of white caught her attention from the back of the cabinet. She felt along the hunk of drywall and wallpaper. Then her fingers touched something smooth. She ran her nail along the edge and peeled it off. It came away easily, held in place by one tab of tape.

She propped the mirror back against the wall on the vanity before holding out the small square of paper into the bathroom's light. Age had yellowed the thick cardstock. She turned it over.

Black ink marked the page in lines and curls, both delicate and bold, that formed the shape of an elaborate *A*. It wasn't the same symbol as the one she'd seen on Leigh and Briggs, but it belonged to the same family. This symbol was graceful, drawn with loose, dripping ink. The thick vellum felt hot to the touch, and the heavy black lines seemed to shiver whenever she wasn't staring directly at them.

Somehow, she knew Gran had drawn it.

It's just Harlan and me left. We need you more than ever.

They'd needed a stranger, more myth than man. Her eyes glazed over until the words were black squiggly lines in front of her.

The night had started with her shooting a man, and it was ending with her questioning everything she'd ever known. How had things gone so sideways in one night?

Until the early hours of the morning, she checked all the mirrors. Every single one had symbols drawn on pages behind them. Some were old, maybe as old as the house. Some were new. Some had been drawn in a hurry, with patchy lines and ink drops. Some had been labors of love, artwork unto themselves. But they were all the *A* shape. The exact placement of the lines and curves never changed from one page to the next. No matter how old the page or new the tape, they were all the same.

She left all the pages in place behind the mirrors where she'd found them. All but the page behind the medicine cabinet. That one she sat on the kitchen table and traced until the ink turned her fingertip black.

She followed the peak of the *A* and the upward curling lines across the letter until she knew them by heart. She traced them until the first bit of sunlight slanted through the dwindling night. Then she stood, page in hand, and went to her truck.

There was only one thing she knew to do at a time like this.

CHAPTER 13

LOEY DROVE INTO TOWN AS the sun rose up from the valley on Saturday morning, the first day of September. The page and her grandparents' letter lay like a live bomb on the passenger seat of her car. She couldn't look at them without feeling a kicking gallop in her heart and a drop in her stomach.

Pulling into her best friend's driveway eased her fears, like everything would be fine if she sat at Dale's kitchen table and bit into a fried egg and gouda sandwich. Dale was a fixer, and fixing Loey over the years had become a not-so-secret project of hers.

Loey opened the front door—she didn't knock anymore; there was no point since she visited so often—and almost ran into Cross, who had his tongue buried in Travis's mouth.

"What the—" she gasped.

Cross, on instinct—an instinct so deeply ingrained in him from years of hiding this very thing—jumped back from Travis, who whirled on her, fists clenched and face red.

"Oh," Cross sighed in relief. "It's just Loey."

Unlike Cross, Travis didn't relax at the sight of her gaping at them in his front door.

Not noticing the building tension, Cross straightened his insurance salesman shirt. "Morning, Loey. Why aren't you at the shop?"

"Get," Loey hissed, and it sounded like *git*, "out."

She shoved Cross back, rumpling his prim suit. His eyes flashed with surprise.

"Hey," he complained. "What's that for?"

"What's that for?" She kept her voice low so Dale wouldn't hear, but it trembled with her short-fused rage. She hadn't had enough sleep—or any—to be dealing with this mess. "You know exactly what that's for. Haven't you two got any sense?"

"Fuck you, Loey Grace," Travis growled, and she'd never hated him more.

He pushed past her, knocking against her shoulder. It was such a high school move that she wanted to shove him down the front porch steps.

"He didn't mean that. You know how scared he is of anyone finding out." Cross reached for Loey's arm like he wanted to comfort her, but seeing the expression on her face, he dropped his hand. "Hey, are you okay? You don't look so good."

"You two have been at this again since you came back from college. Isn't it time to get it out? What's the point of all this running around? You're adults. Your dads can't hurt you if they find out."

Cross straightened away from her, and his face, so handsome it was heartbreaking, shifted into a neutral expression, the one that guarded his thoughts and feelings and shut everyone out.

"That's why you'll never understand," he said. "You think we're scared of our daddies hittin' us, but that's not the hurt we're running from."

He slipped out the front door. Loey didn't know what to say, and she hated that she wanted to give Cross a hug, so she glared at his departing back instead, her eyes saying everything she couldn't.

Not that she cared about Travis kissing Cross. That a man was kissing a man. She cared about Dale's brother kissing

Dale's husband in Dale's foyer.

She slammed the front door and followed the smell of coffee into the kitchen. Dale stood in the bright, white-painted room with her back to the foyer as she piped buttercream icing onto a freshly baked lemon cake.

"Morning, Loey!" she called cheerfully without interrupting her work.

Outside, Cross's big diesel truck roared to life.

Dale kept humming along to whatever song played inside her head. She swayed her hips to the beat only she heard, her sun-spun hair catching the first rays of dawn slipping in through the window. She looked so happy. Glowing, almost.

Every inch of it a lie.

"Doesn't it bother you?" Loey asked.

Dale stopped humming, but she didn't stop icing her cake, spinning it round and round on the rotating cake stand and scraping a spatula along its edge to smooth the icing. The cake was perfect, but still she spun. Round and round. Round and round.

"What do you mean?" she asked as if they were speaking of the weather.

"You know what I mean."

Dale made a noise in the back of her throat. She was so deep in the act today that maybe she didn't realize she was pretending anymore. Loey's heart tugged. She told herself not to. She told herself to shut up and let Dale play her game.

But that was the issue: Loey didn't understand why Dale played along. She knew Dale wanted to protect Cross—she'd die for her brother—but Cross had handled himself fine before Dale married Travis. The act certainly wasn't to protect Travis or because she loved him. She didn't even really speak to the man. Sometimes, Loey caught her staring at him with hatred. No one could win this game the three of them played.

"You know where they're going." The words were out of her mouth before she could hold her tongue.

The spatula stuttered against the cake. It tore into the perfect cream cheese icing as the cake stand slowed to an uneven stop. In a sudden, violent motion, Dale threw the spatula into the sink. White icing splattered against the tile backsplash.

She picked up the cake and walked it to the trash.

"Come on," Loey said right as Dale opened the trash can lid with her sandaled foot. "Don't do that—"

Dale dumped it straight into the bin.

Loey sighed.

When Dale faced her friend, the mask had slipped. Her eyes blazed. "*Obviously*, I know what they're doing. Do you think I'm some vapid *housewife*?"

Loey didn't recoil at the harsh bite of her friend's words. There was nothing Dale could say and no tone she could use that would make Loey turn her back on her friend. They were more than best friends. They were sisters.

"It doesn't bother you?"

Dale's face shuttered with a flash of pain then defeat. She shrugged. "I wanted a life. I wanted a pretty husband and a pretty house filled with pretty things."

Loey waited for her to continue, to say she'd gotten none of those things, to acknowledge she'd married Travis, knowing exactly who he spent his nights with. It hadn't been a surprise. It had been going on since high school, with Travis as the quarterback and Cross as the star running back.

"Dale, you deserve—"

"If you say I deserve someone who loves me, so help me Jesus, Loey Grace, I will *cut* you."

"I was going to say you deserve something real."

Dale's mouth pressed into a slanted line of indifference.

"It's real enough for me."

They'd only talked this much about her marriage the day Loey had tried to stop Dale from walking down the aisle. Dale's marriage, like Leigh and Folton, was a skeleton they'd buried, and only they knew where to dig it up. People didn't speak of such things in the South, especially in Righteous. It was polite to sweep issues under the rug. It was kind to leave people to their own devices, as long as those devices remained behind closed doors and didn't spill over into the light of day or, worse, on the pew on Sunday. But maybe it was what had happened last night. Maybe it was the realization that it wasn't only Gran and Pap who'd thought her too weak to know the truth, but Dale too. Dale had always protected her. She was the stronger friend. The braver one. But maybe the time had come for that to change.

Haltingly, because they—she, Dale, and Cross—never spoke about it as a rule, Loey said, "If it's about him... about what we did to Folton—"

That was as far as she got before Dale erupted. "Don't even say his name! Come off it, okay? Not everything has to be so deep."

"But—"

"Leave it!"

Loey wouldn't. Not after learning her grandparents had known all along that Folton hadn't killed Leigh. "We did a bad thing, and maybe it's time we told someone."

Dale's face blanched. Her stunning blue eyes widened beneath her lashes. She shook her head. "No." She kept shaking her head. "No. We didn't do a bad thing. *He* did a bad thing. And he kept doing bad things. We stopped him. That's all. He deserved what he got."

"He was—"

"He was *not* innocent. All those things he did to you

makes him a disgusting *pig*. So stop telling yourself he was innocent. That shit will eat you up."

"He did it to you too."

"Once," Dale growled, the word so vicious spittle flew from her mouth. "He did it *once*, and it was *planned,* and I was in control. It was *fine*. We had to if the prolonged molestation claim was going to stick."

The air in Loey's chest, and all her fight, left her in one long whoosh. All the bad things she'd done were demons dogging her heels. They kept her up at night. They ate at her. Bite by bite. Piece by piece. She could still feel his too-warm, too-sweaty hands on her skin. Her body. If she thought about it—and she tried not to, but sometimes the thought came anyway—she remembered what it felt like when he'd forced himself inside her. She remembered the way the desk dug into her belly as he'd rutted above her.

Dale's hands were on her shoulders, shaking her. She was right in her face, and Loey couldn't remember her walking over.

"… see what you're doing. Christ Almighty, Loey Grace. What the hell? You're white as a sheet."

"Oh," Loey managed, the word a weak breath wheezed from between her lips. She smelled his skin. His scent. His desperation as he bruised her mouth to hold in her cries.

As if she knew, because she always knew, Dale pulled her into a tight hug. Loey pressed her face into her best friend's hair. Her expensive shampoo filled Loey's nose and exorcised his smell. Dale's touch took away his memory like a salve. With a deep breath, Loey relaxed in Dale's arms.

"He deserved it," Dale whispered fiercely. "I hope he's getting ass-fucked by every skinhead in that prison. It's what he deserves for those things he did. We did what we had to because no one else would."

Loey shuddered, and Dale's hold on her tightened.

"It's because of Pastor Briggs. It's bringing up old shit," Dale said even quieter so Loey had to strain to hear the words. Over Dale's shoulder, she stared at the white icing on the tiles, where Dale would have to scrub it clean. "But some shit should stay buried."

Dale pulled back, though her fingers clenched Loey's shoulders until it hurt.

"We are good people," Dale said. "We are good people who did a tiny bad thing. That doesn't make us bad like him. Do you hear me?"

"I hear you," Loey whispered, her voice cracking.

Was that why her grandparents had let Folton go to jail for a crime he hadn't committed? Because they were good people willing to let a bad thing happen for the sake of greater justice?

Dale studied her, her gaze searching every inch of Loey's soul. She released her shoulders. "Good. Now, I don't want to hear about it again. Let it go." She flashed Loey a perfect white smile and spread her hands wide. "Let it go like I have."

She smoothed down the ruffles of her sunflower-printed apron. When she looked up at Loey again, her pretty and perfect smile spread wider, faker than Loey had ever seen it. "Now, what did you come over for?"

Staring at her best friend, Loey saw a stranger with a mask of glass and bones of air. Dale's fragile existence was one of charades and dagger-sharp smiles. She teetered so close to the edge that Loey pulled her shirt down lower over her back pocket, where the letter and page hid, and offered up a fake smile of her own.

She was done being small and weak. From this, Loey could protect Dale.

"Nothing," she said. "Nothing at all."

CHAPTER 14

OCTOBER 31, 2011

T HE STUDENT COUNCIL STAYED LATE Friday afternoon to decorate for the Fall Jamboree that night. Loey had strung up more ghosts, made from helium balloons and white fabric she'd borrowed from the home economics classroom, than she wanted to count, and her fingers were stained black from painting signs.

Dale had nipped some vodka from her mother's stash and poured it in a plastic water bottle, which they passed between them, taking stolen sips whenever the teachers weren't looking. When the decorations were up and they needed to change into their costumes before the kids arrived for trick-or-treating and games, Loey felt a solid warmth in her bones and a fuzziness in her head. The floor tilted just enough that she had to focus on walking beside Dale as they left the gym to change. She'd rarely drunk before this, and never at a school function, but she felt reckless, like her life was wisps of smoke slipping between her fingers, so why not enjoy it?

In the hall, Dale took her hand as she rambled about her bride of Frankenstein costume. Loey listened with half an ear.

"Hey," she interrupted Dale, "do you hear that?"

"What?"

"Listen."

A banging came from inside the boys' locker room. It was

more rhythmic than a simple closing of lockers, and football practice had ended hours ago.

Dale giggled, pressing a finger to her lips.

Loey smelled the vodka on her breath. She blushed as she asked, "Are people *doing* it in there?"

"Let's find out." Dale pulled her into the locker room with a soft snort.

The air was steamy from the showers, and the smell of too much cologne hung like a curtain Loey had to push aside. She gagged, and Dale choked on a laugh. They swept around the lockers, ready to catch someone in the act, and froze dead in their tracks.

Cross was bent over Travis, whose back was pressed against the lockers, their heads bowed together like they were praying. They could have been, if their tongues hadn't been in each other's mouths, their limbs so entwined they looked like a ball of mating snakes. Travis had his hand down the front of Cross's briefs, his fist pumping to the rhythm of Cross's grunts. Their thrusts against the lockers caused the metallic banging.

They were so consumed with trying to crawl right up inside each other that they didn't even notice that Loey and Dale stood gawking inside the locker room. Only when Loey gasped, her hand slapping over her mouth, did they look up.

Cross leaped away from Travis, stumbling over the bench between the row of lockers. Travis jerked upright, his cheeks flushed, his lips swollen. Their hair was so disheveled it looked like they'd sat through a hurricane. Fear, white bright and tangible, sparked deep in their eyes.

"What the ever-lovin' fuck?" Dale growled.

"Dale," Cross said, stumbling over her name as if he hadn't been saying it his entire life. "Please. Wait. This isn't what it looks like."

"Then what is it? 'Cause it looks like my boyfriend was giving you a handy in the locker room, Cross."

"Hey, maybe we should—" Loey started.

"If you two tell anyone about this," Travis snarled, starting toward them, his face red and growing redder as his fists clenched tight, "I'll kill you. Don't think I'm lyin' either. I'll bury you so—"

"Travis," Cross grabbed his shoulder, holding him back. "They won't tell anyone. Right?"

He was begging, his eyes wide. He trembled too, and he held Travis tight, as if he really was worried about what Travis might do if he came closer to the girls.

"Loey," Cross said when Dale continued to glare and fume in silence as she wound up for a tirade of epic proportions, "please. No one can know. Dad will kill me. Really kill me. And Travis's too. Please. We didn't mean for it to happen …" Cross glanced at Travis, who was withering into himself before Loey's eyes. "We… we love each other."

"Love each other?" Dale shouted. Loey grabbed her hand and shushed her. "Travis, you were talking about marrying me yesterday. Now you're hand-fuckin' my brother?"

"Dale, calm down," Loey soothed.

"Fuck that!"

Loey ground Dale's delicate bones together as she squeezed her hand. Dale hissed in pain.

"Cross, I won't tell anybody. I swear it," Loey said.

Dale fumed silently, twisting their fates up tight in her hands. Finally, she said, "Fine, I won't either, but we're over, Travis. *Over.*"

His eyes flashed wide. "No. We can't. Not right now."

"What the hell?" Cross asked him, shocked.

Loey's gaze darted between the three of them. She felt like she might be sick. Like this was something she didn't need to be watching. It was too private, too raw. It should have been happening behind closed doors.

"Yeah, what the hell, Trav?" Dale snapped. "You're gonna cheat on me with my brother, then cheat on my brother with me? Fuck. That."

Travis pulled away from Cross and stumbled to Dale's feet. He grabbed her hips and looked up at her with so much emotion that Loey dropped Dale's hand and stepped away.

"Dale," he begged.

Behind him, Cross's spine jerked straight. His eyes narrowed as he crossed his arms in a way that said he wanted to hold out the world and hold himself deep, deep inside.

"Dale," Travis said again from his knees, "please. Daddy can't know. Last summer, he found me on the computer with that homo porn and he almost killed me."

"When you broke your back?" Dale asked, frowning. She hadn't pulled away from Travis's clutches. "You said you did it playing basketball."

"It was him. He beat me so hard." Travis looked like he might cry, like he wanted to real bad, but he fought back the tears. Cross sank farther away the more Travis pleaded. "But when we started dating, things changed. He gave me Nana's ring, Dale. He said we would be the ones to fix the rift between our families. He said he was gonna come to my games this year. Please, baby. Please don't say anything and don't break up with me. I'm sorry. I'm so sorry, baby, and it won't happen again. I'm a dirty homo, and I swear I won't do it again. I won't even think about him, and I'll pray real hard at church."

Dale's frown deepened. Her gaze left Travis and lifted to Cross, who wouldn't even look at her. His jaw was so tight Loey worried for his molars.

"You're not a dirty homo," Loey said. Travis's focus flickered to her, but it was Cross's attention she wanted. He cut his eyes toward her. "Nothing's wrong with you, aside from the fact you're cheating on my best friend, which would be messed up no matter who you did it with."

"She's right," Dale said. At the words, Travis let out a sob of relief. Cross's nostrils flared. "Nothing's wrong with you, so screw praying at church. We won't tell."

"And you won't break up with me?"

Dale sighed. "Not today, but I'm sure you'll give me another good reason to in a week."

Travis scooped Dale into a bone-crushing hug, thanking her over and over again as if she'd saved his life. Maybe she had. But behind them, Cross looked like he'd just lost his.

He dropped his arms and walked past them, brushing close to Loey as he gave Dale and Travis's embrace a wide berth. He smiled at Loey. It was a sad thing, a low thing, like he'd never been more lost.

She touched his arm and found his skin ice cold. Her touch was a promise, a pact. He recognized it with a nod.

Their secret, for Cross's sake, would die with her if he wanted it to.

CHAPTER 15

AFTER THE LATE LUNCH RUSH that Saturday, Loey closed the coffee shop and walked over to the police station. She juggled a tray of coffees in one hand and a bag of donuts in the other as she wrestled the front door open. Perhaps it was stereotypical to bring donuts to a cop, but Burl was a sucker for his daughter-in-law's homemade frosted apple cider donuts, and the batch Dale had made for Pastor Briggs's funeral hadn't sold out.

The inside of the station smelled like burnt coffee and stale air, with the faintest undercurrent of overweight, middle-aged man sweat. Loey breathed through her mouth and made her way to the glass cubicle containing the sheriff's office, distributing coffee thermoses and donuts to the various deputies on duty. Fortunately, Matt wasn't among them.

She rapped on the door, and Burl called out, "Come in."

"Hi, Sheriff," she said, closing the door behind her. "I come bearing gifts."

He leaned back in his chair, the springs squeaking in complaint. His face had a perpetual sheen of sweat that couldn't be healthy, and his brows were two slashing punctuation marks across his face as he watched her set the donuts and coffee on his desk. "To what do I owe this pleasure?"

"I wanted to bring my favorite sheriff some treats."

He hadn't served as sheriff for over ten years by chance, and even though he had peculiarities—some of them sexist, most of them downright strange—he wasn't a half-bad sheriff, so it didn't surprise Loey when he didn't take her bait.

"There's been no change in the case, Loey Grace. Not that I'd share those details with a civilian. You know that. You have to let this go."

"This isn't about Pastor Briggs." She sat opposite him, her back to the blinds that kept out prying eyes. She was grateful for them, as she didn't know how this would go.

Bribe or not, he leaned forward and took in his spoils, his eyes lighting up when he peered into the bag. "I thought I smelled apple cider." He ate an entire donut in one bite, murmuring with a happy contentment that only baked goods could produce. "If this ain't about Briggs, what's on your mind?"

What wasn't on her mind? If she thought too long on any one thing, she might have a nervous breakdown right here in Burl's cheap, sticky plastic chair. "It's about Gran and Pap. I have a few questions."

Burl set aside the second donut he'd brought toward his mouth. His jowls twitched as he frowned. He reminded her of a rounder, less cute Dewey. "You having trouble with the will? Or the insurance?"

She resisted the urge to stare at her hands as she spoke. "No, it's about the night they died."

"Loey," Burl said like a sad warning. "You don't need to know the specifics. It, well, it wasn't pretty."

She was a coward because she didn't want to know the specifics, but last night had changed the course of her life, made it much bigger than she'd imagined possible, *if* Jeronimo had spoke the truth. She couldn't deny what she'd seen when she shot him or Gran's letter or the ground shaking after his tale, but it all felt outside her. Like it was happening to her.

She needed a way to take back control. She needed to see for herself, even though she doubted her grandparents' accident report would reveal any truths.

"I have to know, Burl. Please."

He scowled at his desk, his double chin dimpling.

He stayed silent for so long that Loey felt compelled to add, "I need to know that's how they died."

Instantly, she realized her mistake, but the words were already out of her mouth. It had been wrong to suggest Burl hadn't done his job right. She was questioning his police report, his duty to Righteous, and Burl did not take his job lightly—aside from the hookers.

The tip of his acne-scarred nose bloomed a deep purple. "What exactly are you tryin' to say here?"

"I mean," Loey said because she couldn't stop now, "I want to know for myself. Know what you know. That's all."

But the damage was done. "You saw the coroner's report. You know all you need to know." He stood from his chair, shaking his head as he towered over her. "What if your gran could see you asking these questions? What would your pap say? He played Rook with my father for decades."

What *would* Gran have said? She'd always told Loey that Righteous was a special place, and the people of Righteous were made of better stock than the rest of the world. Burl had known her family since the beginning of time, it seemed. But she'd never been shamed into silence before, and she wouldn't let him shame her now.

"I believe you, but I need to know for myself. I have a right to see your report."

He chewed on the inside of his cheek. When he couldn't bear it any longer, he snapped, "Fine. But don't say I didn't warn you. These pictures are gruesome, Loey Grace, and no young woman should have to see anybody like this, much less her kin."

Loey bit her tongue to hold back her retort that her being a woman should have nothing to do with it. "Thank you."

He banged open his desk drawer. She straightened in her seat to see over his desk. He rifled through manila folders, his fingers walking over the tabs until he found the one he wanted. He withdrew it but didn't offer it to her.

"You're sure about this?" His eyes creased with concern, and his hand trembled enough to rattle the folder in his grip.

"I'm sure."

He pressed his lips together and handed her the folder.

She sat it in her lap, her fingers hovering just above it. Her life had been so small, intentionally small, and possibly weak by result. But opening this file, with its corners still unbent and fresh from newness, would surely increase the scope of her life, even more than last night had. Seeing her grandparents in their final moments was something she would never be able to forget. Sitting there in Burl's office, she knew she had no option of turning back. Last night had blown up her small life. She'd have to be eight feet in the ground with two rings of salt around her grave for her to return to how she'd lived before.

She took a deep breath and opened the file.

Burl had been right. No one should have to see pictures of their family in death. The accident had been vicious, and the raw brutality of it would have been better left hidden in Burl's desk. But she flipped through each photograph, trying not to look at the blood or their faces or the way their bodies curled over the dashboard.

Loey couldn't help but look at one picture in particular. It was a close-up of her grandparents' arms. They were holding hands.

She swallowed as her throat thickened with tears. Their deaths had been slow enough for them to reach for each other in their final moments. She didn't know if it reassured her or further broke her that they had comforted each other in the end.

She closed the file and pressed her palm against the cover like she could seal it closed forever. None of the pictures contained symbols or suggested that her grandparents had died in any other way besides a car accident.

She'd been right: there was no turning back from this.

She looked up at Burl.

"Are you okay?" he asked, still the teddy bear of a man who had given her full-size Snickers bars on Halloween.

"Thank you," she choked out. She handed the file back.

He tucked it away in his drawer and closed it with a resounding slam that made her flinch.

He opened his mouth to speak, but she hurried to say, "I'm sorry for doubting you. I thought… I mean, I thought…" She inhaled the scent of donuts and stale sweat. "I'm sorry."

She went to stand, but Burl reached across the desk and put a hand atop hers. She paused.

When he was certain she wouldn't leave, he walked around his desk to the scratched mirror hanging above his file cabinets. She twisted around in her chair to watch. He moved a massive dying plant in front of it, the pot scraping over the metal top. The wilted leaves blocked the mirror from view.

"What are you doing?"

Burl ignored her question. He stopped right in front of her, between her and the mirror. She spotted a donut crumb stuck to the corner of his mouth. Quietly, so she had to lean closer to hear, he murmured, "Stop asking these questions before he hears you. If he knows, he'll come after you and he won't stop. Do you understand me? Let it go."

Loey recoiled. "How do you know about—"

Burl grabbed her arm and squeezed tightly. Loey cringed, but he didn't soften his grip. "Don't. Not here. He watches me."

The big man had fear in his eyes, more fear than Loey had ever seen. His face was clammy with sweat and pale, too.

121

He wheezed, and she wondered if he might be having a heart attack. But he propelled her from his office before she could ask if he was all right and dumped her outside.

"Burl, wait," she argued, spinning around to face him. "Is this about the symbols? Do you have them too—"

"The mirrors," he hissed. "Keep away from the mirrors."

He slammed the door in her face.

She didn't move. The feeling of someone watching her washed over her, prickling her skin into tight goose bumps. She turned around. The deputies and the operator stared at her like she was a madwoman.

Lowering her head, she rushed through the station and burst outside, sucking down the fresh air. Only once she was down the station's front steps and standing beside her truck did she dare glance back.

The cheap bent blinds covering the window in Burl's office twitched as they snapped back into place.

The file of her grandparents' deaths hadn't proved Jeronimo's words true, but Burl's ominous warning did. If she'd needed another sliver of proof to cling to, that was it.

She glanced up and down the street. Righteous moved around her as steady as the revolution of the earth. Mr. Weebly was out delivering mail. Donna Herbert had her flower arrangements set out on the sidewalk. The deli had its front door propped open, with eighties music spilling out. The maples in the town square turned their shiny green leaves toward the sun to soak up the last bit of summer's sunshine before they turned orange for autumn. In the courthouse's bell tower, the bell tolled out three long gongs to sound off the hour. The town was as it always had been.

But for Loey, her steady revolution of life had tilted, shifted, and tumbled straight off its axis.

CHAPTER 16

SATURDAY AFTERNOON, LOEY WORKED HERSELF into a frenzy with Burl's warning flashing through her mind. She'd left ten messages for him to call her back, but her phone had yet to ring. If he knew about Barty and the mirrors, then he might know more about her grandparents, and even though Burl had his problems, she trusted him more than Jeronimo. If he hadn't called her back by tonight, she resolved to drive to his house and question him in person. Away from mirrors.

She finished scrubbing the water trough and turned around. Jeronimo leaned against the fence post in tight jeans, flannel shirt, and brown leather jacket. *"Speak of the Devil,"* Gran had said, *"and he will appear."*

Gasping, Loey fumbled the scrub brush in her hand.

"Sorry, ma'am" he said, lifting his fingers to the brim of his cattleman's hat.

"Don't do that." She pressed her hand to her heart as she caught her breath.

"Did you look at the mirrors?"

She tucked the brush into the back pocket of her jeans and walked past him toward the barn. His boots crunched over the dirt path as he followed her at a distance. She had to raise her voice as she answered, "You could have told me to look *behind* them. It would have saved me the trouble of patching up the drywall. But I'm assuming you knew what I would find."

"I did."

She turned back to face him. He stopped ten feet away from her. "What are those symbols?"

"It's the same ancient magic as the symbol on the bodies. The ones behind your mirrors were protection wards. They keep the beings across the Seam from straying into your mirrors."

Dewey trotted over with a welcoming, happy woof at seeing Jeronimo. Loey shook her head at him as he pressed against Jeronimo for scratches. Jeronimo crouched beside the dog and obliged, hitting all of Dewey's favorite spots.

Loey went very cold as she recalled her conversation with Burl in a new light. Careful to keep her tone neutral, she asked, "What can stray into my mirror? Barty?"

"Yes."

"And whatever else is in there with your brother?"

Jeronimo paused in his scratches. "Nothing else in there is stronger than my brother. Barty is a killer. There's nothing he enjoys more than the hunt. If something else, aside from the unlucky, unsalted souls, had lived in there with him, it would be dead now. Barty would've seen killing it as entertainment."

"He sounds like a pleasant fellow."

Jeronimo stood. His hat cast a slanting shadow across his face, hiding his eyes completely. But his jaw was hard, his lips a grim line. "He had his moments."

"How does he know the symbols to kill people with if it's ancient mountain magic?"

He gave her a sad twitch of his lips. "Back in the day, the line between faith and magic was more blurred. The superstitions of today were unrelenting truths people lived by back then. They, along with the symbols, were passed down from generation to generation. They faded over time, like all things do, and by the time Barty and I learned them, they were rumors whispered by old men too bent to work at Townsend Rose's sawmills."

"Can anybody use the symbol to kill someone else?"

Jeronimo's eyes went far away. "No, I learned that long ago when I tried to use it."

It took every ounce of Loey's will to keep her standing in front of him and not running for her gun. "Who did you try to use it on?"

"Remember when I told you if people found out about what I was, it would be dangerous? Someone found out." He sniffed, his focus returning back to her. "But it didn't work when I tried. There are some symbols that will only work for Tenders, so I think this killing symbol is similar. It'll only work if the person's soul is bent on killing."

"And since you don't have a soul …" Loey guessed because she knew Jeronimo wouldn't have a problem killing if he needed to.

"Exactly."

At least he was honest, even if his honest was unnerving. "What's your plan to stop Barty then?"

His eyes sharpened on her. "You're going to help?"

"My grandparents protected me from this because they thought I couldn't handle it," she said, speaking the words she'd been mulling over all afternoon. "I didn't get to help them when they were alive, but I can now. I want to at least try."

It might have been relief that made Jeronimo's shoulders sag. Or maybe he was exhausted. He raked a hand through his hair. "It's just us. We have to do more than try."

She hoped the fear his words incited didn't show in her voice as she asked, "So what do we do? Go up Shiner's Ridge and write symbols on the ground? Seal up the Seam with an incantation?"

"It's not that simple. Your grandparents spent… likely spent half their lives figuring out how to seal this Seam for good. Few Tenders have accomplished it with their own Seams across the world. We don't have that kind of time."

"This sounds like a conversation that needs sweet tea. Come on inside. We can sit down and talk."

She led him inside through the back door and held it open for Dewey, who sprawled out on the cool kitchen tile. She poured two glasses of sweet tea and set them on the table. Jeronimo took a seat, settling his hat on the chair's backrest. She settled in opposite him and took a long, delicious pull from her condensation-beaded glass. She let out a sigh and said, "Tell me your plan for Barty."

"You won't like it."

If his brother could cause a small earthquake from the other side of the Seam, even if it was just beneath the church, he was strong, but Loey didn't like the worry in Jeronimo's eyes. She even caught a touch of fear in the way his brow furrowed and the wrinkles around his eyes deepened when he squinted at her.

"Tell me."

Jeronimo steeled himself and said, "We let him rip it completely open—"

Horror pulled Loey's skin tight over her bones. "I don't like this plan."

"—and come out—"

"This is a *terrible* plan."

"—then I kill him, for good this time."

She stared at him for a beat to make sure that was his plan in its entirety. "You're going to let him rip this tatter further and escape, and then you're going to fight a … a *being* that can cause earthquakes and kill people from another world?"

"I wouldn't call it an earthquake. More like a localized shake. But yes, that's the plan."

She exploded. "That's the worst plan I've ever heard! My grandparents sent for you to deal with your brother, and that's all you've got? Let him out and kill him? What if he gets away? Then what? I chase after him with my shotgun?"

"Shooting him will do as much good as shooting me did."

She threw up her hands. "That proves my point! This is crazy, Jeronimo!"

"I know."

"Why do you need me? You could go blow something up near the tatter and wait for him with … with … how are you even going to kill him if the symbol doesn't work for you without your soul?"

"There's other magic I can try." He crossed his arms. "As for why I need your help, if he kills me, you'll have to finish the job."

"You mean kill him."

"That's right."

She wanted to scream. "But I don't know any magic!"

"That's why I'm going to teach you."

The tea churned in her stomach. "When?"

He reached into his jacket pocket to pull out his notepad. He flipped through the age-curled pages to the one he was looking for. Then he laid the pad on the table, spun it around, and slid it toward her.

It was another symbol, though this one was more circular and graceful, its lines tying together in the center like an infinity knot. It looked like the diagram for a knot she'd learned to macramé.

She lifted her gaze, and Jeronimo's smirk remained. "I'm going to teach you now."

It took twenty minutes and many arguments before they returned to the table with a piece of Gran's blank stationery and a thick calligraphy pen. Jeronimo all but shoved her back into her seat with the page in front of her. He pushed the pen into her hand and sat opposite her. Beside him, his tea sat untouched.

"I don't—" she started for the hundredth time.

"Come hell or high water, Loey Grace, you're drawing that damn symbol."

"You don't have to curse." She scowled at him. "Don't we need to be near the Seam for this to work?"

"The Seam isn't a linear path between two points. It's much more complex than that. The threads are constantly around us, woven into the world's fabric."

"Can you see them?"

"You're stalling. Again." Jeronimo indicated the pen in her hand. "But no, I can't. Only Tenders can. If I could see where the threads were, I could do this without you, couldn't I?"

The words chafed her. Maybe she was stalling, but she let her anger sweep her up. "Then why did my grandparents need you?"

He cocked a brow at her, the expression devilish on his rugged face. "Sometimes it helps to have something that can't die fighting something bent on tearing its way to freedom and killing anything in its path."

She pursed her lips. He had a point there.

She turned her attention to the page and pen in her hand. "I'll be able to see the threads if I draw that symbol? What if I mess it up? Will I rip the entire Seam open?"

He pinched the bridge of his nose. "Draw the symbol, Loey."

"You don't have to be so pushy. It's normal that I have questions."

130

He slapped his hands on the table, making such a loud cracking noise that she jumped and Dewey lurched to his feet, barking and running to the front door as if the sound had come from there.

Jeronimo watched him go. "You really should get a better guard dog. Least a smarter one."

"Don't talk about Dewey like that," she snapped. "And if you broke my table, I'll skin your hide."

A soft *whoosh* escaped his mouth. It could have been a laugh, but honestly, she couldn't tell. "My mother used to say that to me and Barty when we got into her pies." He shook his head. "I don't know what will happen when you draw the symbol. I'm not a Tender, and I've never watched one work closely enough, but I know this symbol"—he pointed to the one drawn in his notebook—"will peel back a veil and show you the threads."

"And that's all? What holds them together?"

His jaw flexed. "Again, I'm not a Tender."

"But I don't even know what I'm looking for."

"Which is why we're practicing tonight. You're looking around to see what we're working with, and I'm here in case anything happens."

She gripped her pen tighter. "What could happen?"

He leaned forward, fingers splayed in front of him like he wanted to crawl across the table and shake her. "Barty could tear at the threads, reach through, grab you—"

"Okay!" She uncapped the pen. "You don't have to scare me. I get the point. Now, zip it and let me concentrate."

He sat back in his chair and crossed his arms. "By all means."

She practiced drawing the symbol in his notepad, never completing the circles, just in case. She hated all the unknowns and Jeronimo's *let's see what happens* attitude. The more she spoke to him about his plan in Righteous, the more she suspected she was a means to an end for him, and when he reached that end, she wouldn't hear from him again. It didn't improve her ability to trust him.

She pulled the blank stationery in front of her and took a deep breath. As she lowered the pen tip to the page, Jeronimo leaned forward in his seat to watch. She shot him a dark look. He held up his hands in silent surrender and sat back.

She turned back to her work. As she drew, the pen dragged and skipped, marring the ink with empty patches or thick globs. Her first circle was lopsided, but she continued, spiraling toward the inner infinity symbol. The pen slid in her hand from her sweat, warping the line and causing it to almost touch the outer circle. She overcorrected and barely left enough room to finish the final curve. Her finished symbol was sad compared to the one in Jeronimo's notebook.

"Do you see anything?" he asked as soon as she lifted her pen from the page.

The kitchen appeared the same as before. The evening's fading light cut in through the window. Outside, the cicadas and bullfrogs clamored to speak louder than their neighbors in a symphony of summer nights.

"Literally nothing—"

But as she spoke, a flicker in the corner of her eye caught her attention. She glanced to her right, and the motion set off more lights close to her face. Then they flashed away. She blinked and more appeared. Concentrated beads of light flashed in lines, racing up and down a filament of pulsing luminescence. More filaments full of light beads encircled her until her kitchen was completely blocked from sight.

She didn't realize she was scrambling back in her chair until it tipped over and she fell onto the floor, which she couldn't even see through the blinding barrage of lights. She kicked away until her back collided with the cabinets. Through the thick curtain of lights, Jeronimo called her name.

She jumped when his hand latched onto her arm. He pulled her to her feet, but he was lost behind the lights, even as he shook her.

Her world was blinding spots of concentrated light so bright she couldn't look directly at it.

She screwed her eyes shut, but she still saw the lights through her eyelids. Her skull shrank until she thought her head might implode from the immense pressure. Her temples throbbed with pain, and every blood vessel in her brain pulsed along to her rapid-fire heartbeat.

Jeronimo's voice seeped through her panic. "... safe. It's okay. I've got you. You're safe. It's okay. I've got you."

She cracked open an eye. Seeing nothing but part of Jeronimo's jaw and the dark stubble lining it, she opened both eyes.

The lights were mostly gone. A few fluttered with dying spasms in her periphery, but she kept her gaze locked on Jeronimo and didn't search for the remaining filaments.

"What happened?" Her throat scratched like coarse sandpaper.

Keeping a hand on her elbow to steady her swaying, he said, "You tell me."

"You didn't see anything?"

His eyes swept over her face, down her body, and then back to her eyes. "Just you going berserk."

She pulled her arm free from his hand and limped over to the cabinet with her medicine. Her knee throbbed dully, setting her teeth on edge. She pulled out her headache and pain pills and threw back four of each without conscious thought.

"What's that for?"

"My headaches and my knee," she said as she chewed the

pills into a fine powder before swallowing. She walked to the table and used the rest of Jeronimo's untouched tea to wash down the powdery residue.

Already, she felt better.

"That medicine is worthless."

"I have ocular migraines."

"What the hell is that?"

"They make me see weird lights—oh."

"You're not seeing lights because of headaches. You're seeing the damn threads from a tatter even without the symbol. The Seam is practically begging you to do something," he shouted, and the pressure in her head came roaring back.

"I get that now!" she yelled back. Dewey barked behind her. She shushed him with a hand to his head.

She'd been taking the medicine since her sophomore year in high school, when the lights and head pressure had driven her to a breaking point. Gran had taken her to the doctor. She'd helped Loey describe the lights and the headaches and always ensured Loey had her pills with her in case she ever needed them.

And all that time Gran had known exactly what it was that Loey was seeing, but she'd let Loey medicate herself anyway.

"I get that now," she repeated, quieter this time. "But the medicine makes me feel better."

Her skin crawled. How many times had she heard Dale rationalize her pill issues with that exact phrase? How many times had Loey condemned those very words?

"Fine," he growled. "Hide, then. See where that gets you."

She wrapped her arms around herself. He threw open the back door hard enough to rattle the teacups in their cabinet. A wave of night air poured in. The stars twinkled brightly against a clear sky. Above Shiner's Ridge, the moon cast silver-spun moonshine over the farm.

Before he could stomp out, she murmured, "I'm sorry."

She'd hoped he wouldn't hear—the words weren't meant for him anyway—but he paused at the door. His lips were still pulled in a snarl, and his eyes blazed black. She huddled deeper into herself, wrapping her arms tighter around her waist.

"Don't ever apologize," he told her, his mouth easing as he spoke. "Not ever. The world doesn't deserve your regret."

She thought of her grandparents and how they'd died protecting her from this life. They'd Tended threads and Seams and shadow worlds their entire lives, and she couldn't even look at the threads for a few minutes.

"What if I can't do this?"

His face softened, with a kindness that lightened his eyes from their dark hue to a river-rock gray. He almost looked like someone she could trust.

"You're trying to stare into the fabric of the world, Lo. You can't do that if you don't know what you're made of."

Before she could respond, he was gone, the door snicking shut behind him.

CHAPTER 17

DECEMBER 16, 2011

L OEY HEADED OUTSIDE TO ESCAPE the red and green tinsel, twinkling string lights, and incessant Christmas music. The school's side door swung shut and sealed out the sounds of the Winter Formal dance.

She sucked down a breath.

She hadn't wanted to come, but an hour before the dance started, Cross and Dale had shown up, and Gran and Pap had insisted she go. Dale had plied her with makeup and shoved her in a red sequined dress, and Gran had all but pushed her out the door.

For a while, especially when she'd danced the first slow song with Matt Everton, everything had gone okay. She'd relaxed and finally, *finally*, began to have some fun. While getting a glass of punch from the plastic swan-shaped fountain, she'd felt him come up behind her and put his hand on her back.

"You look ravishing in red."

He'd smelled of cheap cologne, the sickly sweet kind, and his voice had curled around the word *ravishing* like he was picturing ravishing her.

If she'd known Folton was a chaperone at the dance, she never would have allowed her friends and family to convince her this was a good idea.

She'd set down her glass of punch on the table, stepped

away from his touch, and walked directly to the gym's double doors. Safely on the other side of the mistletoe, she'd fled.

Now the dark playground stretched out before her. The slide and swing set pointed up into the darkness like hulking giants. The pebbles slipped beneath her kitten heels as she walked farther from the door, her panicked breathing slowing. What had she been thinking, wearing a red dress? But she knew exactly what had gone through her mind as she'd studied herself in the mirror at her house. The curls Dale had crafted with her curling iron accented the Loey's makeup well, and she'd felt pretty.

But one touch from him and she felt like spoiled meat again.

Slut slut slut slut-slut-slut.

The swings creaked with metallic whispers in the breeze. The town's lights winked beyond the playground's fence, and farther away, up on Shiner's Ridge, the clouds hung low with rain or possibly the first snow of winter.

The moon wove in and out of the clouds, sometimes spilling silver light across the ground, sometimes not. Indecisive and fickle, this moon.

Loey took a deep breath and tilted her head back to soak up the darkness. She felt dark and shadowy, full of things better left to the night. She hadn't always felt like this. Before Folton, she'd been a sunshine girl.

As the swings creaked in the breeze, Loey realized she didn't feel a breeze, only the bite of winter. She looked over toward that side of the playground.

A shadow hung between the swings. Its weight caused the swing set to creak as the shadow swayed, heavy and thick. Her skin prickled.

The moon came out from behind the clouds. Moonlight swept over the playground.

A body—a boy—hung from the swing set's top bar.

He was naked, his belly torn wide open like coyotes had gotten to him, though the cuts were clean and gaping. He hung from a noose made from the chain of a swing seat, which was wrapped around and around the top pole as if it had gotten caught in a great wind. On his chest, in drying blood, was a symbol of slashing lines and slender, delicate curves. His limbs were lanky and long, his body twisted in death. At his feet, shards of reflective glass mirrored the moonlight.

His eyes were open. He stared at the ground as if waiting. A lock of auburn hair had fallen over his eyes.

Leigh Parker looked as awkward in death as he had in life.

As Loey stared, frozen, his foot jerked. His body swayed again and the swing creaked.

"Help!" she screamed. "Someone help!"

When the teachers and students spilled out onto the playground, Leigh's foot wasn't jerking anymore. Loey had held his hand, not knowing what else to do, as she'd watched him die.

CHAPTER 18

LOEY'S EYES SPRANG OPEN FROM the achingly familiar nightmare where she held Leigh as he died, his feet jerking as if he were trying to break through to freedom. Her gaze darted around to take in the living room cast in darkness. The drapes whispered across the floor from the night's balmy breeze entering through the open window. Even with the heat, she shivered.

She untangled herself from the blanket twisted around her body. Dewey snored away at the other end of the couch, his head resting atop her feet, anchoring her to reality. Boltz had arranged himself along the top of the couch, his fried body tucked deep into the old cushions.

She was exhausted to the point of desperation, but she gave up on sleeping. She tugged her feet out from beneath Dewey's head and swept her legs over the edge of the couch. She padded down the hall to the bathroom, the only light coming from the glow of the moon sweeping through the hall's window.

She paused at the window. The Golden Girls' hen house was quiet. The barn was dark and peaceful. In the field, the goats dozed in a heap. Her eyes were drawn farther down the hill, toward the church and beyond to the rectory, where, to her surprise, a single light blazed. From the moonlight, she recognized the olive-green Indian parked out front.

He'd made quick work of settling in. She had no reason to mistrust him, yet something about him—aside from his lack of soul and immortality—set her on edge, like a picture frame hanging a tad askew. She desperately needed to understand people and know what to expect from them. A shrink might suggest it was because of her past with Folton, but she needed to feel comfortable with the people around her, and she was far from comfortable around Jeronimo.

As she watched that far-off light, it fluttered from someone walking back and forth in front of it. Hopefully, the figure was Jeronimo, or else he had a burglar in his new home and she was too tired to care. Besides, he was the type who could handle a simple criminal—his type being the kind that couldn't die.

If he was an angel, he likely shouldn't have been riding a motorcycle and wearing those tight jeans of his. But what else did that leave? A demon? He didn't feel that dark, that evil. He felt like …

Heat climbed up her neck, and she forced herself to move away from the window. Jeronimo James felt like trouble. She needed to focus on that disconcerting feeling more and less on the warmness in her belly.

She sighed. She really should have shot him higher up.

She continued down the hallway to the bathroom, with Dewey's rumbling snores drifting from the living room. The old house made sleeping noises—old creaks and groans that had terrified her friends during sleepovers, but to her, they sounded like comforting conversations that lulled her to sleep.

She blindly switched the bathroom light on. As the bulb blazed to life, she lifted her head out of habit to look straight at the mirror.

But it was no longer hanging on the wall. She only saw

the hole in the drywall and the torn wallpaper. Her focus fell to where the mirror sat on the vanity, leaning back enough to reflect herself and the entire bathroom behind her.

A black man-shaped shadow loomed behind her.

With a ripping snarl, it surged forward. She screamed. The thing hit her square in the back, cutting off the sound, and slammed her face into the cabinet's glass. Pain blossomed through her skull. A resounding crack echoed deep through her head. She gurgled blood in the back of her throat. A gnarled hand curled through her hair and wrenched her head back. The mirror was splintered, with dark red blood smeared across it.

She whimpered. Behind her, the thing laughed.

It slammed her head forward again. The shattered glass dug into her face in a thousand tiny stabs that snagged her skin, reluctant to release her. She slumped against the pedestal sink, the hand in her hair gone, and fell backward.

The tender juncture where her spine met the swell of her skull hit the lip of the claw-foot tub. Her neck snapped forward with a crunch that sent a tingling wave down her legs, followed by the icy chill of nothing.

Before she puddled onto the floor in a boneless heap, before the blackness swept over her, before she had time to think *not like this*, she felt the resounding numbness in her limbs.

Then there was … nothing.

CHAPTER 19

BLOOD ROLLED DOWN HER FACE. A rasp raked from her cheek to her temple and into her hair. Puffs of kibble-scented warmth panted against her hair.

Loey groaned. Her eyes fluttered open, and she stared straight up at Dewey's pink tongue. He licked her again. A long string of drool slid off her chin.

"Dew," she grunted, waving off his tongue's assault. She wiped at her face, and her hand came away wet. She expected to see blood, but only slobber covered her hand. Frowning, she shifted her legs beneath her and looked up.

The mirror was intact. No shattered glass. No blood.

She stood on trembling legs. Slowly, she brought her gaze back to the mirror. She checked over her shoulder first, where the shadow thing had stood, and found the space empty. Nothing but her daisy-patterned shower curtain was behind her. Then she looked at her face.

Not a single cut, aside from her old scars. Her cheeks weren't even flushed. Her hair was plastered to the side of her face, but that was from Dewey waking her. Her frown deepened the permanent pull on the left side of her mouth.

Keep away from mirrors, Burl's words rang in her ears. *He watches me.*

Her mouth popped open. The hole in the drywall. She

hadn't replaced the ward that kept the beings across the Seam from straying into her mirror. The page lay by the couch, where she'd stared at it last night as if the fading ink could conjure her grandmother into the room.

"Son of a—"

Dewey barked. Loey screamed at the sudden woofing boom. He raced into the hall. A second after Dewey's bark of alarm, someone banged their fist against the front door.

A muffled voice shouted from outside, "Loey!"

She recognized Jeronimo's voice instantly. Then a crack splintered the air, followed shortly by another. He was trying to kick down her door.

"Wait! Hang on!" She raced toward the door, pulling her shirt and shorts into place. She pushed Dewey aside and unlocked the door, which she'd locked for the first time ever earlier tonight. It swung open to reveal a rumpled, red-cheeked Jeronimo on her front porch.

His black eyes were wide, and his hair was tangled around his face. He wore a flannel shirt, but he must have thrown it on as an afterthought, because it wasn't buttoned, revealing a stack of abdominal muscles that drew Loey's eyes down to the tuft of hair trailing beneath the waistband of his low-slung jeans.

Nothing, not even a scratch, indicated she'd shot him. His stomach's skin was as smooth as butter. She dragged her focus back to his face, her mouth hanging open in stunned disbelief.

He was talking, and she wasn't listening.

"… happening?" His chest heaved from the exertion of having raced up the hill from the rectory. "I heard you scream."

He smelled like cinnamon and a deeper, darker musk. Her stomach swooped like when her grandfather would accelerate over the top of a hill, and as the car dropped beneath them, her stomach would float for a second, and she'd whoop and squeal, and he'd smile in his quiet way.

"*Loey*."

What the hell was happening to her?

She shook her head to clear her thoughts. "The mirror," she said, sounding like she felt: strained and wrung out. "I didn't replace the page and—"

"Where?"

She crossed her arms over her chest, realizing she wasn't wearing a bra and the air was chilly. Worrying about her nipples was ridiculous, but it seemed improper to be standing in her doorway with her nipples hard.

Before she could answer, or possibly because she was taking too long, Jeronimo pushed by and charged down the hallway, his head craning around into her kitchen and the living room, searching the dark corners. Tail wagging, Dewey trotted happily after the man barging through their house.

"Hey!" she called after Jeronimo, but he didn't stop. She glanced outside. The night was calm, the breeze quiet. She closed the door and locked it before scurrying after him. "Do you think he's in here?"

He took a deep breath and held it as he walked toward the bathroom, its door wide open.

"Jeronimo, tell me—"

He froze in the doorway. His eyes flashed to the mirror. From the hallway, she couldn't see his expression, but his shoulders were tense and his fists were balled tight.

After a long moment of staring at the mirror, he backed out of the room. "I smell him," he said and cursed impressively.

Her mouth parted around a shocked breath. "You know your brother's scent?"

"It smells like sulfur in there. It typically accompanies anything connected with the Seam." He raked his hand through his hair and cursed some more. "I thought he'd come to me. That's why I wanted to be in the rectory and near the church. *Shit*."

"I want to put that page back up as soon as possible."

With a nod, he followed her into the living room to retrieve the ward. She got heavy-duty packing tape, and they converged in front of the mirrored medicine cabinet. By then, he'd buttoned his shirt, and she told herself she wasn't disappointed. Jeronimo ran his fingers along the edge of the hole in the drywall before shooting her a questioning glance.

"I was in a bit of a state when I checked behind it. Can you blame me?" She held up the page. "Do you need to say some sort of spell before I tape it up?"

"I'm not a witch, Loey. You're not either. It's the ink on a page that keeps monsters out of your mirrors."

She almost believed he was trying to calm her down with humor. But he didn't strike her as the type to use jokes to reassure someone.

When she hesitated, he took the paper and tape from her and covered the hole in the drywall with it. "Never hang these upside down," he warned, taping down the corners. When that was finished he traced, the upward peak of the *A* shape. "Your reflection can trap you without a way out. Least, that's what my grandmother always told me."

She stared at him, openmouthed, as he finished setting the medicine cabinet back up on its nails. He gave it a firm shake, and when it held, he stepped back and looked at her.

"What?" he asked upon seeing the look on her face.

"This is stuff you need to tell me, Jeronimo." She flung her hand toward the mirror, her mind flashing to how easy it would have been to invert the *A* into a *V*. "What if I had hung that back up myself the night I took it down?"

"You woulda had a 50/50 chance of getting it right, and you wouldn't be in this position."

"Or I could be *in my mirror*."

He lifted a shoulder a fraction. "Or that."

Her adrenaline high crashed so completely that her blood slogged through her veins. She swayed on her feet, her hand to her temple. "This is going to kill me, isn't it?"

"Hey." Jeronimo took her upper arm, sliding his hand down her bare skin, and threaded his fingers through hers. She stared down at their bound hands as if it wasn't her hand he was holding. "Barty's gone. He can't hurt you. Whatever he showed you or did to you was a dream. He can only affect something on this side of the Seam by coming through a tatter, or if a symbol behind a mirror opens it up."

"That's possible?" Her mind flashed to the shards of mirror at Leigh's feet and Burl hiding his mirror from view.

"If you know the symbols."

"Burl warned me about the mirrors when I went to his office earlier today or"—she checked her wristwatch—"yesterday now. He said, 'He's watching me.'"

"Come on." He led her out of the bathroom by her hand. "Let's go make some tea and you can tell me."

She followed him into the kitchen and sat down at the table. The supplies from her failed attempts at magic still cluttered the surface. Jeronimo went right to the cupboard with the tea packets, found her kettle, and put it on the boil. He set out teacups, picking her favorite one with peonies and a chipped navy blue one for himself. He moved around her house as if he knew it as well as she did, which would have concerned her if she'd had more sleep and fewer face-smashing incidents tonight.

As he worked, she told him about her conversation with Burl and the turn it had taken at the end. Jeronimo listened, his jaw tight, his focus never wavering from the task at hand.

Dewey settled his head on her shoes and started snoring. "What do you think it means?"

The kettle whistled, and he took it off the stove. He poured the water into the teacups and said, "The people in this town have seen things in their mirrors for as long as Righteous has existed. Burl could be seeing things, or he might know the symbols needed to open the mirror for my brother."

"Could it be a gateway?"

He took a seat and sipped from his tea, his mouth making soft noises on the rim of the porcelain. "No. Barty can't come through it. It's a line of communication."

"I know he doesn't act like it, but Burl is a decent cop. His family has struggled with money since the iron smeltery went under in the fifties, and after his divorce, things went off the rails for him," Loey explained.

"You don't have to stand up for him."

She watched him set his cup down. "Tell me more about the magic. I want to know everything about what my grandparents were involved in."

He studied her for a beat too long. "Some superstitions are exaggerated notions from a false understanding of science, but others, like the salt rings, have a true purpose."

"How often do souls slip across the Seam?" Her mind went to her grandparents and fear crashed through her. "Can it happen even if the salt is poured correctly?"

"Your grandparents are fine," he assured her. "It really only happens when someone isn't salted in time after their death."

"How do you know all this?"

He weighed his words, tallied them up in his head, and gave her only a penny's worth of his thoughts. "I've had a lot of time to research the magic of this place."

"But is that all it is?" She nodded toward the ruined pages. "Is it magic, or is it God? What if the other side of the Seam isn't a pocket world but Heaven or Hell? What if—"

"What did you see in that mirror tonight? Was that real?"

"It felt real." She shuddered.

He leaned forward, palms pressed against the table. His eyes threatened to suck her into their depths. "Has church ever made you feel the way you felt tonight while looking into that mirror?"

"I ... I don't know."

He blinked, and the intensity in his gaze dissolved. He sat back like she'd disappointed him. "That's the problem with faith in these parts."

"There's nothing wrong with my faith."

His brow twitched. "There is if it blinds you."

"What do you believe?"

He took the last sip from his cup and set it down on the saucer with a rattle. "I think you left the page off a mirror and my brother took advantage. I think mistakes are best left to a world without killers bent on revenge. That's what I think."

He stood as if to leave. Her chair scraped back as she joined him.

"Should we practice drawing tonight? For the threads?" she asked.

"You need sleep," he said, then thinking further on it, added, "Would it make you feel safer if I stayed the night?"

She snorted out a laugh. "Definitely not."

Hs lips tugged into the smallest of crooked smiles. "Fine. I need to prepare my sermon anyway."

She locked the door behind him when he left and retrieved her shotgun. With Dewey beside her, she went back to the couch. Keeping an eye on the front door and one on the back, she laid the gun across her lap and settled in with her blanket.

She thought sleep would be impossible, but almost before her head hit the cushions, she fell into a dreamless, deep sleep.

CHAPTER 20

APRIL 7, 2012

128.

128 days until Loey left for UT with Dale. They'd received their rooming forms the other day in the mail, and, as planned, they were roommates in their second-choice dorm. 128 days until freedom from this town. From the loudness of school and the brightness of the days. From the silence of the night and the pull of darkness. Freedom from him.

Sometimes, all Loey could see when she blinked was that number—when she wasn't seeing Leigh Parker's body dangling from the swing set.

She *had* to get out of this town. Even Gran and Pap were helping her plan and pack, their anxiety to send her on her way almost matching her own. It wasn't that they'd sensed the change in her. They hadn't. In fact, she'd sensed a change in them. They had more conversations that fell silent when she entered the room. Pap was out late at night, and sometimes, Gran never came home. When they spoke to Loey, it was in riddles and circles.

"Bad things are happening in this town," they'd say. *"It's best you get out for a while."*

Since Leigh's murder, much had changed in Righteous, and it wasn't typical small-town fear either. People refused to stay out late; they locked their doors up tight at night; and parents didn't let their kids walk home from school. There was a town curfew; no one could stay out after dark, lest they get arrested. Sheriff Jinks was taking the threat seriously. He'd stand before any reporter who'd have him, which was a dwindling number these days, and proclaim with more confidence than he had any right to that the boy's murderer wouldn't walk free much longer.

Except he was lying. And as the weeks wore on, people clamored for him to solve the case. The police had called Loey into the station time and again to go over her statement about that night. She'd told the story so many times she questioned her memory of the events. She wondered if she might be adding in details she hadn't seen. Like, had there been a broken mirror on the ground, or had she imagined it? Had she heard laughter chiming above the rattle of the chains?

People wanted answers, and they wanted to feel safe again. Righteous didn't feel like home. It brewed a potion of unease and tension, of short tempers and shorter fuses. The sidewalks were vacant, and for the first time in years, the coffee shop sat empty of patrons for stretches of time.

No one spoke about Leigh at school. His locker beside Loey's was a talisman everyone ignored. But sometimes she opened it. His books were still inside, his backpack too, and a mirror was taped crookedly to the back.

She closed her locker and swung her backpack over her shoulder. The school was mostly empty; her student council meeting had run later than usual. Dale had already left to watch Travis at track practice. She'd stuck to her promise of playing the role of the dutiful girlfriend with an earnestness that worried Loey.

A thump sounded from inside the art history classroom.

In the ensuing silence, Loey thought it might have been

a desk moving, perhaps the cleaning staff mopping the floors. But it sounded again. If she listened closely, she thought she heard the murmur of a voice.

His voice.

She had been about to slip away until she heard the second voice. More of a whimper, really. Scared and young. A girl.

Loey's spine ached with tension. Her palms slickened with sweat against the straps of her book bag she clutched so tightly.

She angled closer to the side of the door's window looking into the classroom. On her tiptoes, she could see inside. She found the source of the voices. Found him. Saw her.

She reacted without thinking, moving on the sudden surge of rage. She flung the classroom door open. It hit the wall so hard it cracked the cinder block wall.

Folton jumped away from the girl he had pinned against his desk, in the position he so favored. Her pants weren't down yet, thank God, but her shirt was askew. She slumped against the desk, her face in the papers he'd piled up to grade, and sobbed.

Folton saw it was Loey in his doorway and breathed a sigh of relief.

A sigh of *relief*. Like it was okay. Like because *she* had found him, he was safe.

She hated that because it was almost true.

"Loey." He pulled at the crotch of his pants, adjusting his growing excitement. He'd always toed the line of getting caught. It added to the thrill, though Loey had never been so lucky. "Did you need something? I haven't gotten to your paper yet, though I'm sure it'll be as stimulating as the last one."

For a second, she couldn't speak. The girl, a freshman named Abigail, clung to the desk. The pale skin of her back peeked out from beneath the shirt he'd shoved out of his way.

Loey knew what it felt like to be that shirt, to be the hindrance between him and his pleasure.

"Stop." She didn't know why she'd said that, why of everything she could have said she'd told him to stop when he never would. "Stop."

Abigail pushed off the desk. As she stumbled past Loey, Folton called to her, "Remember what we spoke about, Abigail."

Loey said nothing to the girl as she tore out of the classroom without looking back.

Folton walked over to Loey with his hands in his pockets. His glasses were still fogged up from his labored breathing. She should've raced out of the classroom too, but her legs weren't working, and she had so much to say to him. She needed to let the words out this time.

But she was silent.

He reached around her and closed the door, sealing her inside with him.

He smiled down at her. "I watched you Sunday at church. Did you wear that dress for me?"

She hadn't. But when he asked like that, like it wasn't even a question, she doubted herself. Had she? Was there a sick part of her that had asked for this? One simple question from him and her resolve crumbled as he pulled her to him.

She didn't fight.

128 days.

"What are you doing?"

The brown bottle fell from Loey's hand, spilling teeth-like white pills across the tile. She jerked her gaze up to find Dale and Cross standing in the doorway of one of the many bathrooms in their sprawling house.

Cross's eyes were wide and his mouth was open as he

looked between her and the pills. But Dale looked pissed, her mouth set in a grim line and her arms crossed. She knew exactly what Loey was doing, because she'd learned it from Dale herself.

"I was looking for Tylenol."

"Don't you lie to me." Dale prowled into the bathroom, her shoes smashing over the pills like tiny gunshots. Loey flinched with each *pop*. "You were taking those pills, weren't you?"

"Dale," Cross gasped. "What's gotten into you? Loey would never—"

"I was. I'm sorry. I …" Loey fumbled to a stop. She knew exactly what had gotten into her. If she pulled up her sleeves, they would see the bruises on her skin from Folton. If she closed her eyes, she could recall the feel of his stubble against the side of her neck and the way the cold, overly filtered air had blown against her backside as he bent her over this last time. She knew exactly what had gotten into her, and all she wanted in the entire world was to fade those memories with a few pills.

She blinked up at Dale, defeated. Her shoulders slumped, and though she'd thought she was cried out completely, the tears came anyway. She shook her head at her best friends. A soft whimper escaped her lips, reminding her so much of the one she'd heard from Abigail earlier this afternoon that Loey started sobbing in earnest.

Cross shouldered his big, lanky body around Dale and wrapped his arms around Loey. He smelled fresh from a recent shower. He was so big and strong, and when he pulled her against him, she folded into him like he could consume her.

After a moment, Dale came closer, not bothering to step around the pills. She wrapped her arms around Loey from behind, sandwiching her between her two best friends. She was smothered and locked in tight, even though she'd thought she could never be held from behind again. But she'd never felt safer. Never felt more whole. And in their arms, she lost it completely.

They held her until she stopped shaking and her tears ran dry and she took the first deep breath she'd taken all year.

Only then did they drop their arms, but they didn't move away. They leveled equally beautiful and serious stares at her, and together, like the siblings they were, they commanded, "Tell us."

She thought about the first time and how it hadn't been the last time like she'd prayed. She thought about Leigh and his body and the way his foot had twitched. She thought about Abigail's bunched-up shirt. She thought about all the times in church when she'd felt his eyes on her, and how he'd made her feel vulnerable in the one place she'd always felt secure. In the pews of Blackmore Baptist, she'd begged God to make it stop.

But He hadn't listened so she told her best friends instead. The words tumbled from her mouth in a rush, and she cried again. When she shuddered and hiccupped and choked on her words, Dale guided her to the ground, pushing aside the crushed pills, and together, the three of them sat in the Roses' bathroom until the sun set. She finished with the story of today, with Abigail and how Folton would never stop, how there would always be another girl.

When finished, she expected a weight to lift from her shoulders. Wasn't that how the truth worked? She expected everything to feel easier. But staring back at her friends' eyes, which were darkening with determination and rage, she didn't feel lighter at all.

She felt heavier.

Because now it was time to do something about Folton Terry Jr.

The hard part had only begun.

CHAPTER 21

L OEY ARRIVED EARLY FOR CHURCH on Sunday morning. She needed time to herself before putting on a good face and pretending everything was normal.

The white clapboard building drew her as it often had, a reassuring pull like coming home after a long day. She slipped inside and left the doors cracked open behind her.

Dappled sunlight spilled through the windows, and the old wooden planks gleamed brighter than pennies. The church smelled like cedar and pollen from the freshly cut wildflowers arranged at the base of the pulpit and hung from loops of lace at the ends of the pews. The planks squeaked under Loey's sandals as she walked to one of the low wooden benches along either side of the pulpit.

Here, the wood was worn down to the grain from countless people kneeling over the years. How many times had Loey found herself here with her head bowed to the bench, her fingers clasped, and her knees smarting? How many times had Gran and Pap joined her, their arms around her back to hold her together as she prayed?

What about her mom? Had she found herself here, with these same questions in her head? Had she crumbled beneath the pressure of tending the threads of this little town, or had she taken the first escape route that presented itself to avoid getting trapped? Loey understood all about getting trapped; it was the one thing she had in common with her mother. And now, after discovering she was a Tender, her ties to Righteous had strengthened, ensnaring her further. She'd never leave. Not alive, anyway.

Kneeling, Loey braced her elbows on the bench. She bowed her head against her clasped hands. In this position, the words slipped freely off her lips in a whispered prayer. She lost herself to the cadence as natural as breathing, a precious meditation. Everything else faded away.

"Are you praying for me?"

She jolted away from the bench and whirled around.

Jeronimo walked up the aisle with a smirk on his face. It wasn't a smile, but it was the closest he'd come to a real one, and the way it transformed his face mesmerized her. He looked a decade younger, like the weight he carried wasn't so heavy anymore, like the lines around his mouth from frowning weren't so deep.

"Ah …" She fumbled the words on her tongue. "Maybe."

"Maybe?" He stopped at a front pew and leaned a hip against the wooden end. He crossed his arms, and his brows rose as he waited for an answer.

"I mean, yes, I was."

"Why?"

She swallowed. She had to stop staring at his mouth. "Why was I praying for you?"

His smirk widened. "Yes."

No one had ever asked her that. No one ever questioned why anyone would pray for them, especially in Righteous. "I'll pray for you," was one of those nice things people said to each other. But no one ever questioned it.

"Because," she said slowly, unnerved more than usual by his presence, "I think you need it."

He smiled fully. White teeth and razor-sharp canines, the sharpest she'd ever seen, gleamed in the dust-mote-ridden air of the church. Why was he in such a good mood?

Because he's closer than ever to killing his brother.

"You're wasting your sweet breath," he said happily. "You can't pray for something without a soul. Doesn't your precious Bible tell you that?"

She'd gotten so little out of him—she hardly knew anything about his past or what he did during the day or night—but the way he asked that question, she knew.

"Do you," she started, voice lowering even though no one was around to overhear her, "not believe in God?"

He barked out a laugh. It wasn't a reassuring thing. "You shot me in the belly and watched me not die, and I've shown you the magic simmering beneath all the false pretenses of this town's superstitions." The hint of a smile returned. "But the thing that unsettles you the most is my not believing in God."

"Yes," Loey said, wholeheartedly truthful, "obviously. How can you not believe in God when you know about all this magic? About the threads and the Seam and what happened to you that night the still exploded? That was a miracle, Jeronimo."

"No," he snarled, his mood suddenly shifting, "that was a fucking curse."

His vehemence startled her. But how could he not believe? Even what little magic she'd done, seeing those threads of light in her kitchen and touching the fabric of life, made her feel like she'd seen the fingerprint of God.

"How can you say that?"

"Because I was there, Loey Grace, and every day since then I've paid the price. How can I believe in a god when I know what this magic can do? When I know what's across the Seam?"

"You're about to give a sermon," she said. "They think you're going to preach to them. These people trust you."

"Tell me, after everything you've seen, you can look me in the eye and tell me your faith hasn't been shaken."

"It hasn't," she stated.

His interest sharpened, and he pounced on her rawest wound. "What about your grandparents?"

The words prickled the deepest stirring of pain. "Stop."

"They put rings of salt around the graves so the souls can't escape. Where is that in your good book?"

"Don't talk about them."

"How does the magic from last night fit into your faith? Over half a century ago, this church drank moonshine and called it holy water. They were no better than those they scorned in Little Cricket. But they put a pretty name on it and got three sheets to the wind from the safety of their pews."

"Shut up!" she shouted.

Thankfully, she startled him into silence. He rocked back on his heels and regarded her as if she'd finally said something interesting. She hated that look on his face. She wanted to shoot it clean off.

"Do you think I don't know this place is full of hypocrites?" she snapped. "Do you think I don't know I'm the biggest one? I sit in my pew every Sunday, and every Sunday I pray the same prayer and I listen to the sermon and I nod my head and I wear my pretty dresses and I shake hands and I dole out my smile, even when I want to bash someone's head in. But that's just the South, Jeronimo. Sometimes we have a little bit of devil in us, but most days, we have a whole lot of good and that should count for something."

Jeronimo opened his mouth, squinting as he focused solely on her, but before he could speak, the front doors swung open and the old biddies, led by Ms. Ida May, flocked in, squawking about the September weather and spice cakes and who'd seen the first leaf change.

Loey heaved out a breath, still staring at Jeronimo. He met her eyes for a long moment before turning away right as the biddies roosted in a tight gaggle around him, chirping about how excited they were for his sermon today.

Loey spun on her heel, her hands fisted at her sides. She needed fresh air.

A *thing* existed in Southern Baptist churches. It was a religious thing. A "holy spirit" thing. The most devout believed the holy spirit would come into a church and fill up the souls of its worshipers. People described it in various ways. Some would experience euphoria, others would be overcome and fall to the ground in a fit, and others would speak in tongues.

Loey had never been filled with the holy spirit, unless you counted coffee. But that was probably blasphemous.

That Sunday morning, Jeronimo delivered his sermon eloquently, almost beautifully, captivating the congregation, who all pressed forward in their seats, hanging on his every word. Loey, however, gnawed on her fingernails and slumped in her pew, his words falling on deaf ears.

But even Loey thought the holy spirit was upon them when the church doors rattled and shook from a banging so loud it made Ms. Ida May jump plumb out of her skin.

Up at the pulpit, Jeronimo paused mid-sentence, his eyes narrowing on the church's front doors where the handles clanged against the locks as if someone couldn't figure out how to open the doors.

Everyone twisted around in their seats, as if expecting Jesus Christ to open the doors and stroll inside.

Someone said, "Praise Jesus."

Another added, "Amen."

The doors slammed open, spilling bright Sunday morning light down the church's center aisle like day-old lemonade.

"Martha Lee!" shouted the swaying shadow that stumbled in after the light.

"Well, it sure as shit ain't Jesus," Dale whispered in Loey's ear.

"*Dale,*" Loey hissed. She spun around to better see the spectacle developing at the back of the church.

It wasn't Jesus. It wasn't even the holy spirit. It was Tate Freeman on a bender and pissed as a tomcat with a firecracker duct-taped to its tail.

Cross sighed. "Here we go again."

Tate crashed into a pew and bellowed, "Martha Lee, get your fat ass out here right this second!"

He was drunk as a skunk and smelled worse than one. Around him, the congregation jerked to their feet and retreated from the stinking filth and foul language that always crawled out of Little Cricket Trailer Park.

Martha Lee Freeman, sporting a fresh smattering of bruises on her knobby arms, stood and clutched Emma Todd to her chest. Waylon, her sticky-faced toddler, clung to her bare, skinny legs.

"No shame," Ms. Ida May whispered from the front row. But her whisper carried, and Martha Lee flinched as if the words were blows.

A strong breeze could've blown over Martha Lee. She wore her fear on her body, in the hollows beneath her cheeks, in the dark blooms of her husband's special love. She wore one of her three threadbare dresses she rotated between on Sundays. This one's buttons had recently been replaced, their too-bright thread stark against the washed-out floral print. Her feet were clad in cheap plastic flip-flops, her toes dirty from the walk over from the trailer park.

"Tate," Martha Lee begged, "please. I'm sorry. I'm coming. Meet me at the car."

She moved fast for a woman who looked two inches from Death's doorstep. Emma Todd wailed, and Waylon joined in with his sister. Standing quickly, Loey was at the end of her pew before Martha Lee could skitter by.

"Loey Grace," Ms. Rose snarled, dropping her sweet-as-pie voice, "get back *here*."

"Hey." Loey ignored Dale's mother. "Hey, Martha Lee."

The woman darted a sideways glance her way, not slowing. "Don't. Just don't."

"Stay here." Loey knew it was no use. It never was.

Behind her, Dale pressed forward as her mother hissed more warnings. "Come on back to my house after the service. You can stay as long as you need."

"She ain't going nowhere but home with me," Tate slurred at Dale.

A few pews back, Mayor Goody, in a red dress that made her eyes gleam like polished river stones, with her son clinging to her hand, added, "That sounds like a good idea, Martha Lee. Why don't you stay and finish up Pastor James's sermon then head on with Loey and Dale?"

"Thank you, Mayor," Martha Lee stammered. "But—"

"What's going on here?"

The booming voice from the front of the church could have been God's, considering every whisper and titter ceased in the church. Even Tate shut up. Loey swung her gaze to the pulpit.

Jeronimo stood beside it, his hand holding the wooden lip, his knuckles white. His black eyes flashed like flint striking a flame. Color blossomed high on his cheeks, his ashen hair sweeping across his forehead. A single vein pulsed beneath his right eye. Loey's nose tingled.

"Stay out of this, preacher man. I'm just gettin' my woman."

"I don't think she's going with you." Jeronimo climbed down the two steps into the aisle.

"It's fine, Pastor James," Martha Lee said in such a trembling rush that the words didn't even sound like English. To Tate, she added, "I'm coming. Right now. Let's go."

"I told you …" The rest of Tate's words were lost in a slurring mess.

But Martha Lee nodded like she understood, like she knew those words by heart. When he grabbed her arm, she went to him, keeping her body between Emma Todd and her drunken husband.

"Tate," Loey said, stepping into the aisle so the wayward family would have to stop or shoulder past her, "why don't you stay? You could sit—"

"Stuck-up bitch," Tate growled. He indeed passed Loey, shouldering her out of the way. She stumbled back into a pew to the gasps of indignant old women.

He pushed the back of Waylon's head so the boy toddled in a half run, half stumble in front of the couple. Tate hauled Martha Lee into the churchyard, and they all heard his hand strike her face, that staccato smack of skin on skin, and her surprised whimper.

Loey was moving down the aisle when Jeronimo strode by and blocked her exit with his arm. "Stay inside."

"But—"

"Keep everyone inside. Martha Lee doesn't need this to be a show," he said before striding out to the churchyard.

He should've known there was no way this *wouldn't* be a show. Everyone, including Dale and Cross, flooded out through the front doors and onto the yard to catch the rest of the spectacle. Loey elbowed her way to the front of the crowd.

By the time she made it, it took her a moment to process the sight in front of her.

Beneath the churchyard's willow tree, Martha Lee cried into Emma Todd's dirty curls. Tate, with his nose gushing blood, narrowly skirted another blow from Jeronimo's fist. Tate scrambled in the grass and tore off toward his truck, but Jeronimo moved like a shadow slipping up the wall. His lithe, tall body reacted faster than it should. He clamped his hand onto the back of Tate's shirt, and Loey swore she saw Tate's feet leave the ground as Jeronimo slung the man to the ground. All the women gasped like good Christian women, and Dale cheered. Loey clapped a hand over her mouth.

Tate spit and sputtered, digging his feet deep into the dirt. Jeronimo reared his fist back, his white shirt flashing in the sun, and slammed his knuckles straight down into Tate's mouth.

Everyone fell silent, even Martha Lee. The only sound in the churchyard on that once blissful Sunday morning was Tate's gurgling moans.

Jeronimo wrenched the man to his feet by one arm. He practically carried Tate to his truck and slung him into the passenger seat. After slamming the door shut, he turned to his brand-new congregation. They all stared back at their blood-spattered preacher with open mouths and flushed faces.

"I'm taking Mr. Freeman to the sheriff's office. My apologies for cutting the sermon short."

At Jeronimo's words, everyone looked around for the sheriff in question, but Burl wasn't there. His absence stirred up a wave of whispered explanations, most of them involving sin and temptation and falling off the wagon.

Jeronimo's eyes found Loey's in the crowd. With a dip of his chin, he climbed into Tate's truck. Diesel engine roaring, he slung gravel down the church driveway and onto Devil's Maw with a burst of black smoke from the tailpipe.

Martha Lee swiped at her tears and took a trembling breath. Before she could apologize, Dale was at her side, her arm around Martha Lee's thin shoulders.

"Come on," Dale said, smiling so prettily that not even Lucifer could deny her anything, "let's go to my house. I baked a fresh blackberry cake with lemon custard and vanilla buttercream. Doesn't that sound yummy, Waylon?"

"Maybe we shouldn't get involved," Travis murmured beside her, loud enough for Martha Lee to hear.

Dale swung her warm smile to her husband. When it landed on him, it became calculated and frosted at the corners. "Oh, but I thought you and Cross were watching the game today? Right, Cross?"

Travis coughed, his ears reddening. Overhearing from where he stood beside his mother, Cross's spine snapped straight.

To his wife, his words as calculated and frosty as her smile, Travis said, "You're right, honey."

"Then it's settled," Dale said to Martha Lee.

"Thank you," the frail woman whispered.

"Heavens above," Ms. Ida May murmured near Loey. "Is it me, or is our new preacher a fine man?"

"Very fine, indeed."

"And a Godly man."

"So very Godly."

"And what a nice sermon, yes?"

"So very nice."

Ms. Ida May shook her head at the chipped pavement of Devil's Maw. "Those pants are awfully tight though…"

CHAPTER 22

EARLY MONDAY MORNING, SO EARLY the hens weren't even awake yet, Loey picked up her phone.

Notions of faith and the world's threads and her own substance plagued her. The past week had caught up to her, and her anxiety coiled itself up into a loaded gun that lived in her chest, the trigger waiting to be pulled.

Her grandparents had lived an entirely separate life from her. They'd shielded her from it for reasons only they would ever know, except for one. The main one, the one Loey was certain of, was because they'd loved her. But the smaller reasons that gnawed at her were the ones she conjured up in their absence. *Small. Weak.* They'd known about Folton, and they'd taken her secret to the grave for her sake, at the cost of their souls.

Because Loey did believe in faith and sin, Heaven and Hell, God and the darker things of this world. She'd thought what she'd done to Folton only marred her soul, but she'd sullied her grandparents' as well. She couldn't let Cross and Dale experience the same fate.

It was time to atone.

Dale answered before the first ring finished. "Lo, I can't talk right now."

"Sorry," Loey said in a tumbling rush, "I know it's early."

173

She cradled her phone between her shoulder and ear to better chew on her nails, which formed bloody half-moons on her fingertips. She sat at the kitchen table, which was heaped with every flower that bloomed in the graveyard. Violets and irises, lilies that smelled like blood, bleeding hearts and simple geraniums with pollen coated to their petals, heaps of carnations because they'd reminded her of the boutique she'd found on her grandparents' grave. She'd gathered various cuttings of them all yesterday when she'd spent the entire day tending the flowers, bushes, and vines that adorned Blackmore Cemetery.

"Is everything okay?"

No, Loey wanted to scream, but she swallowed the word back down her throat.

"I just... I just, well, I've been thinking." She paused to gather her resolve. Dale wasn't going to take this well. "About Folton."

The silence on the other end of the line stretched long. Loey couldn't even hear Dale breathing.

"Dale?"

"*No*."

"It's killing me, Dale. It has to be killing you too. Doesn't it keep you up at night?" Loey pried off a chunk of skin from her thumb. Before Dale could answer, she blazed on, "I never told my grandparents because I thought it would change how they loved me, but I found ... I mean, *if* I found out a secret about them, it would never be big enough to change how I loved them. And I should've known that. I should've trusted them. But I didn't and this feels like the only way to make it right."

She heaved a huge breath into the silence.

"Does that make sense?" she asked.

Something slammed in the background of Dale's phone and splintered.

Loey sat up a little straighter, frowning. "What's going on? Are you baking?"

When Dale didn't respond again, Loey checked the screen of her phone, thinking Dale might have hung up on her, but the call was still connected.

"Dale?"

"Do whatever it is you need to do." Dale's muffled voice sounded far away; she must have been putting a cake in the oven. "But don't involve me. I've already paid the price for this secret, do you …" She was too far away from the phone to hear. She cut back in with a ripple of static. "… entire town *judges* me. They watch me walk down the street and all they can think about is Folton Fucking Terry. So do what you need to do, Loey Grace, but I stand by what we decided and I'll never take it back. Not until I die."

Loey dropped her hand from her mouth and said, "I'm going to the station this morning with or without you. But I think you should come. We need to do this."

"You won't."

"I am. I mean it this time."

Dale laughed, suddenly close to the phone again and loud enough to make the laugh like a growl. "One of these days you'll learn to keep your secrets. Because when people know all the truths about you, they can never really love you again."

"Mornin', Loey. What can I help you with?"

Matt's voice was low and rich, like chocolate cake baked with the darkest coffee. Across the desk that separated the front lobby of the station from the desks and offices in the back, where a handful of deputies spoke on phones or drank coffee, Matt smiled at her. His dark hair made his honey-colored eyes seem even brighter this morning. His officer's uniform was crisp and tidy. Loey knew for a fact that his mother still ironed his uniforms for him every week.

Thinking she might puke from nerves, Loey kept her lips closed as she smiled. "I'm looking for Burl. Isn't he in yet?"

"Not yet, but we're expecting him soon."

Matt, too nice for his own good, always covered for Burl; the sheriff had been like an idol to him, a small-town Sherlock Holmes before the hookers and divorce had led the detective astray. Now, instead of playing Watson, Matt kept himself busy putting out Burl's fires.

"Oh, okay." She fidgeted with the strap of her purse. A glance back out the front door confirmed Dale wasn't walking up the sidewalk, ready to meet her so they could unburden themselves together. "I guess I'll come back later."

"Hey, wait," Matt said in a rush as she turned to leave. "I heard you've been seein' the new preacher some."

"I wouldn't say that." That was the way of small towns: telephone gossip and exaggerations.

"I was on duty yesterday when Mr. James brought Tate in."

Loey frowned. "Was he charged with anything?"

"I decided against it since Burl wasn't in." He mulled over his words, his forehead deeply creased in concentration. "Didn't seem right to charge a preacher on a Sunday, and he didn't do nothing we haven't all wanted to."

Loey hesitated to see if he was serious. Slowly, she said, "I meant Tate. Was he charged with assaulting Martha Lee?"

"What?" Matt asked, though she knew darn well he'd heard her from the way his mouth had gone slack with fear. "I mean, I wasn't at the church, and no one filed an official report, so I couldn't exactly charge him. 'Sides no one saw him hit her."

"But she's always covered in bruises!"

"You know she won't press charges. She never does."

Loey's grip tightened on her purse. "Fine. Thanks for letting me know about Burl. Tell him to call me when he gets in."

"Is there anything I can help you with?" he asked with such hope that Loey's queasiness returned.

"I have to get to the shop," she muttered.

She shoved through the station's front door. The sunlight spilled brightness across the freshly cut grass in the town square. The fresh day's cheer directly opposed Loey's mood. She managed a weak wave at the mailman, Mr. Weebly, and Mrs. Herbert, with her flower arrangements outside her boutique, as she stomped up to Deadly Sin and stabbed the key into the front door lock.

The bell chimed overhead, and she flipped on the lights. Today, not even the shop's scent could calm her. The dance of grinding coffee beans and starting the first brew of the morning did little to ease her nerves. The pastries she set out in the counter display only served to remind her of her talk with Dale this morning.

Normally, by this time, her best friend would be in the shop with her, helping to prep for the morning rush. But Dale still hadn't shown by lunch. Loey texted and called but got no response.

Of course they'd had fights over the years. Having a best friend like Dale meant there would be fights. But this one felt different. This one prodded the root of their darkness, their hollow parts. Secrets like that inevitably caused rifts that changed friendships forever.

After closing the shop that afternoon, Loey aimed her truck for home. It wasn't a conscious decision to turn onto the road leading away from Devil's Maw and straight to the Jinks Estate; it was the kernel of strength she'd found in telling Dale it was time to tell the truth about Leigh and Folton. That temporary easement was like a drug, and Loey needed more.

She wondered if she should have called first. Maybe he was sick or had company. Maybe he had *that* kind of company. It would be rude to interrupt.

It blew her mind that, even now, she was concerned about etiquette. But Gran had raised her with the notion that a "please" and "thank-you" could get you much further when said in a sweet voice and with a pleasant smile. *"Especially,"* Gran had always added, *"when dealing with men. But don't tell your pap I said that."* And she'd wink.

The picture of their hands entwined in death blinked through Loey's memory.

Burl's driveway loomed ahead. The roses on the mailbox were dead, their vines black with rot. The hedges that adorned the entrance had turned brittle with weeds. A massive iron sign hung above the road, proclaiming the entrance to the Jinks Estate.

Burl came from a long line of iron barons. All the men of the Jinks family had mined and smelted iron ever since Townsend Rose had purchased thousands of acres of hardwoods from Obidiah Jinks in exchange for providing the wood to fuel their massive iron smelter operation, which made everyone richer until the deal went bad between Townsend and Obidiah. Bad blood or not, their graves were right in the middle of Blackmore Cemetery, alongside the Keenes'. But the Jinkses' old money was as bloody as the Roses'. It had been borne on the back of stealing land from those who couldn't fight to keep it—natives, the poor, and people broken beneath a white man's wallet and politics—and dirty under-the-table deals that kept everyone happy, albeit temporarily.

Nothing had changed. Politics still ruled this town. And at the end of the day, it all came down to who had the most money and who was smart enough to use it like a knife.

But the once-great Jinks property had fallen into disrepair. Weeds choked the grass. Fence boards had fallen from posts and lay on the ground, and the few boards still attached had chipped paint and bowed middles. The twister had uprooted a few old maples; they'd fallen onto the road, over the fence, and, as Loey pulled up to the house and saw the rest of the damage, over Burl's '76 Dodge Charger.

The house had fared worse than the property. Mrs. Jinks had left Burl after the last scandal, when Burl couldn't afford her silence anymore and no one felt inclined to show him charity, and her absence showed.

The flower beds were heaped with twisted brambles. Junk cluttered the sprawling farmhouse's wrap-around porch, which had once contained rocking chairs and lush ferns. The windows were all closed, the drapes pulled tight to seal out all light. It had to be dark as a cave inside.

Loey cut the truck's engine and got out.

She walked to the front porch, her boots crunching over the gravel. The only other sound came from the crickets in the woods near the house and a toad out by the pond in the pasture. The day could have been pleasant if not for the smell. Garbage bags were piled beside the front door and forgotten, a feat given their rankness.

Dale hadn't mentioned the state into which Burl had fallen, but perhaps she didn't know. Or, like most Southern families, she had viewed his troubles as a secret meant to be tucked away and overlooked. The condition of the place didn't match Loey's memory of the proud man who had caused Travis to quake with fear in high school or inspired the worst of Little Cricket to straighten up before he had to bring them to the station.

She glanced into the tall windows flanking the big double doors. Nothing but darkness stretched out behind the glass.

She knocked.

"Burl?" she called but didn't expect an answer.

After a few more tries with no response, she tested the doorknob. It turned. She pushed it open to the hinges' squeaking complaint. Sulfur, as strong as it had been that night in the church, gusted through the opened door.

The rational part of her brain told her to retreat to her truck, where she could safely call the authorities or—given the smell of sulfur—Jeronimo. But the part of her that would always be impulsive and headlong—like running through a twister or after an intruder in the cemetery—won out. Something was wrong in Burl's house, and she had to know, to see for herself, and to help however she could.

She stepped over the threshold and into the dark interior of the entryway. The stairs swept up to the second level, where the reflections of dancing lights played off the large bay window.

The dusty luminescence glittered on bits of glass strewn across the hardwood. Her eyes lingered on the empty frames along the wall with shards of glass still embedded in the edges. As she passed one, she caught her reflection.

They weren't empty picture frames. They were broken mirrors, and there had to be nearly fifty of them on the wall.

Her spine turned to a column of ice. She backed toward the front door. When she was within a few steps of freedom, a hand clapped over her mouth, and a set of strong arms wrenched her out of the house.

CHAPTER 23

LOEY THRASHED AGAINST THE ARMS holding her.

"Calm down," a voice hissed in her ear.

The arms released her, and she whirled around to glare at Jeronimo.

"What the heck was that about? You can't grab me like that," she whisper-shouted.

He squinted down at her. "You don't have to whisper."

"Fine," she ground out between clenched teeth, her fists balled at her sides. "But why are you following me?"

"Because you like sticking your nose in dangerous situations." He lifted his chin toward the open door behind her. "Like this one."

"I need to check on Burl. I saw threads in there right before you jerked me out."

"I didn't jerk you. I gently pulled you back."

She stabbed a finger into his chest, his muscles firm enough to hurt her finger. "You caveman-handled me, and the next time you do it, I'm shooting you again."

He caught her hand and pushed it away. "Then lead the way, ma'am."

She rolled her eyes and strode through Burl's front door with more gumption than she felt.

Dust covered everything, even the chandelier. The wallpaper was faded except in spots where family pictures had hung. There was no furniture, and moving boxes were scattered around as if Burl had been ready to move but hadn't gotten around to it.

"Do you see all the mirrors?" She pointed to wall of frames and shards.

"I see them."

"That's not good, is it?"

"Where did you see the threads?" Jeronimo asked from behind her, his heavy boots clumping across the hardwood.

Loey glanced back. Jeronimo's jaw was tight, his eyes squinted with worry. She stepped aside to let him pass and said, "Upstairs."

With a nod, he started toward the staircase. Loey went to follow him, but her eyes caught on the room off the entryway. From its formal fireplace and sprawling windows, she recognized it as a parlor, but the room was crammed with towering mounds of boxes, with paperwork haphazardly sticking out. A sofa covered in a blanket and pillow was shoved against the back wall. In front of it, a card table acted as a coffee table. Coffee mugs, ashtrays, and more paperwork littered the top. A cursory glance revealed they were bank statements with lots of red overdrawn notices. But one small leather-bound notebook caught her eye. Feathery handwriting filled the pages, which were all dated going back as far as the early fifties, as if it were a diary. She was about to close it when she saw a name that caused her skin to prickle with goose bumps.

Knox.

Her great-great-grandfather. Which meant the book possibly could have belonged to Obidiah Jinks, who'd lived during that same era in Righteous's history.

"Loey!" Jeronimo shouted down from upstairs. His voice sounded strained, with a scratching rasp that turned into a cough. The sound echoed through the empty house.

Without time to think on it further, Loey stuffed the book into the pocket of her jeans and raced out of the parlor. Flickering lights spilled over the upstairs banister and down the stairs. Somewhere out of sight, Jeronimo was still coughing.

Loey ran, taking the stairs two at a time. "Jeronimo?"

She rounded the curved banister and found him on his knees in the reading area that served as an open landing and library. The shelves were devoid of books and coated with dust. The air reeked of sulfur.

She surged forward.

"Wait!" Jeronimo flung up his hand. Blood streamed from his nose, over his lips and chin, and dripped onto the moth-eaten rug.

Loey froze. He pointed to the wall where a large picture had once hung. In its wake, a message was being burned into the wall.

Not al, the entity had finished so far.

As Loey watched, an *o* was added to the message.

"Is that Barty?" she asked without taking her eyes off the letters.

An *n* scorched itself into the wall.

Gran's favorite show to watch in the evenings had always been *Wheel of Fortune*. She and Pap used to compete to see who could guess the phrase fastest. Sometimes, Loey would beat them both.

"He's not alone?" she guessed. "Why would—"

"That tatter," Jeronimo gasped out. "Look at the tatter."

"Oh." Loey glanced around. "I don't have a pen or a page. Are you sure? What if I look at the threads and Barty is coming through?"

"Stop stalling," Jeronimo growled around a cough. He waved her over as Barty finished his message.

Not alone, it read.

185

"He could tell us who's with him," Loey mumbled, giving the message a wide berth as she scooted closer to Jeronimo. "That would be helpful."

"Some other being might be in there with him, but he's the killer. Nothing else matters. Now, the tatter."

"How? I don't—"

He grabbed her hand and dragged her fingers across his face, drenching them in the blood dripping from his nose.

She jerked away from Jeronimo. "Oh my gosh!"

On the wall, Barty began the second line of the message. He wrote an *S* then a *k*.

She gagged and held her hand out like it was ruined for life.

"Loey. *Now*."

On the wall, an *i* and two *n*'s were added.

With her bloody fingers, Loey hurried to paint the circular symbol on a patch of hardwood beside the rug before the blood could dry.

As she drew, she glanced up. The first word was complete: *Skinned*. Next, Barty wrote out an *M*.

She finished her symbol.

An *a* was added.

"Skinned Man?" she guessed. "Who's that? Do you think he's actually telling us who's in there with him?"

Jeronimo didn't have time to answer before her world erupted into a star-studded cosmos.

The threads appeared faster this time, stronger and brighter too. If she hadn't been kneeling on the ground, she would have fallen from the sheer sense of spatial deprivation. Her entire vision was nothing but lights racing up and down delicate threads, but she'd known to expect this. As her heart raced and her blood thundered through her veins, she blindly focused on the tatter near the wall.

The second message was complete; she'd been right. It read, *Skinned Man.*

But that wasn't what made her gasp.

A shadow man hovered behind the threads near the wall. The tatter was only big enough for him to fit his upper body through, and around him, the threads swung loose, snapping and whipping on an invisible wind, their connection points torn asunder. Their lights fizzled, flashing on and off in distress. Most of the colors were white, but closer to the tatter the lights were red or bruise purple or, like inside the pit of the tear, an empty, colorless black that shrouded the man in darkness.

"Barty?" she asked the shadow man.

Beside her, Jeronimo grabbed her arm and asked her something, his fingers squeezing her arm with bruising force.

Loey pulled away and stood without looking at him. He was too weak from his brother's proximity to hold her back. She walked toward the tatter, drawn by a compulsion to hold the threads and knot them together, to fix their torn parts and make them right again.

The closer she came, the more the shadow figure flickered and pulsed. This close, she knew. He wasn't the shadow man from her mirror, the one who'd seeped evil and wrongness and tried to hurt her. She stared right at him and he stared back. His presence felt inconsequential and fleeting, as if she could blink and he'd fade from sight. When she was a few steps away, he pulled back through the small tatter and disappeared. She looked through the tear and saw nothing but blackness, like a void existed across the Seam.

Her attention went to the torn threads. Staring at them in their loosened form, she realized the concentrated pools of light were tightly wound knots that held one thread to the next. She brushed her fingers over the nearest knot and electricity burst across her skin. She shivered.

A thread flapped near her arm and she picked it up. It felt weightless and less substantial than a spider's web against her fingers. She reached for another thread and brought it toward the first one. Like she was working on her macramé, she started tying.

The threads screeched as she tried to bind them together. Before she could even jerk back, the threads ripped apart. They twitched up into the air. Near the ceiling, they shriveled around each other, turned brittle and black, and burned to ash. The debris blew away.

She had enough time to look back at the tatter and see that the threads were flapping more erratically and the hole had grown bigger before the entire vision disappeared. She'd done something wrong, but she blinked, and reality came back into focus.

Jeronimo groaned across the library landing. She turned to him for the first time since she'd drawn the symbol. He was strong enough now to stand. "Is he gone? What happened?"

"He's gone. It's over."

Jeronimo's shoulders eased. "What did you see?"

"Are you sure it's Barty who's making you weak?" she asked instead, her mind puzzling over the clues.

"It's Barty, Loey. I swear it. He's a killer. He won't stop—"

"I know. I know. But what if he isn't alone? What if this"—she gestured to the wall—"is someone else trying to warn you about your brother? He's always covered in shadows, and I can't see his face. We don't really know it's your brother."

"What are you getting at?"

"You said the explosion set Barty on fire, right? Maybe he looks skinned?"

Jeronimo steadied himself on a bookshelf, but he wasn't arguing with her anymore. Instead, he considered her words before quietly saying, "I watched him burn. Those flames shoulda killed him. They'd certainly leave him scarred."

"So maybe it's not Barty making you weak but just being exposed to a tatter and the other side of the Seam."

Jeronimo's jaw clenched. She knew he didn't like considering anything other than the narrative he'd established in his head surrounding his brother. He was blindingly bent on the facts he considered true, but Loey wasn't so convinced anymore.

"I think I know who's in there with Barty," she said. "I think I know who's trying to warn me."

"Who?"

All the puzzle pieces fell into place. "Leigh Parker."

"The kid who was murdered at your high school? Loey"— Jeronimo let out a breath—"he would've had a timely burial. His body would've been salted in time."

"Maybe not," she argued against the logic. She'd gone to Leigh's funeral herself and watched as his mother poured the salt, but she forged on regardless. "What if he's bent on proving what happened to him? Barty killed him all those years ago, and now he's trapped across the Seam with his killer. That's pretty good incentive to get strong enough to warn the people Barty is coming after."

Near the wall with the message, a dusty vase rocked on a side table, slowly building momentum before it toppled off. It smashed onto the floor, and its dusty, dried flowers disintegrated across the floor.

"See?" Loey waved at the mess. "It's Leigh."

"Even if his soul had somehow leaked into the Seam," Jeronimo said, his voice stronger now that his nose had stopped bleeding, "that doesn't matter at this point. Barty is the priority."

Loey crossed her arms. "No offense, but you couldn't even

stand straight while Barty or *whoever* was writing a message on the wall. How the heck do you plan on fighting your brother long enough to kill him?"

Jeronimo snarled and stalked off toward the archway leading out of the library landing and down a hall lined with bedrooms. Rolling her eyes, Loey trailed after him. At the end of the hall, he opened a set of French doors and started inside.

Something caught his eye up toward the ceiling. His jaw clenched. He stepped back and closed the doors.

Loey stopped halfway down the hall, her tirade trailing off. "What did you see?"

"It's Burl." Jeronimo stood at the door as if to block her from barging past him to see for herself.

But he had the wrong idea. She had no desire to see any more dead bodies.

"Did Barty kill him too?"

Jeronimo's throat bobbed as he swallowed. "Burl did that himself."

"Suicide?"

He dipped his chin.

"Are you sure? Barty might have tried to conceal it."

"Barty is proud of his work. He wouldn't conceal what he'd done."

"Oh."

From the opening and closing of the door, a scent had drifted down the hall from the room. It clung to Jeronimo's clothes as he approached. Death. The scent of decay. Like something the wind sometimes carried down from Shiner's Ridge.

"We need to call the cops."

By the time the deputies arrived, the sun had set, and the Jinks plantation was cast in the pulsing blue lights of the cop cars.

Loey and Jeronimo answered their questions and pointed them inside. A deputy who'd been on the high school football team called Travis. Mayor Goody arrived, her face grim. She gave a small wave to Loey before going inside the house.

Loey tried calling Dale but kept getting her voicemail.

There would be another funeral in Righteous. More salt rings to pour. Another pine box to set eight feet down.

Loey caught strands of the deputies' conversation about Burl and the noose hanging from the ceiling fan and a letter written on the back of a photo taken on the day he and Mrs. Jinks were married. When Travis arrived and heard the news, he gave a sharp dip of his chin and set about making arrangements, right there on his father's overgrown lawn as if he wasn't even surprised. He tried calling Dale too, but she didn't answer.

After giving their statements, Loey drove home, with Jeronimo following on his motorcycle.

Outside Righteous, the moon shone behind a thick stack of clouds. Ribbons of fog draped over Shiner's Ridge. Driving up Devil's Maw by the glow of her headlights carried a different weight this evening. As always, she avoided looking at the crosses that marked the side of the road. There were too many, and two belonged to her grandparents.

Loey parked in her driveway. The truck's rumble died as she cut the engine. Behind her, Jeronimo's headlight winked off. Before she got out, she released a breath she'd been holding since walking out of Burl's house.

He'd been a good sheriff who'd made a few mistakes, but no one would remember his good deeds; they'd only whisper about the bad ones.

Roots grew deep in Righteous, and sometimes a war broke out over a few words. Pride was a lucrative currency in these parts. Money came and went as the Jinks family knew better than most, but a man's reputation was all he had.

And in the end, Burl didn't even have that.

CHAPTER 24

JERONIMO HAD ESCORTED HER ALL the way home Monday night. She'd been so exhausted by the time she'd checked on the animals and let Dewey out that she'd stripped her clothes, tossed them in the dirty laundry, and fallen straight to bed, where she'd dreamed of nooses and squeaking swing sets. She'd forgotten all about not hearing form Dale until the next morning, when she opened the shop again without word from her best friend.

Cross couldn't reach her, and according to him, neither could Travis. Dale had disappeared before. Normally, they waited for her to make her way back home, but this time felt different. Even after she'd told Cross about calling Dale and demanding she come to the station, he wanted to wait. If they started asking questions about her, people would take notice, and Mrs. Rose did not want the added attention while Burl's death was making the family look bad.

Loey had promised to wait, but as she made coffee and rang up pastry sales, all the hush-hush gossip her patrons bandied about over Burl's death chipped away at her resolve. Thoughts of murder and magic and Tenders and threads zigzagged through her mind, and by the afternoon, dread had settled like wool over her skin. Dale's chair sat empty, and every time Loey's gaze landed on it, the sense of wrongness spread further.

It positively erupted over her flesh when the bell over the door chimed and Martha Lee Freeman skittered into the shop, holding Waylon's hand.

She wore too-short jeans with dirt stains spread over the denim and a shirt that billowed around her bird-bone frame. Waylon's bare feet slapped across the floor as Martha Lee tugged him toward the counter, and his eyes lit up at the goodies contained inside.

The few customers Loey had fell silent as Martha Lee stopped at the counter.

Loey sat aside the sieve she'd been cleaning. "Martha Lee, it's good to see you. What brings you by today?"

Martha Lee grabbed Waylon's free hand before he could plaster it against the glass counter, his mouth watering at the chocolate donuts.

"I, um …" Martha Lee stammered. Her eyes slanted toward the other patrons pretending not to be eavesdropping. She lowered her voice such that Loey had to lean over the counter to hear her. "It's Dale. She's, well, she's in Little Cricket again. I thought you oughta know."

Loey pressed her hands against the countertop to keep from swaying. "You're sure?"

"Dale helped me out last Sunday. She was real nice to me, and you've always been kind to us. I wanted you to know, givin' the sheriff's untimely, well, you know. I wanted you to know. Yeah, that's all. Just that."

Before Loey could respond, Martha Lee jerked Waylon back toward the door.

"Wait," Loey said too loudly.

Martha Lee froze. The shop fell silent.

Loey reached inside the counter and pulled out a chocolate donut. She put it in a bag and came around the counter, offering it to Waylon.

"You don't have to do that," Martha Lee said as Waylon snatched the bag. Martha Lee tried to take it back, but he screamed and twisted away from her to protect his prize. "Give that back, Waylon. We can't pay for nothin' here."

Quietly, so no one else heard, Loey said, "It's the least I can do. Let him keep it. And thank you."

Martha Lee stared at her so openly it was like seeing a raw nerve. Loey wondered if anyone had ever thanked the woman before. She nodded jerkily. "Say 'thank you,' Waylon."

"Tanks," the boy said, sniffling.

After they'd left, Loey waited anxiously for the shop to clear out, and then she slapped the Open sign to Closed. She didn't clean the coffee maker or espresso machine. She didn't wipe up the spilled grounds or errant coffee beans scattered across the floor. She paused long enough to lock the register and take off her apron. Pulling her cell phone from her jeans pocket, she hit a number in her contacts list.

"Loey?" Cross answered on the first ring. "Have you heard—"

"She's in Little Cricket again."

"What?" Something muffled scraped across the phone as Cross readjusted himself. Voice low, he asked, "How do you know?"

"Martha Lee Freeman came by the shop."

"Son of a bitch."

"Come pick me up?"

The fact she was asking for backup meant she intended to search the one place in Righteous she didn't feel completely safe.

Cross groaned. "She wouldn't go to Little Cricket. Not after last time."

"Cross, don't be naive. There're storms coming this evening, and I want to get out there before the creek rises and blocks us off."

Cross sighed through his nose. "I'm on my way. Don't call anyone else."

Little Cricket Trailer Park was mostly full of good people down on their luck, but in the trailers with tinfoil-covered windows and old hounds skinnier than a tick in October sleeping outside, there were folks who didn't care about changing their luck. They had all they'd ever want in a double-wide and a bottle of pills.

Some called them pill houses, but most people didn't speak of them.

Cross parked his truck outside a once-white trailer with trash strewn outside and a rocking horse discarded beneath the porch. A dog lay in a patch of dirt, its chain snaking out from the tree beside the house. It growled as Loey jumped down from the truck, ready to tear off into the house, but Cross rounded the hood and caught her arm.

"Stay in the truck."

"I'm gonna ring their necks," Loey snarled. "All of 'em."

"You're going to wait in the truck."

He went to haul her back to the passenger seat, but that was the thing with Cross: he was too gentle a soul. Loey kicked him in the shin, and as he bent over, howling, she dashed for the front porch.

The dog lunged. It hit the end of its chain with a full-body jerk and a ripping snarl louder than Pap's old chainsaw. Loey paid it no mind. Her boots rang off the steps as she pounded up them. From the yard, which was all weeds and rocks, Cross was cussing at her.

She didn't pay no heed. She'd pray for him.

She ripped open the front door and *Alice in Wonderland-*

ed into another world.

The haze of countless cigarettes and joints hung thick in the trailer's air, which was twenty degrees hotter than outside. The heat alone sent Loey reeling. She coughed on instinct, her hand to her nose as she took in the rest of the trailer.

Too many couches filled the small space, and every seat was taken. Arms and legs mingled together, bodies piled on top of each other. Through the smoke, pale faces squinted back at her. No one moved. No one cared that she'd barged into their drug dungeon or when Cross stormed in behind her, bowling her straight over.

He grabbed her arms but didn't push her out of the way. She had the feeling he was using her as a human shield, and she didn't blame him.

They tiptoed along the wall, skirting around the trailer's happenings, eyes locked on the people sprawled across the couches.

"I swear," Cross hissed, "she'll pay for this."

"Come on."

She took his hand and tugged him past the kitchen and down the hall where the carpet had been rolled against the wall like a body was tucked inside it. The wood beneath was wet and made a sucking noise as Loey walked over it, and she worried she might fall straight through.

Cross opened the first door they came to and promptly closed it again.

"What?" Loey asked, reaching around him to push it back open.

"She's not in there. Trust me."

"You barely looked!"

"I saw enough, and it made me gayer. Let's go."

Loey guessed the next room was the bathroom. The door stuck, and she had to throw her shoulder into it. It finally opened enough to squeeze through, and she discovered the reason it had refused to budge.

Someone had been propped against it. That someone being Dale.

She was spilled across the dirty laminate, limp, her hair cascading over her face.

Cross said a foul word and pushed by Loey to crouch beside Dale. Loey froze, terror reducing her body to dagger-like stillness. Cross flipped Dale onto her back, her limbs flopping like the Raggedy Ann doll Loey had played with as a kid, and pushed her sweat-stiffened hair out of her face.

She could be dead. She could—

Her eyelids twitched, and relief washed over Loey like a baptism. She moved in beside Cross, their shoulders touching in the claustrophobic bathroom that reeked of pee and puke.

"Dale," Cross was saying, "wake up or I swear to God I'll tell Mother."

Dale moaned, her lips moving. Against the laminate, which was peeling in unfortunate spots, her hand twitched.

"We should call 911," Loey said, already reaching for her phone.

Dale moaned louder, and Cross almost shouted, "No! She's fine. She doesn't need a hospital."

"Cross, she can't move. She probably overdosed."

"If she'd overdosed, she wouldn't be responsive. She's fine. Nothing an ice shower won't fix."

Dale mumbled something again, her movements more agitated.

Loey took her hand and squeezed. "It's okay, Dale. We've got you."

"... the mirrors."

Loey almost dropped her hand. "What about the mirrors?"

"She's high," Cross said and positioned himself to pick his

sister up. "She's out of her head."

"... in the mirrors."

"What was in the mirrors?"

Loey leaned close to Dale, close enough to smell her sweat and the soured smell of her perfume. Her dark lashes fluttered against her freckled cheeks. Dale had always hated her freckles, and without her normal full face of makeup, she looked far too young to be in this dirty bathroom.

"Dale," Loey said, ignoring her pounding heart, "what was in the mirrors?"

"Him," Dale whispered. But Loey heard.

Loey pictured the shadow man, the tall presence standing behind her when she'd looked in the mirror those few nights ago. She felt the evil, the stale musk of wrongness in the back of her throat.

"Enough," Cross growled.

He lifted Dale off the floor as if she weighed nothing, and indeed, Loey spotted the knobs of Dale's ribs pressing against her thin shirt. When had she lost so much weight? Loey couldn't recall. Ever since Dale was a girl, people had expected much of her. She was expected to dress well, and be thin, and have her hair curled. It all went hand in hand with "belonging" to Dale, with being wanted and appreciated.

Loey had never had a mother like Mrs. Rose. Gran had only ever wanted Loey to be a good and kind person who put other people first. Gran never minded if Loey left the house without a full face of makeup.

That hadn't been the case with Dale, especially when people learned about Folton.

Forcing thoughts of mirrors and shadow men from her mind, Loey followed Cross back through the smoke den and out into the evening's clean air. The dog didn't bother with them this time, his pocked lips huffing against the dirt as he lay there, his eyes tracking them as they walked to Cross's truck.

Now that she didn't have to worry about the dog ripping out her throat, she got a better look at the tree he was chained to. Pieces of glass and white porcelain hung from the branches. Loey paused. The other pieces weren't porcelain at all.

They were polished bones.

Squirrel skulls and thin bones twinkled between darker curled bits that could have been pieces of furry flesh torn from road kill or a hunter's spoils. The wind whistled, and the home-made wind chimes played a macabre song that transfixed Loey.

"Hang on a second," she mumbled to Cross. She left him with Dale and walked as close to the tree as she could, given the dog's chain.

She stared up at the bones, recognizing the ribs and vertebrae and femurs. On a smooth, curved bone, smudged black ink caught her attention. She twisted to see the back of the bone and gasped.

It looked identical to the style of symbol she'd seen on Briggs's chest and on Leigh. It differed in small ways, like the slant of the lines and the number of curves, but it was the magic Jeronimo had taught her.

Without thinking, she snatched the bone from the thin piece of twine it hung from. The dog surged to its feet, snapping against the end of its chain and barking its head off.

The trailer's front door slammed open. The sound of a shotgun pumping punctuated the air.

"Loey!" Cross shouted. "Let's go!"

She ran.

"Hey!" someone shouted behind her.

Cross dumped Dale into the backseat as Loey scrambled into the cab. The man fired a warning shot into the air.

"Sonovabitch!" Cross shouted, revving the engine for all it

was worth. They tore out of Little Cricket on two wheels and a prayer.

Only after they'd reached the main road and he had slowed did she say, voice trembling, "We should take her to the hospital, Cross. She's not okay."

"We almost got our asses blasted. We're going home."

"Cross."

"She's *fine*."

The engine obliterated the stillness of Righteous's outskirts. Streetlamps turned on as the sun set.

"It's never been this bad. She needs help."

Cross's grip tightened on the steering wheel. He took the twisting back roads in favor of the straight shot through the heart of Righteous on Main Street, where someone might recognize them coming from Little Cricket. "Not from a hospital. Not like that."

Loey told herself to bite her tongue, but the words simmered behind her lips. "That's ripe coming from you."

Cross's head jerked toward her. Headlights played off his features as they headed up toward Devil's Maw in an unspoken agreement that Dale would sleep it off at Loey's.

"What's that supposed to mean?"

Loey crossed her arms, the piece of bone cool in her hand. "You know exactly what I mean. You sound like your mother when you talk like that. You want to sweep Dale's problems under the rug and make sure she keeps a pretty face on for the neighbors."

The truck swung onto Devil's Maw and accelerated toward Shiner's Ridge and Loey's house, which shone warmly a few miles away as the crow flies.

"I'm protecting her *from* our mother."

"No, you're saving face. Don't you ever get tired of all your secrets?"

The soft snores coming from the backseat filled the long silence. Loey dropped her arms and opened her palm. The bone gleamed in the night's fragmented light. She flipped it over to trace the ink on the back. Bits of black stained her thumb.

"You don't know a thing about secrets," Cross said. "You don't know what it's like to hide from your parents. You don't know none of that, so you don't get to say shit about how I or Dale choose to deal with our problems."

"You're not dealing with them." Loey had probably said too much, but it was too late now. She spoke the words to the bone like it was listening to her. "You're praying no one finds out."

She was ready to apologize when he finally said, "We all pray for something."

Thunder rumbled deep as a man's voice over Shiner's Ridge. The air smelled of dirty pennies, the scent sharp in Loey's nose. Their rocking chairs creaked over the porch's uneven planks. Beside her, Dale took an unsteady sip of tea. She couldn't hide how her hands shook.

"Dale …"

Her best friend shuddered.

"You said something about mirrors," Loey ventured.

"I don't remember anything about mirrors. I was out of my head."

The storm rolled down the ridge, and the smell of rain inched closer with each breath. The storm cloud flashed with lightning, and she sent up a quick prayer for Boltz. Thunder clapped closer. Always closer.

"I'm sorry I haven't been around much lately," Loey whispered.

"It's okay. I know you're dealing with a lot."

"We don't have to tell anyone about Folton if you don't want to. I'm sorry I pushed you so hard when I called."

"I'm sorry for what I said about people loving you when everyone knows the truth," Dale murmured. Both women stared out toward the mountains glinting in the rain-promised darkness.

"I know you've suffered because of what we said Folton did. That wasn't fair to put it all on you."

"But I would do it again to keep you from going through it."

Fat drops of rain splattered directly on the metal roof like gunshots. Loey's heart ached for her best friend who was so brave and so broken. Love came at a cost in Dale's life, and she'd paid hand over fist until the price had started to exact a deeper toll.

"Maybe it's time."

The words were horrible to say. Loey wanted to take them back and hide them away because it was the way of things. It was how you put on a pretty face and smiled when you didn't mean it and said "bless your heart" convincingly enough that people thought you meant it.

But Dale had a problem. She needed help. And Loey couldn't call out Cross for trying to hide Dale's problems, and then do the same thing herself when it came time to talk to Dale about them. She bolstered the best of her courage and forged on.

"I can't find you in that trailer again." The thunder rumbled, drowning out Loey's whispered words.

She waited for the "I'll stop," or the "I'll change," or the "You're right." But they didn't come.

"This time scared me," Dale said. "With what Burl did and everything, I've … I've …" She watched the storm, unblinking. Her grip was white-knuckle tight on the mug. She was trembling. For a horrible, terrible moment, Loey thought Dale was going to say she wanted to die too, like Burl had, but then she whispered, "What's happening?"

Out in the field, a flash of lightning burst hot and bright. A yowl pierced the air. From the tall grass, Boltz skittered out, smoking and singed, his eyes wild as he tore off toward the barn.

Loey didn't want to lie and say she didn't know, but the truth wasn't an option either. Dale was in no condition to handle the madness of everything Loey had learned. So, she said, "The answer isn't in a bottle of Oxy."

Dale bowed her head as if in prayer, but Loey knew better. Dale asked no one for help, not even God.

"Something's out there. I feel it. Don't you?" The rain should have stolen the words Dale had spoken toward Shiner's Ridge, her eyes lingering on the fog-shrouded mountain where the tops of the pines poked through like old, bent men, but the wind shifted and blew the rain onto the porch.

Something was out there, tucked behind threads barely holding together. How many more needed to rip before shadows with teeth and claws spilled down the ridge and into Righteous?

Loey stood. "We should go inside."

Dale nodded and followed her, the screen door slapping shut behind them as the thunder rolled deep overhead.

CHAPTER 25

MAY 23, 2012

S PRING SLIPPED BY WITH A whisper. Temperatures in Righteous went from the last sputters of winter, with frost and freezing nights, to a few wet days of spring, to the blasting heat and humidity of summer in the foothills of the Appalachians. When no one was looking, summer had crept up, and though the calendar claimed it was spring, everyone was complaining about the heat, fanning their faces, and pulling at the backs of their shirts like it would do them any good.

If it wasn't the heat people were complaining about, it was Leigh Parker's murder. Specifically, the lack of suspects. Try as he might, Sheriff Jinks couldn't find a suspect if the killer walked up and waved a white flag in front of the police station.

At graduation, as Righteous's senior class paraded across the stage in their white gowns and silly hats, the school had done nothing to honor Leigh's memory. Not even a mention from the principal. The people of Little Cricket were easy to overlook in Righteous because their side of the tracks wasn't the "cleaned up and smiling on Sundays" kind of side. As Loey sat and listened to everyone's name being called out, along with a bulleted list of their accomplishments, she found an asterisk beside the class's graduating number. There, in the footnotes, he was mentioned in memoriam.

The font was barely big enough to read.

The ceremony hadn't even ended before seniors were pulling out flasks, their efforts to hide their actions as pitiful as their shallow swallows and answering coughs. Trucks roared out of the school parking lot, kids whooping and adults shaking their heads. Everyone knew about the Little Cricket Creek grad party that happened every year, but no one stopped it because kids would be kids, and they were good kids, and they deserved to blow off some steam.

Or that was the expression Loey read in the eyes of the older generation who'd done the same thing on their graduation day.

Trucks pulled up to the creek with their tailgates down. The seniors took turns swinging from the rope swing and flailing into the shallow waters. They shouted and screamed; they made out behind the trees; and they stuffed their faces with hot dogs between long pulls from the cheap liquor they'd stolen from their parents. And when it got too dark for swimming, they lit a bonfire and sat around it, daring one another in a series of escalating pranks.

The party was frenetic, and it felt like the last thing Loey would do in this town, so she'd agreed to tag along with Dale, Cross, and Travis, who was busy flexing his muscles by the fire.

From the tailgate, perched between Dale and Cross, Loey kicked her feet and enjoyed the pleasant heat residing inside her collarbones as the moon cast silver light over the creek. Her belly felt like she was floating, even though she was almost certain she was still sitting. Beside her, Dale laughed at nothing. The half-empty bottle of vodka sloshed in her hand.

"So 'diculous how—" Cross swallowed a burp or puke, Loey couldn't tell which. "How they ain't caught no one."

"If Mother heard you saying 'ain't,' she'd skin you alive." Dale took another long pull from the bottle and passed it to Loey.

Loey considered it. At this point, it tasted dangerously like water. Likely, it was too late for reason anyway, so she took another swig and handed it off to Cross.

"Too bad it wasn't Folton who diced up Leigh. That would have been convenient." Dale shot Loey a narrow-eyed look. "He hasn't touched you again, has he? 'Cause I'll rip off his—what?"

Dale dissolved into genuine confusion as she stared at Loey. Even Cross cocked his head at her, but a crazy idea spun in her mind.

"What if it was him?" she asked, treading carefully.

"Didn't you see him at the dance? That's why you went outside, right? He wouldn't have had time to hang the body and get back inside. You would've literally run into him if he'd killed Leigh."

"You're right, he couldn't have ..." She let the words trail off.

Her eyes locked first with Dale, then with Cross. Slowly, they caught on.

Dale's mouth popped open. "Are you saying what I think you're saying?"

"Burl will never catch the actual killer."

"And he's going to keep on hurting girls long after you're gone," Dale added.

"Hey," Cross said, shaking his head, "you two need to slow down."

"No. No, she's right." Dale was warming to the idea. "It wouldn't take much."

"An anonymous tip," Loey said, thinking aloud. "A few of Leigh's books maybe. They're still in his locker. We could plant them in Folton's house. Hide them real good."

"But not too good. The cops need to find it. This is Burl Jinks we're talking about."

"That's not nice," Cross objected on principle alone. Burl was Travis's father, after all.

Dale ignored him. "Burl would be all over it like a fat kid on cake. Folton would go away for years."

"For *life*," Cross hissed. "You two are talking about sending an innocent man to jail, if not the electric chair."

"Oh, please." Dale waved off his words. "No one gets the chair anymore."

"He's a bad man." Loey stared down at her hands. The calluses on her palms from the reins were thinning; she hadn't ridden Tempest in weeks. She was too scared, too worried about what she might do with that much speed. "If anyone deserves it, it's him."

"I'm not saying what he did to you wasn't bad. You know that. I'd kill him myself if I could. But this is a boy's murder you're talking about. Think about Leigh's momma."

Loey grimaced. Cross had a point. But Dale was a dog with a bone.

"Cross Semper Rose," she snarled. "Do you remember when Loey and I caught you with your dick in my boyfriend's hand?"

Cross's body jerked. His eyes flashed wide. He wasn't drunk enough for this, and Dale was speaking too loudly.

"Dale, don't," Loey added.

Dale held up her hand to Loey and addressed her brother. "She's our best friend. Practically our sister. And when you needed her most, she stayed silent for you. We both did, and don't think I don't know you and Travis still hook up. I smell you on him. I see how you two talk to each other like no one can hear you. We stayed silent for you, and you won't do this for Loey? For all those other girls—"

"Stop," Cross pleaded. "Just stop. Please."

"This was a bad idea. We should—" Loey interjected.

"*Cross.*"

At his name on his sister's lips, in that tone that meant Dale wouldn't back down, Cross's face went blank. It reminded Loey of his expression in the locker room, when Travis had begged Dale to stay with him.

"I'll do it," he said. "Whatever you need."

"Good boy," Dale said, dismissing her brother now that she'd reined him back in line. To Loey, she said, "That notebook is all we need."

"It's circumstantial."

"Not if we tell the cops he likes to get off on young kids."

"No." Loey shook her head hard, making the woods spin. "We can't do that. No one can know. It would break my grandparents' hearts if they knew."

Dale considered her. "We can download some stuff onto his computer. Delete it. Make it look like he tried to hide it. Then"—Dale lowered her voice, smiling and truly terrifying now—"we turn a closet into an altar to the devil. Pentagrams, upside-down crosses, and a dead bird or some shit. Nobody, and I mean nobody, in this town will let a Devil worshipper go free."

"You think it'll be enough?"

Dale shrugged. "If not, he'll have to move. At the very worst, somebody will shoot him in the back one night and leave him for the crows. No one will care, and he'll have paid for what he did to you."

They sat in silence on the tailgate of Cross's truck as the creekside grad party whirled on around them, but the vodka and the night made it easy to hide in the shadows. Maybe all sinners felt that way. And Loey had no doubt that framing an innocent man was a sin. It was the biggest sin. She was committing murder as sure as if she were to cut Folton's throat herself.

But no one else would pay for Leigh's murder, that much

was clear.

She wished she were a better person. She wished she hadn't started nodding. She wished she didn't feel horribly *free*.

She'd put a bad man behind bars, and the people of Righteous would feel safe again.

It should've been harder to ruin a man's life. Certainly harder than speaking a few words.

"I'm sure," she said. "Let's do this."

CHAPTER 26

LOEY LISTENED TO THE STORM tire itself out, the last of the rain petering on the metal roof while Dale slept beside her in bed. She eased out from under the covers and slipped on the tattered sweatshirt Matt had left at her house the last night he'd stayed over. It said "Righteous PD" across the front and smelled of him. On nights she was really lonely, she wore it to feel like someone was in bed beside her.

She'd discovered quickly she didn't want someone beside her. She just didn't want to feel lonely. There was a difference, which was why she hadn't returned the sweatshirt or washed it.

She passed Dewey at the foot of the bed. Before he could rise from his beloved pillow, she gestured for him to stay. He lifted his head, not happy to be left behind, but he didn't move.

She left the bedroom door open a crack and made her way downstairs, careful to avoid the creaky steps on the staircase. In the kitchen, she pulled out the piece of smooth, curved bone from her purse and turned it over in her hand. She had no clue what part of the body was curved like that, almost like a shallow bowl.

It looked like a piece of a skull, but she didn't know what animal was large enough to have a skull this size.

Human.

She shuddered.

215

She'd heard stories of what happened in Little Cricket, but she doubted anyone would hang human skulls from the trees. Surely not.

She tucked it in her pocket and glanced out the window over the sink.

Sure enough, the rectory light was on, which was fortunate, because Loey had a task to do and she needed Jeronimo's help. With the bone in her pocket, she went out through the back door. She locked it behind her.

The night had a bite after the storm that made her huddle deeper in her sweatshirt. Fall would be here soon, bringing with it the sharp tang of autumn, russet-hued leaves, and the crackling cold.

Loey had always loved the fall in the South, but it would be her first without Gran's hot chocolate and pumpkin pies and chicken 'n' dumplings on Thanksgiving.

After Thanksgiving came Christmas, and how would she get through that without Pap sitting in his rocking chair, his steady smile in place as Loey pretended she liked the modest clothes Gran had bought her for Christmas?

She would have been in tears if not for the brisk wind drying out her eyes as she picked up her pace down the hill.

Jeronimo opened the door before she even reached the front stoop. He looked like hell with dark circles beneath his red-rimmed eyes. Shadows deepened the hollows beneath his cheekbones, and his hair was more unruly than usual.

"You don't look so good. Is this still from being near the tatter?" she asked him.

His focus slipped from her face, down her chest, and settled on her sweatshirt's logo. Something about the intensity of his gaze as he cocked his head made her cheeks burn. "What's that?"

She too glanced down as if she'd forgotten what she was wearing. "Just an old sweatshirt."

"That deputy who follows you around like a puppy?"

"Matt doesn't follow me around like a puppy. Anyway," she said to bring the conversation back around to why she'd come over. "Are you going to invite me in? I have something to talk to you about."

"No."

"Ah," she fumbled. "Okay?"

He stared emptily at her, and she again wondered if he was hollow inside, the husk of something incorporeal, perhaps. Was he dust and air, thin skin and sad words? If she shot him again, would he blow away?

"Do you ever sleep?" she asked.

"Never."

She laughed until she realized he was serious. "But aren't you tired?"

"Always."

"Why don't you go to bed then?"

He shook his head, jaw clenching. For a second, he looked away from her, deciding on his words. He picked them tactfully, one by one, as if he were compiling an entire lifetime into one explanation.

"My soul." The words dragged out of him on a tight-throated rasp. "Without it, I'm cursed. I can eat and drink and sleep and fuck all I want, but without my soul, it doesn't fulfill the ache of hunger or thirst or fatigue or longing. I remain as empty as I was before."

Her shock made the silence between them stretch out too long. When she'd recovered, she asked dumbly, "Are you serious?"

His chest heaved with the effort of telling her his secret. She wondered if he'd ever said the words aloud before. *I'm cursed.*

"That's why you can't bleed unless you're near a tatter?"

"I still don't know if I believe your theory on that."

She brushed off his doubt. She expected nothing less from him. "But you feel nothing? Even when you …" She raised her eyebrows at him to silently finish her question.

"Nothing."

Their eyes locked. A vision of her rocking onto her tiptoes and pulling him into a kiss to test his theory flashed through her mind. If she let it, the vision could magically morph into reality. He might have been considering the same image because he'd held his breath, his body tense with the effort, his eyes dark as the night around them. Her body rocked toward him on its own accord. He answered her body's call by releasing his breath, his lips parting like an open invitation to lay hers on them.

She was the first to look away, because she had to.

She cleared her throat so it wouldn't crack from the longing that was making her nose tingle as if on fire. "I found a piece of bone at Little Cricket tonight. It has a symbol on it."

She pulled it from her pocket and offered it to him, but he didn't pick it up. He simply stared and breathed in deep as if he were smelling it. His eyes traced the ashy lines of the symbol, which looked burned into the bone. "You shouldn't touch bone with this symbol on it. It's very dangerous."

"I didn't have much time to think about it. What does that symbol do?"

Without answering, Jeronimo went inside. Loey didn't follow. He came back holding a scrap of newspaper and used the crumpled page to pick up the bone from her hand. He folded it and tucked it into his pocket.

Once finished, he said, "It invites communication with Barty."

Her focus flashed to his pocket. "Are you serious? Shouldn't we burn it or something?"

"I'll take care of it."

218

"How do you know whoever hung this is talking to Barty?"

Jeronimo held her gaze for a long moment. "Because he's the only one strong enough to respond."

Now didn't seem like the time to press her disagreeing theory. Instead, her mind returned to Burl's house and the broken mirrors. "Is that what Burl was doing with all the mirrors?"

"It would seem so."

"But why?"

"Why do you pray?"

The question threw her off completely. "What?"

"You pray because you think God is listening. Burl and whoever hung this symbol were doing their own sort of praying."

She had no clue what Burl could be saying to Barty, but then she hadn't known the sheriff as well as she'd thought. He'd been suffering for months. She'd served him coffee almost every day and every day asked him how he was, but she'd never once actually meant how he *really* was. He was lost right in front of her and she hadn't even known. How often had she accused the other people in this town of doing the exact same thing she'd done?

Jeronimo's voice made her jump when he asked, "Does she go there often?"

Loey stiffened at the sudden change of subject and its swooping trajectory toward something she never spoke about. "How do you know about Dale?"

"It didn't take me long to catch up on the town's business when I returned." He squinted, and his eyes appeared blacker. "And everyone in town talks about her problem when you or Cross ain't around to hear."

It didn't surprise her, but Loey hated the taste of the truth about her best friend. "Even Travis?"

"Especially him."

Loey fought back all the hateful words her dislike of

Travis stirred up. "She'll be fine."

"You sure about that?" The question sounded like a challenge, like he knew something she didn't.

"What are you saying? Of course she'll be fine."

"Being 'fine' is a thin lie we tell ourselves to keep from looking too deeply. Dale won't be fine any more than you and I are fine. This entire town is not fine, and the sooner everyone stops lying to themselves, the better."

Loey wanted to argue, but what could she say? She felt compelled to stand up for the townspeople, but maybe Jeronimo was right. Instead, she mumbled, "You don't know her."

"You two spiral around each other like this elaborate dance. You're never out of each other's sight for long, and when you speak, she watches you, like she can't trust your words. Sometimes you look at her like you don't know who she is."

The words he spoke were eerily on point, and it unsettled her that he'd seen such fine details even she avoided noticing. But Dale was her best friend, and Loey would go to the grave defending her. "She's protective, is all."

His brows twitched as if they wanted to rise but didn't have the heart.

She amended her words. "She's *very* protective."

"Tell me what you did," he pressed, and she knew he wouldn't let it go. The resolve to hear her answer sat squarely in the corner of his hard-pressed lips.

Maybe it was the truth of his curse, or maybe it was the stars like confectioner's sugar dusted across the sky, but her biggest sin, the reason God would never love her, snapped free from her mouth like coiled-up barbed wire.

"I killed a man."

He waited, staring at her. His stillness was so absolute she imagined he could stand there for days, waiting for her to answer.

She expected him to laugh. To recoil. To raise his brows. To blink. He did none of those things. He looked like he was still waiting for her answer.

"Well …" Now that she'd started, she couldn't stop. "Technically, he's still alive, but I sentenced him to death as surely as if I'd shot him in the face."

Still, there was nothing.

"Say something. Please. This is one of those moments where you need to pretend to be normal, okay? 'Cause this"— she waved a hand at him—"isn't."

The angle of his head—of his consideration of her— deepened. "This is about the man in jail for Leigh's murder, ain't it?"

"Yes," she whispered her darkest sin, though it wasn't her dirtiest. That one belonged to Folton and the things he'd done to her in his classroom.

"Tell me. Tell me all of it."

He was magic. The ancient mountain kind, stronger than any ink on a page. Loey couldn't tell him no, couldn't hide from him and didn't want to.

She told him everything, even the darkest details about what Folton had done to her, details she didn't even tell herself no more. He got it all, including how they'd framed Folton and how Dale and Cross had executed it that horrible night.

When she finished, he said, "You're not going to hell."

She was crying. She didn't remember when the tears had started. Sniffling, she said, "How can you believe in Hell if you don't believe in God?"

He wiped away her tears with a stroke of his thumb. His touch stole her breath clean out of her lungs. Perhaps he couldn't feel a thing, but right then, with his hand cupping her cheek, she felt enough for both of them.

"I believe," he murmured, eyes on his hand on her cheek,

"hell is what we make it. This place ain't yours, not even with what that man did to you."

Turning her face into his touch, she whispered, "How can you be sure?"

"Because," he said, dropping his hand and making her silently scream with longing, "you saved yourself from it. You saved other girls and you saved this town. That's not your hell, Loey. That's survival, and sometimes it feels like hell, but most of the time that's life being life."

CHAPTER 27

"I WAS AFRAID OF THIS," JERONIMO said as Loey drove them to Dale's house.

She'd explained Dale's issue with her mirrors and asked Jeronimo for help warding them. Before leaving, she'd picked up Dewey and called Cross to make sure Travis wasn't home. Cross had it on good authority that Travis was at a bar in a nearby city and wouldn't be leaving anytime soon.

"You were?" Loey asked sharply. Her eyes cut to him. In the darkness, his profile was a mere shadow, but he smelled like rich spices and expensive coffee. He smelled like something she wanted to taste.

"Frankie, the girl Barty loved and killed? She was a Rose just like Dale."

"I remember. You think Barty is visiting Dale because she's a Rose?"

"It makes sense."

"Why didn't you suggest we ward her mirrors before if you thought he would do this?"

Jeronimo finally glanced over at her, his eyes dull and far away. He looked worn thin and tattered, his threads loose and flapping in the wind. Now that she knew about his curse, she couldn't unsee his hollowness; she wondered how she had never sensed it before.

"Jeronimo?" she asked again when it was clear his attention had wandered. "Why didn't you think to ward her mirrors? Seeing Barty might have been the reason she nearly overdosed."

His gaze traveled to the dark night beyond his window. "Because she would have anyway, and I'm not the best at thinking about other people."

She was taken aback by his unabashed words. Not because they'd floored her, which they had, but because, for the first time since she'd met him, she felt like she was seeing the rawest version of him.

It astounded her to the point where she couldn't respond as she turned into Dale's driveway.

Loey let them in through the front door with the hidden spare key. Dewey padded in first, tail wagging happily. Dale's house was pristine. Perfect in every way. The carpet and authentic wainscoting were white. The walls were a deep, cool gray. Side tables and bar carts were all in gleaming chrome. Fresh pink peonies were delicately arranged in crystal vases.

"Smells like no one lives here," Jeronimo said as he walked in behind Loey and Dewey, who trotted straight into the kitchen to inspect the floor for crumbs.

There weren't even footprints on the carpet. "She likes the house kept clean."

"This is more than just clean."

Loey hated to agree with him, but he was right. Though she wouldn't betray Dale and her weaknesses by agreeing aloud. Instead, she said, "We can work in the kitchen."

On the breakfast table, she laid out the supplies: thick paper she'd taken from Gran's stationery box, heavy calligraphy pens, and the single paper with the stark black *A* on it that Jeronimo had supplied from his research for them to copy.

"You take half and I take half?" she suggested.

Jeronimo gave her a questioning look. The dark circles accented the bloodshot hue of his eyes. "How many mirrors does she have?"

"She's a former pageant queen," Loey said by way of explanation.

"I see."

They divvied up the pens and paper before sitting opposite each other. Dewey chose Jeronimo to lie beside, and Loey told herself she didn't take it personally. Wrinkling her nose, she studied the A-shaped symbol. It wasn't overly complicated like the circular one to see the threads. She'd brought along enough paper in case she messed up, but once she'd selected a thick black pen, she hesitated.

"What's wrong?"

She looked up to find him watching her. He already had one completed symbol in front of him, but she noticed, as he held the pen, his hand trembled.

"You never told me what these symbols are. You called it old mountain magic, but where did it come from? And what *is* it?"

"Magic is like religion—"

"Are you trying to get God to strike you down with lightning?" She put pen to paper and started on the first parallel line.

Jeronimo snorted. "Let the Good Man try. As I was saying, magic is like religion. No matter where you are in the world, religion exists in some way, whether it's Righteous's Baptists or Italy's Catholics or India's Hindus or Iraq's Muslims. Magic is similar. Its interpretation changes depending on geography and culture." Paper rustled as he picked up a blank sheet. "Here, in Righteous, Tenders have always used these symbols to funnel the magic. Like a rip in the Seam, you're giving the magic floating along the threads around you a way into the real world."

She lifted her pen from the page. The line looked dense and jagged, far less effortless than the one on her example page, but she moved on to the next line. "Which Keene helped you after the explosion?"

She completed the second line, which was marginally better than the first, and focused on the curving hook in the middle.

"Your great-grandmother, Ruby Keene. She was the youngest of Knox's daughters, and when I came into the fold, they were just dealing with his death. Knox was the patriarch of all this, the most famous Tender in Righteous." Jeronimo laughed a bit. "He was king around here. Anyway, your grandmother was just a little girl who liked to play dress-up with her mother's shoes." His pen squeaked against the page as he drew. When he spoke again, his voice was soft, almost tender. Surprised, she looked up. "I wish I'd known your Gran and Pap, though. They sound like they were the good kind."

Loey felt the air around her heat to a pleasant, enfolding warmth. She could almost smell Gran's perfume. Before she started crying, she turned back to her page and finished the curving line.

"They were," she whispered, staring down at her symbol. How many such symbols had Gran and Pap drawn? How many more would she? How did she Tend to something she didn't understand? "I wish they were here to teach me all this."

"They are. They're with you."

Her attention snapped to him. "How can you say that if you don't believe in God?"

He set his finished symbol aside and started on another one. "I believe in a grandparent's love for their granddaughter. That energy never fades from this world. It only changes. They're with you, I promise. They're in the threads closest to your heart."

Loey's mouth fell open as she stared at him. It was almost scary how unguarded he was acting, how open and *caring*. It unnerved her.

"Are you … okay?" she asked.

He lifted a shoulder but kept on drawing. "Seeing him like that, my brother, it drains me. It feels like he sucks me dry."

She still wasn't completely certain it was his brother they saw at Burl's, but it reminded her of something else.

"The threads," she said, thinking about the filaments of light. "I saw them more clearly at Burl's. They're held together with knots, like the ones I macramé."

"See?" He still hadn't looked up, his pen squeaking across the stationary to produce perfect lines. "Your grandmother was teaching you how to Tend the threads through your macramé. All your tapestries were practice for Tending. Every single knot. Every single thread. You just didn't know it."

Tears sprung to her eyes. He continued to draw as if he hadn't spoken the words that had given her the narrowest margin of peace in the last few months. She pressed her hand over her mouth to hold in her whimpers. He'd finished three more symbols by the time she pulled herself back together. She swiped at a few stray tears and took a deep breath.

"Thank you for that," she said, meaning every word.

He shrugged. "No thanks needed. I know they struggled with you being stuck in Righteous after the accident on Tempest, especially when you were so desperate to leave because of Folton. It's not fair the surgeries ate up your entire tuition fund."

Her spine stiffened. She sat very, very still.

Distantly, she heard her pen hit the tabletop.

Across the table, Jeronimo looked up and frowned. "What? What's wrong?"

"How do you know about Tempest?"

229

His frown vanished. "You told me."

"I never told you that. I never talk about her."

Hit the ground. The words echoed from deep in the back of her mind. *She don't need to see the mare hit the ground.*

"Your … your grandparents told me," Jeronimo fumbled.

"You said their letter was the first time you'd heard from them, and the letter mentioned nothing about Tempest." Her words were hollow, droning things that sounded spoken from someone else's mouth.

He blinked as if thinking back, or maybe his eyes were dry. Realizing his mistake, he scrubbed a hand over his jaw and sighed.

"I lied," he said with another shrug. He made an *oh well* face and spread his hands wide.

"You lied," she repeated deliberately, because this mattered. This mattered more than anything. "About what?"

"About hearing from them. That wasn't the first letter they'd sent me. It wasn't even the first time they'd asked for my help."

"What are you *saying?*"

He rubbed his temples as if she were giving him a headache. "I'm saying they'd been after me for years to help finish Barty off and seal the Seam. I … I wasn't ready. I thought they understood. But when I saw the news about their deaths, I realized it was probably connected to their last letter. I came back to make it right."

Trembling all over, she jerked to her feet so fast Dewey jumped up with a bark. "You didn't come," she choked out, "when they asked you for help."

He stared up at her, and understanding dawned through his exhaustion and pain and whatever the hell he was dealing with after his encounter with his brother. "Oh," he said, then louder, "Oh. Oh, Loey. Wait. No. I mean, yes, but you have to understand—"

"I don't have to understand anything," she snarled, biting off the words like they burned her mouth.

"I can explain—"

"You bastard!" She picked up all her pages and pens and threw them at him. He let them pelt him in the chest and face.

"They didn't need me, Loey. If they were sealing the Seam, then they were going to kill Barty anyway—with or without me."

She trembled so badly her teeth chattered. "They were asking for your help."

"They didn't need it."

"How dare you? My grandparents wouldn't have wasted their time asking a stranger for help if they didn't need it. They were proud people. If they asked for help that many times, they were desperate."

She hated him for making her say the words, but it was the truth. Gran and Pap had needed him; their last letter had been raw with their fear and desperation. Pap had never asked anyone for help in his life. And Jeronimo had turned his back on them.

"I was busy—"

"They were desperate and you left them stranded. They're dead because of you." Her voice rose as she glared down at him, her hands shaking so badly she balled them into fists and pressed them against the table until her knuckles ached.

"That's not—"

"Your brother killed them because you wouldn't come home and finish what you started."

"I—"

"These people—Leigh, Briggs, Burl—they're dead because of you. The people of Righteous are suffering because of you."

"Just stop!" he yelled, surging to his feet. He slammed his hands onto the table. The fine china in the dining room cabinet rattled in protest.

Dewey barked and didn't stop until Loey signaled for his silence. Her ears rang.

"Just stop," Jeronimo said, quieter this time.

She shook her head, the fight draining out of her. "Afraid to hear the truth? You've been running from it for a long time."

"I've been researching. To help Tenders—" He clapped his mouth shut. His cheeks bloomed with angry red splotches. The vein beneath his eye thrummed against the thin skin.

Loey gathered the pages on the table and smacked their edges against the top to line up their corners. Jeronimo flinched as if the sound were a gunshot. She picked up the pens next. The tidying applied a balm to the raw gash of her anger. Her seeping rage.

She wanted to unfurl it on him all at once, but Gran had taught her to always hold in her bigger, messier emotions. To lock them down tight and only let them out when it was safe. Jeronimo wasn't safe anymore. So Loey arranged pages and stacked pens.

"What're you gonna do, Loey?" The question sounded more like he'd asked, "Who're you gonna be?"

The problem with faith was that you couldn't believe in a god without believing in a devil. There was no Heaven without Hell. No faithful without sinners. There were angels and there were demons, and though Loey accepted this, she'd always preferred to look at the pretty, simple aspects of being a good woman of faith. She averted her attention from the shadows and chose not to read the darker parts of the Bible because, to be completely honest, she was scared.

She chose not to read those parts of the Bible because they tested her faith in herself.

But her faith had never been tested more than in this moment as she stared across Dale's breakfast table at a man she could hate with every fiber, every thread, of her existence.

Because of him, her grandparents were dead. Because of him, she was alone and doubting everything she'd ever known. Her faith was being tested, and though she knew he was the worst sort of evil—the kind that hid behind a face you considered your friend or family—she was willing to work with him to accomplish something greater. Her morals should have demanded more from her, but she needed him, and for now, she would use him.

"I'll help you kill Barty," she said, "and you'll teach me everything you know about Tending. Then you'll get the hell out of Righteous and never come back."

His relief was so great, so instant, she immediately understood his desperation for her help.

He didn't need her help as a Tender, much like he'd assumed her grandparents didn't need him, but he needed her there. He needed not to be alone. He needed someone to point at his brother and say, "It's time to kill him," because he couldn't do that for himself.

"What are you going to do?" he asked.

She'd been so lost in her realization that she almost hadn't heard him. She locked eyes with him, her gaze unflinching. "I'm going to finish what they started and seal the Seam."

He nodded. "Okay then. So we—"

"*We* don't do anything. There is no 'we' anymore. You're going to leave, and I'm going to finish protecting my best friend, and then, after Burl's funeral, we're going to finish this once and for all. Then I never want to see you again."

He took a deep breath. Maybe it was his exhaustion from enduring the pain of being near his brother, both physically and emotionally, but Loey thought he looked lost.

Good, she thought, *he deserves it*.

"For what it's worth," he rasped out, "I'm sorry, Loey. I never thought they would die."

All that rage and hate swelled back up inside her, and there was no holding it down or sealing it in with a smile.

"You're a coward, Jeronimo James. You're a coward of the worst kind, because it's not fear of dying or losing someone you love that's making you hide from the fight. You're the worst kind of coward because your fear is selfish and ugly and grown from the blackest part of your soul." She huffed out a laugh. "But you don't have a soul, do you? That's how you justify all the bad things you've done. All the damage you've wreaked. Maybe you're cursed. But you are a hollow man, Jeronimo. You're a hollow man with black rot inside you. You are a coward, and I will hate you until the day I die."

CHAPTER 28

L ATER THAT WEEK, AFTER THE autopsy had been
completed, Jeronimo officiated Burl's funeral. He delivered
eloquent words about the sheriff, about a life lived for
service and an afterlife meant for men who had done more
right than wrong. It was tactful in a way that Burl's penchant
for hookers barely came to mind.

Loey had overdone it again decorating the church for
the funeral. Flowers, freshly cut from the cemetery, adorned
every surface, hung from every pew's end, and spilled out
from a massive copper urn in front of the pulpit. She'd used
peonies, English roses, gardenias, baby's breath, and bunches
of lavender with abandon. If a flower was a prayer, Loey had
atoned for every sin ever committed in Righteous. At least,
she'd tried.

Dale looked fresh as a daisy for her father-in-law's funeral.
She sat beside Travis in the front row, with the other Jinkses
filling out the pew. Burl's ex-wife sat on Travis's other side.
None of Burl's closest kin cried for him, not even his ailing
father or uncles. Behind their pew, the Roses sat stiffly, backs
ramrod straight. Mr. Rose had come in from the city for the
occasion, and Loey hadn't seen him speak yet. Mrs. Rose
wore a felt hat that dipped low over one eye. Beside her, her
sisters and their husbands, with their children and cousins,

sat. Everyone had their place, and the church was filled to the brim. Loey sat at the end of the first pew in her place as a Keene on a funeral day. In her pocket, the salt weighed heavily. She'd give it to the family to pour for Burl beneath her watchful eye ensuring the circles were perfect. The town coroner had estimated Burl had only been dead for less than a day before she and Jeronimo had found him, which meant he would be salted in time.

But even after decorating the church with the tedious precision of making every arrangement perfect, the rage from Jeronimo's lie made her feel as though she were losing her mind, especially when she let herself think too much about how scared her grandparents must have been to send that letter. Her fingers quivered as they had all morning. She sweated beneath the simple black dress she wore, the one that kept her tattoo covered.

Her grandparents had asked Jeronimo for help countless times over, and he'd ignored them. He'd abandoned them and his hometown when they'd needed him most. Because he was a coward. Because he was afraid of facing the brother he'd tried to kill. Rage and hate filled up Loey's heart until they were something she could taste on the back of her tongue, rancid and burning, like day-old coffee.

She dug her fingernails into the fleshy part of her palms. Dale cast another questioning look over her shoulder.

Before Loey could offer her a reassuring smile, a soft vibration hummed up her leg, but it was gone before she could pay it much attention. She uncrossed her legs and adjusted her dress. It was then, looking down at her sandaled feet, that she saw it.

A forked tongue flicked out from the end of a pointed, pale brown nose sticking out from between the wooden slats of the old floor.

Loey gasped and jerked her feet up. Her dress slipped up her thighs, and it would have been scandalous if not for the scream that pierced the air from across the aisle.

Ms. Ruth leaped to her feet, her Bible flying into the back of Mr. Weebly's head. For an old woman with a stooped back and blue hair, she moved fast as she sprang up onto the pew, screeching at the top of her lungs.

Up at the pulpit, Jeronimo froze. His words hung unfinished as more screams joined Ms. Ruth's.

Staring up at him, Loey saw the first few threads illuminate. Their white-bright knots flashed pulsing hot. They flickered in and out of sight, racing up and down their threads. The lights spread around the tatter. The loose ends slashed into the air, their knots black and sooty. The stench of sulfur built.

A hiss drew her attention back to the floorboards. The copperhead at her feet slunk up through the gap, its skinny but long body pouring upward. Beneath the pew, it twined around Cross's boot.

He was too busy half standing, mouth open as if he might help the congregation who were all leaping onto pews or running into the aisle or screaming or staring in confusion like Dale, to notice as that light brown tail disappeared up his pant leg.

"Cross ..." Loey's stunned voice was too quiet. He didn't hear, but he felt it soon enough.

His eyes stretched wide. He glanced down, blinking in shock, and that shock grew to horror.

"Oh, shit," he began, reaching for his belt. "Oh, fuck. Oh, fuck. Fuck!" he shouted.

"Cross Semper Rose!" his mother hissed in a whisper as if people weren't shouting and screaming all around them.

He tore his belt from the loops and didn't bother unbuttoning or unzipping his pants before he ripped them over his hips.

Everyone froze. They all stared at Cross's underwear. They weren't briefs or boxers. Instead, he wore red lace.

A woman's red lace thong.

In that frozen moment, nothing but the sight of that red lace was more important, not even the venomous snakes. Mrs. Rose toppled clean over in a dead faint. Mr. Rose didn't even try to catch her. Dale snorted out a laugh from where she'd half climbed up Travis's body to escape the snakes. She looked down at the ground, where more copperheads slithered about and laughed some more. Travis just stared at Cross, his face growing redder and redder.

Half wrenching his pants back up to cover his underwear, Cross grabbed the copperhead twining up his leg before it could strike and slung it against the wall. It hit with a solid thud.

The sound stirred everyone back into motion. Bodies clogged the aisle as the congregation shoved their way to the front doors. Atop its rest, Burl's casket wobbled. Men pushed women, and old ladies threw their fists with abandon. Everyone screamed. From a pew, young Riley Goody wailed. A red and black snake slithered toward his bare toes.

Loey snatched him up and swung him onto her hip. She swatted the snake away before joining the churning mass trying to escape the church.

Someone knocked into her, and she would have gone down if not for a hand grabbing her elbow.

She twisted around. Jeronimo stared back at her grimly, but he kept his hand on her arm, keeping her and Riley upright as they flooded out the front doors on a wave of terrified Baptists.

As he pulled her through the crowd, Loey glanced back in time to see the tatter's lights dim and then disappear. When she turned back, Jeronimo's eyes were on her. His jaw clenched, and he looked away. His nose wasn't bleeding. The color in his cheeks was bright and healthy. He moved without stumbling or falling, which did little to bolster her theory that the tatter made him weak, not Barty.

Once outside, people shook out their hair and purses, swatted at their pant legs, and rustled their skirts. Some ran straight for their cars and tore out of the parking lot on a cloud of dust.

Mayor Goody swooped down on Loey and pried Riley from her arms. "Thank you, Loey. I got separated from him. Oh, thank you so much."

"Sure," Loey said numbly.

Jeronimo hadn't taken his hand off Loey's arm. She jerked away from his touch without glancing at him.

"Holy shit." Dale came up beside her, wide-eyed and mouth gaping. A hysterical laugh bubbled out as she took in the bedlam unfolding in the churchyard. "This takes snake handling to a whole new level, huh?"

It had taken nearly three hours and all the men Jeronimo could wrangle to poke around every nook and cranny of the church for remaining snakes. The thought of burning down the church had entered everyone's minds more than a few times. By noon, the men had cleared the church of snakes, and Burl's casket had gone on to the cemetery for a harried graveside service.

Once Burl was eight feet in the ground and surrounded by salt, and after his final sweep of the church for snakes, Jeronimo walked toward Loey. She perched on the rusted metal railing of the church's front porch to take pressure off her knee, which ached in time with her heartbeat.

Jeronimo raked a hand through his sweat-dampened

hair. He'd untucked his white shirt and rolled up the cuffs. His black slacks were coated with dirt and dust, and he had a gaping snake bite in one hand.

Loey pointed at it. "I hope that hurt."

"Mr. Weebly made me promise I'd go to the hospital."

"Don't think he won't check to make sure you did."

"I know."

"Why didn't your nose bleed this time?."

His jaw clenched tight as he forced out the words. "He wasn't close enough."

"Seems to me he would've needed to be close to call those snakes into the church, especially since I saw the threads without even having to draw a symbol."

Jeronimo sighed. He stopped in front of her knees. Her dress had slipped up again, exposing more of her thighs than was decent, especially when he stared at her skin like that. But Loey didn't move to put herself to rights.

Let him stare. Who cares? It's not like he feels anything or has a soul or even cares about anything other than himself.

She knew her thoughts were reckless, but she felt out of control anyway. His opinion of her meant too little for her to care. Let him think whatever he wanted. He was a bad man of the worst sort, and he could stare all he wanted.

She'd spent her entire adult life being prim and proper. Where had that gotten her? Nowhere.

She shook off the thought. Without her thinking it, her knees parted enough for the breeze to whisk up against her thighs. Jeronimo's gaze fell lower, toward dangerous territory. Her heart kicked up to a gallop against her ribs.

He lifted his hand, and it hovered above her leg as he decided.

She smacked it away, hopped down from the railing, and growled, "Coward."

He didn't argue. Instead, he said, "The tatter is stretching."

"If Barty keeps this up, the whole town will know something wrong is happening around here."

"He won't stop. Not until I pay for trapping him in there."

Loey couldn't reconcile the shadow that had left a message on the wall in Burl's house with a brother bent on revenge. Though she struggled to argue against the logic of Leigh being salted in time, she still believed he could be the shadow man leaving warnings behind. But she couldn't deny something from across the Seam had slammed her face into a mirror. If Barty was strong enough to send snakes through the floorboards of the church, then he was strong enough to create a legion of shadow men.

She crossed her arms. "Do you think you can kill him first when this thing tears open? Before you fall apart in a puddle of your own nose blood?"

Jeronimo didn't answer. Sweat beaded along his brow. A smudge of dirt created a shadow over his cheekbone. He looked tan and tired, his breathing shallow in his throat. Finally, he looked back at her.

"J," she pressed, because he could do this forever: stare at her and never answer, as if his silence was enough. And that wasn't okay. Not after the letter. Not after his denying her grandparents help. It wasn't okay, and she didn't care if he stared at her like she stirred up some precious wind in his hollow, dusty, soulless insides. She *did not care*.

His eyes fell to her mouth. "I like that."

"J? I don't know, it just came out." She shrugged. It meant nothing. He meant nothing. "Sometimes you act like you're not in the same world as me when I'm talking to you. It's annoying."

He huffed out the weakest laugh Loey had ever heard. "Sometimes I'm not. Don't take it personally."

She scowled at him. "It's hard not to."

He held out his hand, palm up. She didn't take it. He dropped it back to his side.

"Come on," he said. "We have to ward the church."

He paused when she didn't follow him toward the church doors.

"Right. I would hate for you to have to spend an extra second in this town before you leave me to Tend all this alone."

"Do you remember when I said hell is what we make it?"

"How could I forget?" she said dryly.

"Righteous is my hell."

He went back inside the church, and the pine doors swung shut behind him.

In that moment, she could almost—almost—imagine why he hadn't returned to Righteous when her grandparents had begged for his help countless times. Because if her hell was Folton's classroom, she would never return, no matter who begged her. No matter what price she had to pay.

CHAPTER 29

AFTER WARDING THE CHURCH, LOEY had left Jeronimo to take care of her chores at home. She returned to the rectory as night fell and discovered his motorcycle missing. The cottage was dark and closed, the doors locked.

Loey checked the cemetery and the church, but Jeronimo was gone. It wasn't like he had a cell phone she could call. Her only way to contact him, aside from face to face, was through the rectory's ancient rotary landline.

The Seam had weakened enough for Barty to create another tatter in the church without needing something as destructive as a tornado to tear at the threads. They needed to eliminate Barty before he did any more damage.

With a growl of annoyance, Loey trekked back up the hay pasture to her house. She was halfway to the back door when Cross's truck rumbled up the drive.

The silhouettes of two people sat behind the dash, and from the big hair of the person in the passenger seat, Loey reckoned Dale had come with her brother. Dale had left Loey's and returned home after Burl's funeral; it wouldn't look right for her to be absent from her husband's side while he grieved, though Cross had mentioned Travis was spending more and more time at the bar than at home.

The truck pulled to a stop. The diesel engine shut off, and

the night's quiet returned. Loey made her way over as the doors opened.

"Evening," she called to the Rose siblings. She met Dale with a hug.

"Hey," Dale said into Loey's hair.

"How are you?" Loey asked.

Dale straightened away from Loey and gave her a soft smile. "That's why we came by."

Loey shot Cross a look as he rounded the truck's hood to join them. He put a hand on Dale's back. Loey's stomach turned over with sickness.

"Is everything okay?" she asked, looking between the siblings.

Cross squeezed Dale's shoulder, and Dale released a long breath. "I've decided it's time."

Dread washed over Loey. "For what?"

Dale swallowed, emotion swimming in her eyes. She ducked her head.

For her, because she couldn't, Cross said, "Rehab. She said it's time to get help."

"Oh, Dale."

Loey pulled her best friend into a crushing hug. Cross kept one hand on his sister's shoulder, and his other went to Loey's. It reminded her of their embrace so long ago, in high school, when she'd told them about Folton. She wished they could go back to a time when they weren't falling apart, when their hugs were rooted in happiness and not brokenness.

"I have to try," Dale said, her words muffled against Loey. "I feel like I'm going crazy."

"I'm sorry," Loey whispered, her throat tight with tears. She didn't want them to come, not when Dale needed her strength, but they came anyway and poured down her cheeks. "I wish I'd never asked you to help me. I wish we had never done what we did."

Dale pulled back and took her hand. Cross tucked Loey against his side.

"I'll *never* be sorry," Dale said, feverish with conviction. "Not ever. He deserved what he got, and we didn't do a bad thing. But I'm sorry for forcing your silence. I felt like I could never feel pain over what happened that night because he'd done it more often to you, and it's been eating away at me. Like, I *hate* him. I hate him so much for what he did to you."

"And what he did to you. Just because you knew it would happen when you went to his house that night doesn't mean it wasn't horrible and awful. We never should have put ourselves in that situation."

"It's time," Cross said gently. "It's time to tell the truth about what we did."

Dale nodded. "I wanted you to know that before I left. The truth is important to you, and I understand that now. You should tell it if you want to, if it'll help you. I think it'll help all of us."

"I think," Loey said, "it's time to move on."

"It is." Dale wrapped her arms around Loey and her brother.

They stood like that until their arms ached and their backs went stiff.

When they released each other, Cross said, "We should hit the road. Dale picked a facility in South Carolina, and Mother wanted us to stop and see Grandmother Helene on our way."

Loey cringed. "Good luck with your grandmother."

"Pray for me," Dale sing-songed. She tried to smile.

"I will," Loey murmured.

Cross went around to the driver's side, and as Dale climbed back into the passenger seat, she said to Loey, "I feel like I'm leaving you at the wrong time. I think you're going through something really big, and I won't be around for you."

Loey held the truck's door as Dale buckled in. Across the cab, Cross clambered in and slammed his door.

"I'm handling it. More than I ever have before, I'm handling myself."

Cross started the truck, and Dale smiled. Over the diesel's roar, she said, "You're stronger than you know, Lo."

"I'm learning."

"Good."

"Get well, Dale."

"I'll try."

"I love you."

Dale blew her a kiss as Loey stepped back. "I love you too."

CHAPTER 30

JULY 4, 2012

GRAN CONVINCED HER TO COMPETE in the Fourth of July rodeo. Loey hadn't wanted to, but the look on Gran's face when Loey told her she didn't want to run the barrels had done her in.

Pap had hitched the trailer before Gran could ask, and Loey loaded her tack without a word. Tempest pranced all the way from her stall, walking on her tiptoes, buzzing with so much energy it threatened to zap Loey if she got too close.

Tempest was breathing fire, and in the pit of Loey's stomach, a seed of fear took root.

When they arrived at the county fairgrounds, the sun had set and the arena's massive spotlights cast vast pools of illumination over the stands filled with sweat-kissed crowds in cowboy hats and boots, kids with cotton-candy mouths, girls wearing too-short shorts, and boys with their shirttails coming untucked. The announcer gave the last call for the silent auction and mentioned a cakewalk later. In the parking lot, where Pap stopped the truck, trailers sat with horses tacked up and tied off. Loey hopped out of the truck as Gran wished her good luck and said she would watch her event from the baked goods table.

Pap saddled up Tempest while Loey changed into her good rodeo shirt, a pink and blue button-up that matched her saddle pad. With her hair tied back in a tight ponytail and her cowboy hat pulled down low, she took over for Pap and wrapped Tempest's legs, checked her tack, and put on Tempest's bridle.

She reached the arena right as the barrel-racing event started. As she watched the riders, mostly kids her age on hay-fat ponies, tear around the three metal barrels positioned in a triangle formation in the arena, Tempest jigged beside her. The horn blared every time a rider raced home after the final turn, kicking their horse to run faster, to signal their final time. The fastest duo won, and Loey and Tempest were always the fastest.

She mounted up. The announcer's voice droned into the background. She had to focus solely on keeping Tempest contained beneath her. She pranced and pawed, skittering to the side at every noise. Pap grabbed onto the reins to help Loey hold her still.

"She's awful full of it tonight. You sure you got her?"

He sounded worried. He pulled on the reins to tug Tempest's head down. She tried to bite him and struck out with her front hoof in frustration.

Loey most certainly did not have her, but it was a matter of pride now. She hadn't lost a barrel event since her grandparents had found Tempest at a county auction and bought her for a hundred dollars. There was no backing down.

Loey got Tempest into the chute, a row of metal gate panels running down either side of the alleyway, a twenty-five-foot stretch of dirt that led out toward the parking lot. On either side of the alley, rodeo volunteers, parents, and friends hung off the panels or had a leg slung over the ten-foot top bar. They all waved and wished her luck.

Control was an illusion, and Tempest was a dragon ready to take flight beneath her. When the rider before Loey came down the chute, slowing his horse from a gallop to a steady lope to a calm trot before reaching the end of the red-dirt runway, Loey pointed Tempest toward the arena and sent God a prayer.

Please be able to stop.

She released the reins and Tempest bolted.

The length of the chute passed in a metal blur. Without needing guidance, Tempest angled for the first barrel. She slowed her gallop enough to whip around the outside of the barrel, her legs bunching beneath her, leaning so far to the side that Loey's boot touched the ground. They righted by a miracle alone and flew toward the second barrel.

Tempest brushed it as she careened around it, but it managed to right itself. To the third and last barrel they went, and Loey clutched the saddle's horn, her body pressed low to Tempest's neck. Into the mare's flying black mane, Loey prayed.

Please be able to—

They'd rounded the last barrel before Loey could even finish. The end of the arena and the narrow opening to the chute loomed ahead.

They flashed by the timer and the horn blared. The announcer erupted in a flurry of excitement over Loey and Tempest's time, possibly a new county record.

Loey heard none of it because she was trying to slow Tempest so they could stop before they reached the end of the chute.

But stopping was an illusion, as was steering. Loey tried to rein Tempest back or tug her off balance so the mare would have to readjust her headlong dash toward the narrow chute. But it was no use, and Loey gave in and held on, hoping if Tempest didn't stop by the end of the chute, she'd stop by the end of the parking lot.

A few feet from the chute's opening, Tempest stumbled. She caught herself, but Loey slipped forward off the mare's left wither. Her imperfect balance further disrupted Tempest's faltering stride, and the mare swerved—straight toward the chute's edge.

There was no time for anything but a dull acceptance, and certainly no time for a prayer, though even if she'd had minutes, Loey doubted she would have prayed.

God wasn't listening to her anymore.

They hit the chute's ten-foot double-paneled metal gates at a full-tilt gallop, the fastest Loey had ever gone. First, Loey only saw metal, then she only saw red dirt as Tempest tried to jump the panel before impact.

There was no time.

They flipped over the gate but not enough to clear it. Tempest's legs tangled, and she screamed. With her boot caught in the stirrup, Loey's left knee took the brunt of Tempest's fall. Metal screeched and wrapped around them like chains on a swing set. Tempest thrashed against the metal rods, and the saddle's horn stabbed into Loey's belly with blinding pain. When the gate finally broke and Tempest fell, Loey's head snapped forward and her face, mainly her mouth, slammed straight into the jagged metal edge of a freshly snapped pole.

Sometime later, Loey blinked her eyes open, but she saw nothing but the hazy outline of bodies silhouetted against the arena's huge spotlights. A rag lay over her face, dripping warm liquid into her hair. The drops rolled into her ears and collected there like tears.

Sirens wailed in the distance.

"Get her to the damn ambulance," someone snarled. It sounded like Burl's gruff baritone. "She don't need to see the mare hit the ground."

Hit the ground? Loey wondered. *What does he mean, hit the ground?*

The sirens grew louder. Vaguely, she heard the announcer

telling everyone to remain calm, to stay in their seats and give the professionals room.

"Get her on!" Burl shouted.

"I've got her."

Loey would have recognized that voice from the grave. Even through the din of sirens and Burl's shouted instructions, Loey knew that voice, which sounded from right above her. She screamed.

He scooped her up as if she were air.

The rag clung to her nose, turning her breathing into a wet, sucking effort. Folton's fingers dug into her skin. The pain of his touch rooted her back to reality. She wasn't the one screaming.

It was Tempest.

Her cries of pain punched the air and shredded it to fine, bloody ribbons in Loey's ears. The sound pitched to an octave that punctured Loey's heart and turned it to ribbons too as Folton's bouncy, half-running stride made all her shattered parts stab into her few unbroken pieces.

He settled her onto a gurney. Above her, the paramedics spoke to Folton in quick, staccato sentences. Somewhere far away, she heard Gran's shouting getting closer.

But all that faded, and the real world melted away. She felt Tempest's gallop beneath her. Felt the air streaming by her. Felt the ground churning beneath them. Smelled Tempest's special scent. Heard her deep breaths. Felt the way she took the bit and ran and ran and ran, as if she would never stop. As if the world had no end, and life was merely finding your place on the back of a good horse.

Reality crashed back into focus behind the wet rag covering her face. Gran was shouting overhead to *"Just end her, Harlan,"* and Loey's body jerked and rocked as they loaded the gurney into the back of the ambulance.

The gunshot echoed loudest. Everyone fell quiet.

Then Tempest's resounding silence.

It was … nothing.

She don't need to see the mare hit the ground.

Hit the ground, as in dead.

Loey opened her mouth against the wet thing over her face and sucked in a mighty breath, nearly swallowing the rag deep into her throat.

She screamed and didn't stop.

CHAPTER 31

FOR THE FIRST SATURDAY SINCE the day Burl had called, harried and breathless, to tell Loey her grandparents had crashed through the guardrail up on Devil's Maw, Loey did not open the coffee shop.

Instead, she headed to the library. When she asked Delilah, the head librarian, if she could flip through microfilm newspaper articles, the woman actually laughed before realizing Loey was serious. Only then did the librarian escort her to the basement.

Delilah helped Loey familiarize herself with the machine, which probably hadn't been dusted since well before they were both born, and then lingered to catch a peek of what Loey was investigating.

"Does this have something to do with Briggs's murder?" Delilah burst out in a whisper that was too high-pitched with glee.

Before Loey could answer, she went on. "Are you about to catch the murderer? I can help, you know, if you need it."

"Sorry." Loey gave the librarian her most regretful smile. "I'm looking for old articles about the coffee shop."

Delilah soaked up her words, and then, as if realizing something, she snapped to attention. She winked. "Coffee shop articles. Right. I'll leave you to those coffee shop articles."

She winked again, even though they were the only ones in the library basement. "Let me know"—another wink—"if I can help."

When she finally left, Loey flipped back through endless pages of *The Righteous Daily* to the fifties. She found three news articles of interest, two of them about the day of the explosion.

The first and largest article took up the entire front page of the paper. Loey skimmed it until it mentioned her seventy-four-year-old great-great-grandfather's death, which had happened earlier that month in 1956. Knox Keene had died and left the entirety of Shiner's Ridge to Townsend Rose, who, in an unexpected turn of events, had deeded the land to a protected nature reserve, where the timber could never be cut. As the South's richest timber baron, the decision wouldn't come close to affecting his countless sawmills, but without the formerly promised lumber to burn in his smelteries, Obidiah Jinks's iron mills were undercut.

Loey knew from her own history lessons of Righteous that this decision would lead to the Jinks family's ruin and the bad blood between the two families. It wouldn't be until Dale married Travis that a Jinks and a Rose would even be in the same room as the other. The wedding had been a tense affair, to say the least.

The second article covered the moonshine still's explosion. It listed nothing Loey hadn't already heard from Jeronimo. It spoke of Jeronimo being on the lam in the woods from a famous West Virginian revenuer and his brother's past with the law. The article was shorter than an obituary and seemed to serve as one, because Loey couldn't find another reference to either James brother after April 7, 1956.

The third article was written on April 12, 1956, when Frankie Rose's body was discovered in Little Cricket Creek.

Townsend Rose, her father, had fought the District Attorney's autopsy request, but her involvement with the James brothers and her injuries had necessitated one. Her funeral was listed for the following week.

Loey's skin pimpled with gooseflesh as she read the article. She knew from Jeronimo's story about the night in '56 that Frankie had been killed on that night. But her body hadn't been found until nearly a week later.

She hadn't been salted in time, which meant there was only one place for her soul.

Loey's stomach cramped. Frankie was stuck across the Seam with her killer. Jeronimo kept telling her loose souls weren't strong enough to make the messages they'd been receiving, but Loey knew the power of a scorned Southern woman. If anyone could find the strength, it would be Frankie Rose.

She had to find Jeronimo and tell him. She grimaced at the thought. She knew from how he spoke of Frankie that he'd loved her, even if he didn't know himself. She couldn't imagine how hard it would be to hear her soul was trapped across the Seam with his brother, who'd killed her.

It was messed up, even for a small town in the South.

After taking pictures of the articles with her phone, she left the library with those three articles spinning in her head and her eyes dry from the dust in the library's basement. She started up her truck and headed toward home.

On her way to Devil's Maw from town, she looked up to the ridge and sighed.

Fog hung like a moth-eaten tapestry off the pegs of Shiner's Ridge. Above the wall of gray, the mountains floated, their black peaks molting strands of curling fog. The sun must have forgotten it was supposed to shine, because the evening's light was sepia-toned with dankness.

As the truck trundled across the bridge over Little Cricket

Creek, Loey struggled to see beyond the truck's nose. The fog slipped free and rolled down above the pines and into the fields and across Devil's Maw, reducing the world to seeping, moist grayness. The hood of her truck peeked through the wall of fog, along with the faint outline of the white line on the road, but that was all she saw.

She slowed the truck to a crawl on the road. The sudden blindness was almost absolute, the fog so thick it felt oppressive. With her windows down, she imagined she could open her mouth and the fog would dissolve like fresh cotton candy on her tongue.

Muttering under her breath, she accelerated by faith and memory alone. She took the switchbacks slow as she wound her way up the ridge, the tires passing over the white line and kissing the chipped shoulder more times than what was comfortable. The wheel tugged in her hands when she hit the shoulder again, and she corrected with a sharp jerk that left her heart racing and pressed the brake again.

Ahead, the battered guardrail of the sharpest turn of Devil's Maw gleamed like a demented smile with all those white crosses marking its bend like bad omens. She eased toward it, inching up the pavement slower than Ms. Ida May in her old Cadillac.

Halfway around the deadly bend, the truck stalled and died. She fumbled for the ignition as the vehicle rolled back toward the flimsy guardrail separating her from the straight drop to the valley below.

She jerked her foot over to the brake, missed, and hit the clutch. When she finally found the brake in a blind panic, the truck heaved to a stop in the middle of the road.

Fingers shaking, she reached for the ignition. The engine sputtered.

In the cupholder beside her, her phone rang, a shrill sound

that made her jump. Her foot slipped off the brake. Like it had been waiting for such a mistake, the truck rolled back a few more feet. She pumped the brake so hard her leg shook from the effort.

She grabbed her phone.

After the murky illumination from her headlights in the fog, the screen's light blinded her.

On her phone, in plain white letters, the caller's name was displayed.

Gran.

Her hand spasmed. The phone fell to the floorboard, where it slid partially under the seat, still ringing that shrill sound.

Gran was calling.

But Loey knew the old flip phone with large buttons for Gran's ailing eyes was dead in a junk drawer in the kitchen. Gran had barely used it while alive. Loey didn't even know if it could power on.

The sound stopped. In the silence, Loey trembled.

It was Barty. It had to be, which meant she had to get out of this fog.

She tried the ignition again. The motor turned over without a problem.

She accelerated up the turn, switching gears quickly to keep from stalling again. The engine revved. The tires spun and caught on the loose gravel that had washed up from the ditch during the last rainstorm. She twisted the wheel hard to the left to follow the white line up the steep grade, her headlights not even reaching the pavement beyond the truck's hood.

Her phone rang again.

Loud. Urgent. Even though it should have been muffled beneath the seat.

With one hand on the wheel, she shifted in her seat and reached down, fingers stretching in search of her phone beneath the seat.

The truck bounced beneath her right as her fingers brushed the edge of the slim case. The tires skidded into a ditch. She jerked upright. The wheel twisted in her hand. The truck tilted to the side as the back wheel lost contact with the ground.

All along Devil's Maw, the shoulder had fallen away. The road was one hard rain from caving in. She'd driven into one of its gaping holes, those big patches of nothing.

She hit the gas, praying the other three tires would pull her out.

Her phone continued to ring beneath her.

The truck heaved out of the hole, found solid pavement again, and surged forward. Loey spun the wheel, making the next turn as the guardrail glinted into view through the fog. She pressed the gas harder than she should have. If she was near a tatter, she had to get away from it.

Her phone still rang. She shouldn't have, but she reached again for it, stretching lower so her eyes dipped below the dashboard. She connected with the phone, grabbed it, and jerked upright, all within two seconds.

Her headlights illuminated a man standing in the road, silhouetted by fog.

His eyes locked on her right as she hit him with a sick thump, her foot never leaving the gas.

He struck the hood as she screamed, as her phone rang in her hand, as the metal of her hood creaked beneath his weight. He hit her windshield with a mighty crack and rolled up over the top of her truck.

She hit the brakes too hard.

He was flung back forward and tossed onto the road. Even from inside the truck, she heard his body collide against the pavement with a thick slap of flesh.

He'd disappeared below the line of her headlights. She

trembled in the driver's seat, both feet on the brake. Her left knee screeched in complaint. Her knuckles were white. Her cheeks were wet. She was crying. She was still screaming.

Her phone was still ringing.

On the screen, Gran's name was still displayed.

She stopped screaming. Of its own accord, her finger swiped across the screen to answer the call. She pressed the phone to her ear.

"Hello?"

CHAPTER 32

HEAVY BREATHING SOUNDED ON THE other end
of the call. Heavy and panting, like the person had been
running.

From the hood of the truck, the glow of the headlights
fluttered. The person she'd hit was stirring.

"Barty, is this you?"

The breathing turned shallower, gasping.

The man staggered upright.

In the light, against the fog, Jeronimo stared back at her
with his shirt torn half off his body.

"Frankie?" Loey whispered into the phone, her eyes on
Jeronimo.

He cocked his head as if he could hear her, the motion not
at all humanlike.

From the phone, the breathing stopped. Silence poured
into Loey's ear.

The call ended.

She threw her phone onto the floor of the truck and
watched it bounce back under the seat. When she looked back
up, Jeronimo was gone.

A finger tapped on the glass near her head.

She screamed.

Jeronimo stood at the driver's window. She rolled down

the window, a silly gesture. She should have been out of the truck helping him. She should have been doing more. Doing *something*.

Before the window was halfway down, he shook his head, and a piece of hair fell across his forehead.

"What happened?" he asked roughly. "Why were you screaming?"

She raked her eyes over his body, processing his strangely bloodless injuries. Habit, she figured, since he should be dead. "What happened? Has the Seam ripped?"

"Loey," he warned.

She knew the call had been one of Barty's tricks, but she couldn't help how it had rattled her. She stuffed it down.

"The fog," she answered. "It has me rattled. What happened to you?"

His expression suggested he didn't believe her, but he let it go. "I was up at the old still—"

"Tonight? You went alone?" Loey shouted. "Do you want to die?"

She noticed then how rattled and wide-eyed he looked, like he'd received a phone call from his dead grandmother and not her. "You were right."

"About what?" she asked.

"I'm a coward."

He stared at her so blankly, as though he'd never been more lost in his life. It terrified her. She knew vague, hiding-secrets Jeronimo, and she knew cocky, my-plan-or-the-highway Jeronimo. But she didn't know this uncertain, wavering version, and it worried her.

"Let's talk about it in the truck," she said slowly, "before you get run over. Again."

"Yes, ma'am."

She cranked up her window as he limped around the hood

and climbed into the passenger seat.

"Is he chasing you?" she asked.

"You're awfully calm if he is."

"Stop dancing around the truth," she snapped. "I'm not moving until you tell me where your brother's at."

"He's not loose." He grimaced as if in pain, but Loey saw no gaping black holes in him.

"Then what happened? Did you fight him at the still? Why did you say you're a coward?"

He leaned his head back against the seat and sucked in a long breath, but getting a solid gulp of oxygen seemed beyond his grasp. She'd considered him all but immortal since she'd shot him, but seeing him like this, so weak, unsettled her.

"J, what happened to you?" she said louder as he drifted toward unconsciousness. "Are you okay?"

"I was in the middle of the road because I was looking for you. Barty followed me from the still's tatter. He brought the fog."

"And the still? Why the heck did you think it was a good idea to go alone?"

"Good. I was worried you would be bitter."

She blinked at him. "Did you make a joke?"

He flung his hand toward the road in front of them. The fog was lifting; Barty must have gotten bored with their bickering. "Can you drive and stop giving me a hard time for once? I'm exhausted and everything hurts."

"First you make a joke, and now you're whining."

"Loey," he warned, growling her name in a way that, she was reluctant to admit, made her nose tingle.

"Fine." She shoved the truck into drive and accelerated up the steep road. "But you better tell me everything before we get there. By the way, where are we going?"

"The cemetery. The plan's changed."

She shot him a sidelong glance. "Why?"

271

"I had my chance to kill him. He was right there. He took my hand and *pulled*. There was a second when I thought he would yank me across the Seam."

"He can do that?"

"He's strong. Stronger than I thought. Shoulda known. He was always better at this than me," he mumbled incoherently.

She lightly slapped his arm. "Stay with me. Why has the plan changed?"

"Because I couldn't kill him. I can't. You were right. About everything."

She wound her way up Devil's Maw, twisting closer to the faint lights of her house and the rectory. "And the new plan?"

"I'll help you seal the Seam. We need to look at the tatter in the cemetery tonight before anything else happens. It's the biggest and most dangerous one. If we can figure out how to stitch it up temporarily, then we can buy ourselves some time to find a more permanent solution."

Her fingers clenched around the steering wheel so tightly it hurt. Somewhere in the back of her mouth, she thought she heard her teeth crack and crumble from the force of her clenched jaw.

"I know what you're thinking."

"You should."

"I'm sorry."

She pressed the gas down farther and roared up the last stretch of Devil's Maw.

"I shoulda come when they first asked. It's my fault they're dead, and you're right to hate me."

His words conjured the memory of the fresh bouquet on her grandparents' graves. They were just flowers. They couldn't be an atonement, couldn't right the wrong he'd done. But they were flowers. They were something.

"Was Frankie salted in time?" she asked since they were

both thinking about things they were sorry for.

Jeronimo's resounding silence was answer enough. He knew. In his silence, Loey sensed that he'd spent his undying life thinking about that very fact. He'd lived every day knowing Frankie was trapped with Barty. No wonder he looked like a hollow man. He was cursed in every way.

"Do you think she's the one warning us about Barty?"

"I think, in the end, it doesn't really matter."

His response came out sharp enough to warn her not to ask more questions. If she wanted to discover who was leaving the messages or confirm it was Frankie, she'd have to do it on her own.

When she tore past the church's gravel road, the soft edge to Jeronimo's voice hardened as he said, "I told you to go to the cemetery."

"And I have to feed my horse and the chickens and let Dewey out before we go waltzing through the cemetery, so sit there nicely and don't speak to me in that tone of voice, unless you want to get shot again."

When he barked out a laugh, she practically jumped out of her skin. He shook his head, a smile spreading clear across his face. It was so wide his teeth gleamed between his lips. A dimple appeared in his right cheek.

"I could love you," he said, and the words shook her to her core. As if he hadn't gotten the point across, he repeated, "I could love you, Loey Grace Keene. If you didn't have every right to hate me and want me dead, I could love you."

Her palms went slick against the wheel. In a split second, her body flashed ice cold, then scalding hot, then back to ice cold. She didn't know whether to shiver or pull at her shirt collar.

I could love you.

He was still chuckling beside her, finding the notion truly hilarious. But to her, and her hammering heart and flipping belly, those words meant something. They meant, as Gran would have said, that she'd been busy taking wooden nickels from handsome strangers.

With one hand on the wheel, she slugged him hard in his arm. It cut his chuckling right off.

"What the hell was that for?"

"Listen here, Jeronimo James. You don't say things like loving someone unless you darn well mean it. You hear me?"

"Yes, ma'am," he said, his smile vanishing.

She released a blustery sigh. "I miss the days when I thought you were a serial killer. Those were good times."

CHAPTER 33

TRAIPSING THROUGH BLACKMORE CEMETERY AT midnight was an experience Loey could have lived without.

She followed Jeronimo as he picked his way down the brick-lined path toward the center, and oldest part, of the graveyard. He moved through the cemetery like it was his second home. Maybe it was. He was buried here, after all.

Or an empty coffin was.

She clutched a few pieces of Gran's thick stationery, the black calligraphy pen, and the last of her patience.

They reached the poplar in which Briggs had died far too soon. Jeronimo sat his bag at the trunk's base and pulled out a container of salt and a slender knife. He unsheathed it and check its curving edge before he laid it aside. He next produced a jar of moonshine, which he opened and took a hearty gulp, followed by two more, each one longer than the last.

When he handed it to her, it was a quarter gone, and the lines around his eyes were less deep.

She took the offering. Though she stopped at two big sips, she felt the familiar heat spread through her marrow.

"Ready?" he asked.

She pursed her lips, tasting the last few drops of bitter medicine. She inclined her head in answer.

Jeronimo stepped back to give her room. "You can do this."

"I know," she snapped, but the pages in her hand grew foreign. The pen between her fingers could have been a viper. If she listened closely, she could hear a swing set's chain rattling in a breeze.

Don't think about Briggs. Or Leigh. Or Folton. Or anyone.

"Loey?" His voice rang out across the cemetery.

She kept her back to him and pretended to prepare her page. "I'm fine."

"I know," he murmured, "but your grandparents would be proud of you."

She let his words roll off her back like they didn't mean anything to her, when they meant far too much. She lifted her face toward the highest branches. The memory of Pastor Briggs's bare toes flashed strobe-light bright through her mind.

"Don't talk about them," she said instead of the "thank you" she'd wanted to say. She needed her anger. She needed to hate him. Otherwise, everything felt wrong.

I could love you, Loey Grace Keene.

She crouched close enough to the base of the tree's wide trunk to smell the nutty spice of its bark. Beyond the scent, she caught something sharper, like an old burning fire.

Pushing the thought away, she focused on the page in front of her and the pen in her hand. Gran and Pap needed her. Dale, Cross, and all the other innocent people of Righteous— who might be hypocrites sometimes, just like her, but had the best of intentions—needed her. And those who weren't here, like Briggs and Leigh and Burl, needed her. Even Jeronimo, the coward who could love her, needed her.

Holding her breath, she started to draw.

The circular symbol reminded her of a snake eating its own tail. Her hand was steady and her line came out loose. Her circle closed perfectly. She dragged her pen to the center, keeping the dark line continuous, and drew a loose knot in the shape of an infinity sign.

When she lifted her pen, she released her breath and waited for the threads to appear. When they didn't, she thought it hadn't worked, that she wasn't a true Tender after all.

Before she could stand up fully to face Jeronimo, the stars fell.

Except the stars were pinpricks of dancing light around her. Instead of falling to the ground, they undulated, vibrating in a rhythmic, mesmerizing dance around her. Like so many fireflies, these stars flickered and flashed with colors that ranged from white to pastels to bright, vivid, brutal reds.

She gasped.

The tatter was *huge*. And its destruction was terribly beautiful.

The lights from more threads and knots than she'd ever seen engulfed her, sweeping around her as far as she could see. Even up toward her house at the base of Shiner's Ridge she saw the faint flicker of knots. She turned in a slow circle. Her sight was so consumed by the threads and their knots that she couldn't make out Jeronimo through the magical display.

Magic.

She'd done nothing but draw a few curved lines. These threads had always existed, had always been there; all she'd needed to do was open her eyes. Maybe some would call that magic; she could be okay with that. This wasn't magic to be feared, but beautiful and delicate and utterly perfect in its design.

Lifting her hand, she brushed her fingers down a pale yellow thread. Its knots chimed a song beneath her touch. They felt like sparks against her fingertips, as if she was brushing against the pulse of the world.

"Loey."

She turned toward the sound of her name. Now that she wasn't focusing on the threads, she spotted Jeronimo through the luminescence, where he stood beside Townsend Rose's headstone. When she saw him fully, she let out a whoosh of air.

"Oh."

She hadn't had time to look at him while trying to fix the tatter in Burl's house, but she saw him now, and the sight took her breath away.

The knots around him were dark as onyx. They didn't pulse with light but absorbed it from nearby threads. It should have been terrifying. It should have suggested his darkness, his wrongness, but she found his threads beautiful. She'd always turned away from the shadows in her life, needing desperately to only believe in the bright and shiny, the easy truths, the bits and pieces of life that were easy to swallow.

But Jeronimo James was all shadow, and she would never look away.

"Loey," he said again.

She couldn't breathe. "It's a shame you can't see this."

See you, she amended in her thoughts because she didn't dare say the words aloud. He was stunning. His threads were the most beautiful thing she'd ever seen.

He took her hand, perhaps to ground her or perhaps to tether her to him. "Can you find the tatter? How bad is it?"

The question pulled her from her reverie. Keeping his hand in hers, she turned back to face the poplar tree where Briggs had died and the epicenter of the tatter's destruction.

Threads hung in unconnected strands that desperately flailed in a nonexistent wind. They had no knots, nothing to bind them to the other threads. They were unanchored and lost. Loey sensed the wrongness in the pit of her stomach.

"Bad," she murmured.

"Can you knot them back together?"

She ran her hand down the sundered threads, and they stilled. She imagined them taking a breath before resuming their rattling dance. Focusing on the remaining knots around the ripped threads, she saw where to knot the loose threads together. In Burl's house, she'd just grabbed random threads to tie together, but when she looked closer, she saw how the threads wanted to weave together. She saw them as if they already formed a tapestry and she just had to tie the knots to make it so.

"I can try."

"Do it." Jeronimo's voice came out tense behind her, his breath hot against the back of her neck.

It should have bothered her after Folton; it should have been easy to recall the scrape of his dry mouth on her skin. But she felt safe with Jeronimo at her back, guarding her. But what was he guarding her against? What was happening beyond her world of fractured starlight?

"Quickly," he added.

Dropping his hand so both of hers were free, she reached for the first knot. Her fingers traced its solid wrappings. Jeronimo was right; Gran had been preparing her for Tending knots her entire life. She knew this knot, a square knot, because she'd tied millions of them over her lifetime. She could form it with her eyes closed and tighten it as easily.

She worked in silence. Once she started, she had to keep going, or else she'd lose her place in the infinite lights. Unblinking and mostly unbreathing, she moved her fingers at lightning speed, dancing from one knot to the next.

"Loey."

She ignored him and kept working, but he pulled her back.

She swiped at her damp forehead. "What?"

Jeronimo spun her to face him. He swept his eyes over her from head to toe as if convinced she was hurt. "You've been working for an hour. What's happening?"

"An hour?" she breathed out, shocked. It had felt like seconds.

"*Loey*, what's happening?"

"It's big. I feel like I could tie knots forever and it would never end."

The more she talked, the more she came out of the trance.

"Are you making any progress? Do you think it'll hold?"

"It's tight enough so Barty can't pull you back through." She smirked at him.

"Don't bull-crap me," he said, aiming for a light-hearted tone but landing closer to sad. "I drive you crazy. You wouldn't mind if I was gone."

As if his words had conjured their own magic, the threads around her erupted in pulsing glimmers. Millions and millions of tiny stars. A galaxy of her very own. She almost couldn't see Jeronimo through the glow of pulsing knots.

But she took his hand. "I'd mind."

"Lo." He stared at her like he was seeing the threads around her, like he was staring into the sort of miracle he didn't believe in. "You'll never know how sorry I am for your Gran and Pap. I'll never forgive myself."

She squeezed his fingers, but he didn't look away from her. It hurt. His words hurt. Because she knew it was partly his fault, if not mostly. There would always be a part of her that would never forget that a decision he'd made had contributed to them being taken from her so suddenly. But Gran had raised her better than to hold grudges, to live with hate. Gran had preached forgiveness and faith in mankind's better angels.

"You were the one who put the flowers on their graves? The grocery store carnations?" she asked.

He nodded, his lips twisted up in anguish. He didn't speak, and his silence seemed like he wanted to say more but he didn't trust his voice.

"You put flowers on their graves. It's something."

"You should hate me," he told her.

She offered him a simple lift of her shoulder, a tiny shrug, and a soft smile of forgiveness. "And you could love me."

There was a moment, a lifetime that stretched into infinity, as if Loey were watching it happen from a place far, far removed from herself. One second, Jeronimo was *there*, his lips *there*, in *his* space. And then, a mere breath later, he was *here* against her, his lips on *hers*, in *her* space.

She crashed back inside herself as he breathed into her mouth. Her lips parted against his. His mouth hovered against hers.

For that lifetime, they breathed each other in, and Loey knew what it was like to soar through the air, miles above land, untouchable and lost to the pure sensation of *living*.

Then he was kissing her, and she had no clue how it happened or why it had, but it was like no kiss she'd ever experienced and never would again.

And heavens above, how he *tasted*.

He was sweet and bitter, bite and salve. On her tongue, she tasted cinnamon and something darker, like aged bourbon, like the rich smoke of an expensive cigar, like leather and sweat and a time long past.

He kissed like he tasted. Dichotomous and paradoxical. Ironic and perfect. He kissed the way Loey had always dreamed of being kissed.

She took his face in her hands and kissed him back with everything she had as the threads strobed around them.

Dampness touched the sensitive valley beneath her nose. She pulled back, her fingers brushing at her skin. They came away wet.

"What's wrong …" Jeronimo's question trailed off as he also brought his hand to his face.

Darkness welled beneath his left nostril. A stretching shadow. A line of nighttime terrors. It glistened in the moonlight and then dripped off his upper lip.

She brought her tongue to her upper lip and tasted it. Salt, darkness, and an earthier spice that tasted ancient.

Blood.

"He's coming," she managed to say before the smell of fire filled the air and a cracking shot echoed through the graveyard. Another shot followed the first, like gunfire but louder, and echoed across the valley. The noise was sure to call attention to them from town.

Jeronimo instinctively grabbed her to protect her, even though the origin of the sound wasn't immediately clear.

But they figured it out soon enough.

The giant poplar's bark burned in ragged lines. The lines formed letters, spelling a single word.

Run.

CHAPTER 34

R UN.

"Why is he telling us to run?" Loey's hands trembled, but her voice was strong.

But Jeronimo wasn't listening. His eyes had never been so empty. Loey stared into them and knew he was gone.

"J," she said, her voice harsher this time, harsher and full of fear, "J."

He angled his head. He gazed at the word on the tree, his eyes glazing over. He swayed.

Loey whirled away from the tree to face Jeronimo. Blocking his view of the message, she slapped him. Hard. "J!"

His head snapped to the side from the force of the blow. Granite eyes locked on hers. He blinked her into focus. When he spoke, he sounded like a stranger. "You need to go. You need to go now."

His voice echoed across the silent graveyard. What was the phrase? Silent as the grave? It rang true now.

"I'm not going anywhere!"

Behind her, the threads let out a blast of chimes. Something was ripping its way through and undoing all her previous work.

"That's not my brother," Jeronimo said, his eyes slipping to focus on something over her shoulder. "That's *not* Barty."

Loey turned around. A man, whip-thin and distorted, stepped over the Seam. A shroud of shadows undulated around him. It was the creature from her mirror, the one that had bashed her face. She knew him by the evil weeping from his darkness.

"Go," Jeronimo spoke into her ear. "Go now."

He didn't wait for her answer before hauling her behind him, causing her to stumble into Townsend's headstone. He pulled them farther away from the tree and tatter until they were deep into the oldest graves in the cemetery. Together, they faced the thing pulling itself free from the last of the tatter's loose, torn threads.

"We should run," she told Jeronimo, her eyes locked on the creature-man.

"I'm going to draw it toward the church. When it follows me, get back to the tatter and start tying it back. When you're close enough, give me a sign."

"What if he just rips it again?"

Jeronimo glanced over at her. "Then we need to figure out how to kill him."

The creature's head snapped toward them, and the shadows clinging to it streamed through the air like distorted black ribbons. It sucked in deep gulps of air, scenting them fully, and snarled.

"Go!" Jeronimo shouted to her.

He raced off toward the church, and the creature followed in a fast lurch as if its legs didn't work right. The farther away from the Seam it chased Jeronimo, the more its shroud of shadows fell away to reveal a mottled face with yellowed eyes and jagged teeth.

Forcing herself to move, Loey raced through the headstones back to the tree. As she passed Townsends's headstone, a scream split the air.

She froze. The creature had leaped onto Jeronimo, who took the impact with a growl as he hit the ground.

Loey forced herself to look away as he grappled with the shadows clinging to the creature. Jeronimo was okay. He could handle a fight. She had to take care of the tatter.

Giving them a wide berth, she circled around the poplar and the tattered threads pulsing with angry-bright colors.

After another quick glance behind her—Jeronimo was on top of the creature and had landed a solid punch to its face, knocking loose more shadows—she started on the closest knot.

The creature had ripped the tatter further when it burst through. She had more threads to tie up than she'd anticipated. She tried to move quickly, flashing from knot to knot, sealing up the Seam enough so Jeronimo could toss that thing back in there and she could quickly finish mending the tatter, trapping the creature inside, but every time she heard a fist strike flesh, her fingers faltered.

A moan snapped her focus. She butchered a knot, and the thread trilled in complaint. She whipped around and saw the creature kick Jeronimo's prone body. He tumbled through the air and landed with a teeth-clacking smack against the earth.

For a long moment, he didn't move. Then, slowly, he got his arms beneath him, pushed up onto his knees, and shakily regained his feet. He'd barely managed it before the creature was on him again.

Loey's heart roared in her ears. She couldn't move. She didn't know if she should be helping him fight, running for help, or tying up the tatter.

One thing was for certain: she had to decide and quick. This thing was going to kill Jeronimo, and she was supposed to be his backup.

The creature's limbs were stretchy-man long and wispy, but it threw Jeronimo clean through the air.

His back collided with an oak tree, shaking the thick lower limbs. The creature advanced farther into the moonlight, and its shroud separated completely.

Loey gasped at the sight.

Without the cloak, she saw the creature for what it was—a man. His skin was nothing more than thin ropes of white scarring stretched bone-tight over a naked, withered frame. Where his manhood should have been, there was nothing but snarls of skin lashed up tight between his twig-thin legs.

He looked like he'd been skinned alive.

The Skinned Man.

The Skinned Man who certainly wasn't Barty, which meant Barty had been warning them all along.

Jeronimo hesitated a beat too long, caught up in his surprise at the man's skin—or the same realization Loey had just had. The Skinned Man grabbed Jeronimo by the throat. He squeezed and kept squeezing as he lifted Jeronimo off his feet.

Jeronimo grasped at the Skinned Man's gnarled hands, his feet kicking.

Loey clapped a hand over her mouth to keep from screaming. A rustling noise drew her attention toward the tatter, but she only found pulsing shadows.

Jeronimo was still in the Skinned Man's grip. His efforts to free himself dwindled. This was it. He needed backup.

"Hey!" she shouted. "Hey, over here!"

The Skinned Man's bare head snapped toward her. He paused. His eyes flicked up and down her body. He released his hold, and Jeronimo fell to the earth. Intrigued, he turned away from where Jeronimo lay at his feet.

The Skinned Man lurched toward her.

From the ground, Jeronimo struggled onto his elbow. He opened his mouth to speak but choked and coughed.

Now that she had the creature's attention, she didn't know

what to do. Step into the Seam and hope he followed? She didn't relish the idea of getting trapped in there or losing her soul.

He kept advancing on her, and every step brought him closer to the tatter's edge.

Think, she told herself. *Think!*

Unarmed, all she had were the loose threads whipping around her. She doubted the Skinned Man could see them since only Tenders could. It was her only advantage.

She grabbed the closest thread and waited.

When he was a couple steps away, she smelled him. Ash and smoke and the bitter tang of chemicals. And decay. His head twitched, his nose—half gone—flared as he pulled her smell deep into his lungs. He smiled with a lipless mouth, speaking words lost to its garbled speech.

One step away, close enough to touch, he reached for her.

She lashed out with the thread, wrapped it around his throat, and jerked it tight.

The Skinned Man screamed like a dying rabbit.

Loey didn't stop long enough to examine the complexity of his inhuman scream. She grabbed thread after thread and whipped them at his arms and legs, his torso and face, pausing only long enough to aim.

He flailed and screamed. Ensnared, he fell deeper into the threads' tangle. Loey ducked out of the way to keep from being trapped with him. She swung around behind him and waited for her opportunity to kick him back where he belonged.

Back here, she saw what she couldn't before. In middle of the largest cluster of strobing white lights, the Skinned Man tried to claw his way free, but behind him, at the edge of the Seam, a shadow hovered.

"Barty!" Jeronimo shouted, seeing his brother too. His effort reduced him to a heaving and coughing mess, and he fell to one knee then the other. He braced himself against the ground as if his guts were trying to turn him wrong-side out.

At the edge of the Seam, the threads' light illuminated the shadow man as he stepped over the Seam and around where the Skinned Man thrashed against the threads' hold. The shadows shrouding Barty fell away as they had from the Skinned Man, but instead of revealing a monster, they unveiled a young man. Barty's face had a youthful bounce despite his weary eyes, which darted between the killer and his brother. His hair was a lighter blond than Jeronimo's and curled above his ears. His mouth was bow-shaped and lush, softening the harder angles of his jaw and cleft chin. His sad eyes locked on Loey.

A high-pitched whine split the air.

The Skinned Man grabbed another thread and ripped it clean in half. Its light flickered then went out.

"No!" Loey shouted. She had no idea what ripping the worlds' threads would do, but it couldn't be anything good.

She moved close enough to whip another thread at the Skinned Man. She realized her mistake as soon as she moved. But it was too late. She was too close. The Skinned Man lashed out, striking her across her side. The impact sent her flying backward.

"Loey!" Jeronimo yelled.

She hit the ground and her head snapped back against the hard earth. The world spun, and she was nothing but searing pain and pulsing lights. As she straightened off the ground, her ribs stabbed her insides, stealing her breath and threatening to level her again. In her head, a wailing started up in time with the pulsing lights going off behind her eyelids. She shook her head to clear it. The wailing screech didn't stop, because it wasn't in her head. Cop cars were racing up Devil's Maw from town.

The shooting sounds the Seam had made when it ripped must have alerted the cops; they didn't have long now.

Barty watched her from the tatter. Close to him, the Skinned Man was nearly free.

"Barty," Loey called, her voice cracking around his name.

Jeronimo's brother found her again. His stillness was otherworldly. His eyes were so sad.

"Help," Loey mouthed, pleading. Her eyes flicked to the Skinned Man.

Barty looked between her, the Skinned Man, and his brother. If he'd considered his freedom for longer than a second, Loey had missed it. Like his brother did when he decided something, Barty clenched his jaw. He grabbed the man from behind, tangling them both in the Seam's tattered threads, and dragged him back across the Seam.

"Stop!" Jeronimo crawled forward. "Get out while you can. Barty!"

Loey stumbled to her feet. Her knee threatened to buckle beneath her, but she limped to the tatter. She got close enough to meet Barty's eyes. As she started tying the tatter back together, he gave her a solemn nod and jerked the killer farther inside.

"Get him," Jeronimo shouted at Loey. "Loey, help him!"

Loey didn't help him. He'd made his decision, and she'd made hers. Her fingers flying on instinct alone, she tied knot after knot until the tatter was small enough to keep everything safely inside, or so she hoped. When she'd done all she could in a hurry, she stepped back. Something rattled at her feet. She glanced down and found the jar of salt Jeronimo had brought in his bag. Thinking of souls and rings, she grabbed it and dumped a thick line across the front of the largest hole in the tatter.

When the jar was empty, she spun dizzily around, lost in the lights. Jeronimo was standing a few feet behind her.

"It wasn't him," he mumbled. "He wasn't the killer."

He swayed away from her. She grabbed for him too late.

He fell to his knees, his head drooping in exhaustion. She sank to the ground beside him, her arms around his waist. It took all her strength to keep him from falling completely flat.

"Come on. Look at me. *Look at me.*"

She had to grab his chin and lift his face toward hers. The way he leaned fully into her, the way his eyes were sunken, his face ashen, his lips and chin bloody from the nosebleed that wouldn't quit, shook her to the very foundation of her soul.

"J," she whispered, "what's happening?"

He groaned. There were words of defeat in that noise that Loey couldn't catch. She leaned closer to him, closer than she'd ever been before, even when they'd kissed. The kiss, which had literally pulled Loey's world apart, felt like a lifetime ago.

"… thing in there with him." Jeronimo coughed. Her breath lodged in her throat. "He's trapped in there with that bastard. I … doomed him … *again.*"

He sobbed, and Loey's heart sundered straight in half.

"He tried to warn us." He coughed again then moaned as if his insides were crumbling. "I thought he was killing people this entire time because I've always thought the worst of him."

He sagged again, but Loey couldn't catch him. Jeronimo fell back flat on his back and Loey hovered above him, her arms useless around his limp body. He blinked up at her, his lips turning blue.

She needed help. *He* needed help.

"We have to save him."

"Your brother will be fine, but you have to hold on. You have to stay alive, because you're not making me do this alone, okay?"

"You'll help me?"

She looked him in the eye and vowed, "I will. No matter what we have to do, I'll help you."

"No matter how much you hate me?"

"I don't hate you, J."

Down the road, the sound of sirens neared. Their whirring scream dimmed, then grew louder, then dimmed again as the cop cars wound their way up the serpentine road.

Jeronimo's hand wrapped tighter around hers, drawing her attention back to him. His black eyes dulled to a smokescreen gray. His pupils stood out stark against the whitewash of color. His eyes fluttered closed.

She clutched his hand. "Hold on," she whispered desperately. "Hold on. Just hold on. Help's coming." She repeated the words—useless things—over and over as she held on to him with all her strength, grinding the bones in his hand.

The police sirens were close enough to hurt Loey's ears. She glanced back. Through the trees and headstones, she spotted officers piling out of their cars. Guns drawn, they advanced toward the church.

The wrong way.

"I need to signal them over here so they can get you to the hospital before you die."

Jeronimo groaned. He tried to open his eyes. He murmured something that could have been, "No," but she couldn't make it out, and she needed to get the cops' attention.

"It's okay. I'll be right back."

She jumped to her feet and whirled around. The motion caused her vision to slant drunkenly, and white-hot pain blossomed out from her ribs and pulsed like a million threads across her vision. She wove toward the clearing, where she could make out the nearest deputy.

"Hey!" she shouted. "Over here!"

The deputy spun in her direction, looking too far over to the left. The trees behind her cast her in shadows. She limped forward, closer to the church and farther from Jeronimo.

"Over here!" She waved and swallowed down bile as her ribs screamed in pain.

The deputy caught sight of her with a jolt. He shouted back to the others and ran toward her.

She opened her mouth to shout for him to bring paramedics, but a soft chiming stopped her. The chiming grew to a mighty clamor she'd heard before. She whirled around.

All the graves' bells were clanging hard enough to snap their strings, though it didn't stop their trilling.

The dead are talking. Are you listening?

Her eyes fell on Jeronimo, lying in the middle of the gonging bells. As she watched, a gnarled, white-scarred hand reached through a smaller, unsalted rip in the Seam's tatter and gripped Jeronimo's ankle. The torn threads it touched flashed in alarm. The hand gave a mighty jerk.

His body jolted, and the Skinned Man dragged him closer to the glimmering tatter.

Screaming, Loey sprinted forward, right as Jeronimo's body bounced over the tree's roots, half his body disappearing through the tatter. She caught his arm right before he could disappear and hauled with all her strength against the Skinned Man's hold.

Inside, a shadow fluttered. A distinctly feminine voice screamed out a war cry. All at once, Jeronimo lurched back toward her and she fell, Jeronimo landing on top of her.

To the sound of the Skinned Man's fading wails, the tatter and the threads and the pulsing knots blinked out. From the church, the deputies ran over, shouting and swinging their flashlights.

"I've got you," she told Jeronimo, clutching him tight to her chest. "I've got you."

Twice, she thought, *in case the first should fail.*

CHAPTER 35

NOVEMBER 19, 2012

DALE VISITED LOEY OVER THANKSGIVING break. She spoke of college classes and droning professors and the parties where beer was like a token of acceptance. When she ran out of stories to occupy Loey's semi-dark bedroom, they fell silent.

"Does it hurt?"

Loey lay on her bed, where she'd been for the past four months. Six surgeries on her knee, twelve on her face—and they hadn't started on the dental reconstruction yet—three titanium plates to hold her pieces together, countless screws, and there was nothing that never hurt.

"I'm sorry," Dale said when Loey didn't answer. "That was a stupid thing to ask."

Loey shrugged. Words were hard with the deep stitches holding her cheek in place.

They sat silently for so long that Loey wanted her best friend to leave, even after waiting months for Dale to return from college so she could hear the stories and pretend like she'd been there.

Her college fund, all the money she'd saved, all that hope—128 days—had gone toward the endless surgeries and to pay the bills that came in thick white envelopes with pages full of astounding numbers printed in stark black ink next to dollar signs.

There was no end, and Loey watched her grandparents bend beneath the weight of insurance claims and helping her to the bathroom and wiping her mouth when the soft liquids oozed from her lips. And at night, she heard Burl's voice speak those words.

Hit the ground.

Loey was in free fall, and she wanted nothing more than to hit the ground.

"We did it."

She almost missed the whispered words. "Did what?"

"Leigh's old school books. The computer searches. The devil-worshipping closet. All of it. Cross even used real goat's blood to draw the pentagram on the fucker's wall."

Loey frowned as much as she could with her too-tight face. "But Dale, *why?*"

"You should've seen his eyes. The way he was staring at you as he carried you to the ambulance." Dale gritted her teeth, perfect straight rows that Loey would never have again. "He likes you broken. You can't run away from him then."

The temperature of the room dropped. Loey wanted to sink deeper into the blankets, but Dale held her hand so tightly that her manicured nails dug into Loey's palm.

With mangled words, Loey asked, "What did you do?"

"What we had to."

She shook her head. Things hurt in stark relief as she tried to sit up in bed. "How did you get in? How did you get away with it?"

"We needed a story that physical evidence could back up so Cross set everything up while I distracted him." Dale lifted a shoulder. Her hair was lighter now, blonder. Her eyes were deader now too. "It was easy. I had it under control the entire time. I'm going to have Travis take me to the hospital, but I wanted to tell you first."

Loey's heart thudded against her sternum. "Dale …"

"Nobody will allow a child molester to go free. Not in this town."

Loey tried to speak, but the words fell apart in her ruined mouth. Her breath turned ragged from the pain.

"It was fine." Dale shushed her efforts. Her hand tightened around Loey's. "Really, don't worry about me. Honestly, it was easier than trying to do stuff with Travis. I just laid there."

Loey had never seen her best friend's eyes so empty. It was like Dale had vanished. The decision Loey had been so quick to make, of punishing a bad man for another man's sin, had dug out hollow parts in Dale. Loey felt those same parts being dug out of her now. Deep, dark places in her heart echoed emptily. She stared at her best friend and knew, in those empty places in her heart, that things would be forever changed in Righteous, just as they were forever changed in them. They'd done irrevocable damage, and if Loey's lack of tuition savings hadn't already anchored her to this town, then this thing, this grave sin, had trapped her for good. She'd never leave Righteous. Didn't deserve to no how.

Loey whimpered. Dale brought Loey's hand to her mouth and kissed it.

"We made him pay. He's a dead man walking."

"Dale …" Loey was close to tears. She would have been crying if the pain meds hadn't dried her eyes and mouth right up.

"I have good news, though." Dale's fake smile ratcheted up a notch. "I'm entering the Miss Tennessee Pageant. Oh, and Travis asked me to marry him."

"What?"

"I said yes."

"Why?"

"Why not? Even though he's a Jinks, I could have a good life."

"But you'll be stuck here. You should leave while you can. Get out of here."

"There're worse places to be trapped. Righteous is safe, you know? These people, they only want to see the surface. They want a show, and I'm good at that. Besides, if you're stuck here, I want to be stuck with you. We can be hostages together. Wouldn't that be nice?"

"Dale," Loey rasped, "he's gay. You're not the one he loves. It would be a lie."

Dale sneered, and life returned to her eyes, but it was the bad kind that spoke of cynicism and bitterness. It didn't make her face pretty. It made Loey's beautiful best friend ugly in the worst way.

"Righteous is built on lies. These people lie every day, especially on Sundays. They do it straight to your face and you don't even know because they wrap it up all nice and say, 'Bless your heart.' Lying is more of a religion down here than God. I'm giving in, Lo. I'm spinning pretty lies too."

CHAPTER 36

LOEY TOLD MATT A COUGAR was in the graveyard. When he asked how the big cat had broken her ribs without shredding her skin, she told him she'd fallen over a headstone in her dash to escape the animal.

Matt, bless him, had looked between her, with her dirty face and terrified eyes, and Jeronimo, who was unconscious and looking every inch dead. In the end, Matt had simply shrugged and called for the wildlife guys to come check out the church's property.

No one would know the truth about tonight. No one would look too closely either.

The trip to the hospital with Jeronimo and her screaming ribs felt all too familiar. So familiar that it made her scars ache. Her breathing turned to thick, sucking efforts. Her vision slanted. Somewhere beside her, Matt had taken her hand. He called her name out over and over.

When she woke back up, she stared up into the emergency room's circular fluorescent lights like an antiseptic sun. Someone rustled in their chair beside her bed, which had a thin curtain pulled around its perimeter to shield it from the silent emergency room beyond.

She hoped it was Jeronimo she'd find in the chair when she looked. It wasn't.

"I've called Dale," Matt said, his face tired and concerned, but handsome in his wholesome, try-hard way. "I know you would want her here. Cross said they got back into town earlier, but I can't get an answer. He's out in the waiting room though."

Loey frowned. Dale was supposed to be at rehab, not here. "Where's J?"

"Who?"

"Jeronimo."

Matt's face went carefully blank. Cop eyes. He was too young for that, and Righteous was too soft a town for such a quick, deadening expression. "The doctors released him. Nothing was wrong with him. Loey Grace, I don't know if you should be spending so much time around him."

Loey pushed herself up a little straighter on the bed. She grimaced at the flash of pain. Matt was half out of his seat, reaching for her, when she said, "I have something to tell you, and you'll need to write it down."

Something in her voice alerted him. The chair squeaked as he sat back. "What is it?"

Loey took a deep breath. She knew, as she hadn't known the last time she'd told the truth, that this would only be the beginning. That the hard part hadn't even started yet.

"It's the truth about Leigh Parker's murder."

OTHER BOOKS BY MEG COLLETT

FEAR UNIVERSITY SERIES
Fear University
The Killing Season
Monster Mine
Paper Tigers
Dead Man's Stitch

CANAAN ISLAND NOVELS
Fakers
Keepers
Hiders

END OF DAYS TRILOGY
The Hunted One
The Lost One
The Only One
Days of New (An End of Days Serial Collection)

WHITEBIRD CHRONICLES
Lux and Lies

ABOUT THE AUTHOR

MEG COLLETT is from the hills of Tennessee where the cell phone service is a blessing and functioning internet is a myth of epic proportions. She's the author of the bestselling Fear University series, the End of Days trilogy, and the Canaan Island novels. Find out more at her website www.megcollett.com.

ENJOYED BLESS HER DEAD HEART?
Please consider leaving a review!

CPSIA information can be obtained at www.ICGtesting.com
Printed in the USA
LVIW011450020220
645575LV00007B/108